TEN
WOMEN

TEN
WOMEN

MARCELA SERRANO

translated by Beth Fowler

amazoncrossing 🌐

Text copyright © 2011 by Marcela Serrano
English translation copyright © 2014 by Beth Fowler

Ten Women was first published in 2011 by Alfaguara as *Diez Mujeres*. Translated from Spanish by Beth Fowler. Published in English by AmazonCrossing in 2014.

Epigraph from "Here" by Wisława Szymborska translated from Polish by Clare Cavanagh, published in the collection *Here*, reprinted by permission of Houghton Mifflin Harcourt.

Published by AmazonCrossing, Seattle

ISBN-13: 9781477849453
ISBN-10: 1477849459
Library of Congress Control Number: 201391225

Life on Earth is quite a bargain.
Dreams, for one, don't charge admission.
Illusions are only costly when lost.
The body has its own installment plan.

—Wisława Szymborska, "Here"

The madwomen, here come the madwomen, the workers on the grounds will be saying, spying on them from behind the trees.

Natasha can't decide which she finds more entertaining, observing the confusion of those burly men holding picks and hoes, or the women, who at that moment are filing out from the enormous minivan. One by one they get out and tread hard on the gravel-scattered earth, as though they'd like to plant their feet firmly in it.

Perhaps one or other of them would enjoy the idea of being an object of observation or suspicion, she thinks, recalling Andrea saying happily as she left last Thursday: Make sure they know, Natasha, that we're just a little bit neurotic and not completely crazy!

Unashamedly, the men have stopped working and, leaning on their tools, are watching the women. There's something for all tastes. Those who prefer dark hair have the greatest choice. Short, tall, young, old, slim, and heavy with flesh and with time. They are nine women. They are many women. The lawns have been cut, the black plastic bags brimming with Bermuda grass rest against the trunks of two huge avocado trees. The fresh aroma reaches the institute's main house, and for Natasha the scent of grass mingles with that of the nearby mountains. When he loaned her the place, the director warned: They do the gardens on Saturdays. To Natasha's eyes, this isn't a garden so much as a park. She would like to find out the names of many of the trees; only the magnolia, the sweetgums, and the jacaranda are familiar to her, she has seen them at her country home in the Aconcagua Valley. But here she is in the suburbs of Santiago where the Andes brazenly show off their attributes.

The women walk toward the house rather hesitantly. Some gaze entranced at the park and the colorful flowers, others talk among themselves. Mané has taken Guadalupe's arm, leaning against her shoulder. They make quite a pair: the eldest and the youngest. Natasha thinks that Mané will always be saved by her curiosity; no doubt she already has discovered everything about her companion's nose and ear piercings and passed her hand over that near-shaven head. Guadalupe will have enjoyed it, prone to laughter as she is. They've all been together for at least a half hour since they got into the minivan at the exit of Tobalaba subway station. Natasha reckons that somewhere around Avenida Ossa, Juani or Simona will have broken the ice and, coming into Peñalolén, they will have managed to put even the shyest women at ease. Perhaps they dragged a smile out of Layla. Or a few words out of Luisa. Andrea has dropped behind, what's she doing? Natasha smiles: she's signing an autograph. The gardener, who a moment ago was pruning roses, has dropped his shears to the ground and set off after her in a fit of daring. The same thing happens in the doctor's office or hospital—Andrea is always signing autographs, it's her karma. Ana Rosa lingers on the path; she should be walking with the others but she is spellbound watching Andrea. Francisca, terrified she won't be allowed for the rest of the day, lights a cigarette, her crocodile-skin purse hanging open—she never closes it. She looks less pale, how tempting to leave her out in the sun instead of shutting her in a room. Today she is wearing jeans; this is the first time Natasha has seen her dressed casually. Simona, wrapped in a white alpaca poncho, approaches Francisca and asks for a light. The sun on their faces, they inhale with pleasure, making the most of their last opportunity to do so. The two patients I've been seeing longest, Natasha says to herself, and it's the first time I've seen them together. Irrationally, she thinks how much she would like them to get to know one another after today, for them to have each other.

From behind the window, clutching the voile curtain, Natasha attentively watches them all. All morning long, she has been trying to visualize each of them preparing to attend this meeting. Although her plan is to maintain a certain distance, it is difficult for her to ignore the bursts of tenderness that strike her when it comes to these women. She imagines some of them abandoning a bed, and leaving it empty, when it was still dark outside, others leaving a warm, familiar body. They would be tired after the week, a bit more sleep would have done them good. They prepared breakfast, a strong coffee in Simona's case, watery tea for Ana Rosa. Francisca just had a piece of fruit, as usual; Juani ate a roll with butter and jelly. One might have eaten standing at the kitchen counter as she prepared the house for a day in her absence, another sitting at the dining table, perhaps one of them took the cup or tray to bed with the newspaper that was waiting for her by the front door. They probably all felt a certain degree of anxiousness. The minivan would be waiting for them at nine. No one would want to let down Natasha, or make the others late. They took the medication they take every morning, in the hope of fighting such and such malady. For almost all of them, an antidepressant prescribed by Natasha. All making an effort to be a bit happier. To heal themselves. All of them genuinely dedicated to living the best kind of life within their means. Some took a shower and washed their hair, some might have bathed. They all looked at themselves in the mirror because a special day was awaiting them. They know that what is coming will be more than mere words. One woman wanted to put on a bit of makeup, to show her best face. Another thought it inappropriate. When it was time to get dressed and decide what to wear, that time when so many women hate themselves, how many of them changed their outfit because they didn't like what they saw? From La Dehesa to Maipú, was it any different during that minute in front of the mirror? Bring on the blindness, Natasha says to herself, bring it, anything to prevent the unavoidable, brutal contamination to which every woman falls victim on a daily basis. From Guadalupe's nineteen years to Mané's seventy-five, did any of them think twice about making an effort to look as good as possible? Each bringing with her the person she inevitably is. With a slight pain in some part of the body, a discomfort, something she's used to bearing, tired muscles and ligaments. Beneath the black vest or pink blouse, wasn't each woman endowing herself with resolve, gathering courage for the day ahead? Their appearances today are certainly honest, there's no interference from jobs, offices, or formalities that might pigeonhole them; the way they have come today is the way they truly are.

And they are all so beautiful, Natasha says to herself.

How these women move me. How they sadden me. Why did half of humanity take on such a great burden and leave the other half to rest? I'm not afraid of sounding like an idiot, Natasha thinks, I know what I'm saying. I know why I'm saying it.

The women are no longer visible on the path. They have entered the building. Natasha releases the voile at the window through which she has been watching the nine women and leaves the room. The time has come to go out and welcome them.

FRANCISCA

I hate my mother. Or I hate myself, I don't know. I suppose that's the reason I'm here. Hatred is tiring. Getting used to it doesn't resolve a thing.

You never get used to it.

I don't know why Natasha has asked me to begin, I'm quite embarrassed to be the first. Perhaps because I've been her patient for the longest. No one has been in therapy longer than me. Let's be honest: jealousy runs amok in here. We should all be quite jealous of one another. I noticed the way we looked at each other when we got into the minivan, our tense greetings, as if we were Olympic athletes all entering the same race, all of us competing against one another. Perhaps I'm exaggerating, pay no attention. That's one of therapy's cruel aspects: the therapist is unique to you, but not the other way around. How unfair. It's the most unequal relationship you could imagine. I'd love to think that Natasha doesn't like anyone as much as *me*, that no one entertains her like I do, that she doesn't have as much pity or compassion for anyone else, that she doesn't get as involved with others as she does with me. After all, every shred of intimacy I'm capable of dealing with is in her hands. My dream would be for her to receive it only from me. How can I bear the fact that she also gets it from all of you? Does she make you all feel as loved and valued as she does me? Does she create that warm space, that bulletproof shelter in her office for everyone? Does she really have room inside to love us *all*?

One day, I read this headline in the newspaper: "Couple leaves daughter in car to go drinking." The article explained how the twelve-year-old son of a couple from Lleida called the police because his parents came home drunk and without his sister. That story stirred up something in me and I came to see Natasha. Until then I had always thought why change, why move things when you can live in paralysis? I was convinced that a frozen heart was a great virtue.

When I arrived at Natasha's I knew my therapy would be life or death: I had to cut the maternal line at the root, halt the repetition. Let's be clear, this isn't an issue of genetics or DNA, it's a matter of transference during childhood. Everything was plotted out for me to become perverse, to abuse or mistreat. But without knowing it, I resorted to an immense source of internal energy, I married and had children, fighting every day because of it, every day. Sometimes I wonder where this energy came from. From my father? From God, whom I love and pray to in spite of everything? From the grace of my brother Nicolás, who, somehow, helped identify my own dangers for me? I think it was instinct, pure instinct. I had no sense inside me of what a normal family was like. The truth is, I'm a miracle.

I was naked when I came to Natasha.

My name is Francisca—even my name is common. How many Franciscas do you all know? I recently turned forty-two, a complicated stage of life. You're young, but not very, you're not elderly, but you are a bit old. Neither fish nor fowl. It's the transition from one thing to the other, the real start of deterioration. Sometimes I feel like I want to have aged *already*, to be an old woman who has resolved all her expectations.

I'm a partner at a real estate developer and I do quite well for myself. I work a lot, a whole lot. I took the classic path. I started out as assistant to an important architect until I became his right-hand woman and ended up being irreplaceable. We have an office in Providencia with a permanent staff of fourteen and we're pretty busy. I'm also an architect and my great passion is space. I married Vicente, a construction engineer, and we have three daughters. What a curse, all girls. Everyone says my husband is a difficult man and that's probably true, but I get on wonderfully with him. I love him and I'm faithful to him.

But I find daily life to be a form of paralysis: getting up early each morning, dropping the girls at school, swinging by the gym and doing Pilates, going to the office, being lucid in my discussions with the company lawyer, keeping an eye on the whole staff, checking on our buildings, arguing with the new head of sales, whom I don't get on with. If I'm lucky, I have lunch with a friend rather than just a hurried sandwich. I check email, deal with clients, visit ugly properties, agonizing over the unimaginative matchboxes they build nowadays disguised behind pompous words like *walk-in closet, loggia, home office*. On a good day, I close a deal. No matter what, going home I'm tortured by Santiago's shitty traffic. I chat with my husband for a while, go over the girls' homework, heat up something quick and easy for dinner, watch the news, cursing a bit at such and such a statement, trying to understand the economy. I hug my daughters, give them lots of kisses, and go to bed. Sex some days, although hopefully only when I don't have to get up so early. I realize that it isn't always going to be unbridled passion. Sometimes I'm in a really lazy mood when I make love, but I do it anyway.

How many women have that same routine? Thousands upon thousands around the globe. All of us fortysomethings carrying our own little lives on our backs, insignificant and inoffensive deep down, some a bit more intelligent, others friendlier, others more ambitious, others more fun, but all the same in the end. Immersed in a ferocious fight to stand out as someone special, legitimately combative in order to mark the difference. All quite exhausted. You could make an exact template from them. You tend to think that once you've seen one you've seen them all. Some days you have nothing to say to your husband, your children's stories bore you, and you dream of going to bed with George Clooney. Other days, you simply don't feel anything at all. You go through the motions, as best as you can, but entirely on autopilot. If you get run over as you cross the street perhaps you won't even realize it. You don't suffer, you're a block of ice. When those days become more frequent, I call them "The Days of Paralysis." Although, believe me, it takes me a while to realize I'm having them because I'm blinded by my own inertia.

One day my husband accused me of being cold. Poor thing, it took him so long to figure it out. I denied it, to appease him. I never wondered whether or not I was cold, nor was I concerned about being defined as such. I only knew that I entered into states of utter indifference. But like everyone, I'm also familiar with other states: those of passion, of indignation. I die of love and gratitude and masochism when I'm not paralyzed. I can explain.

There are two males in my life, no more. My husband and my cat. I have come to the conclusion that they were both shaped in the same mold and that there's something insane about the way I love them.

My cat is unfriendly. He's enormous and pudgy, with red and yellow stripes. I call him "my tiger," although my daughters mock me. I have no doubt that he loves me, but he's always escaping, as if he's going to find that everything's better away from the house. I struggle to keep him there, it infuriates me that he lives the best of lives at my expense. He has a house with food, affection and warmth and he also has an entire block of rooftops to walk along and carouse. He's a born fighter. He always comes home wounded, with scratches, blood, or missing fur. I care for him more than I do for myself. I apply disinfectant, I take him to the vet for the slightest thing. Every night I stand in the middle of the street and start calling him, sometimes quite late, in pajamas, and my daughters swear they don't know me. I can't get to sleep if he doesn't come home and I get up a thousand times until I can hold him in my arms. Some might say that loving this cat is useless, but they'd be wrong. Once he surrenders, he's the sweetest cat in the world. The first and most surprising thing about him is that when I call him he answers. He only responds to me, no one else. He always answers me, that's why I always find him in the end. Put it this way: if it wasn't for this peculiarity of his—because no one will disagree that it *is* a peculiarity—I'd have lost him long ago. It's a combination of my tenacity and his singular behavior that has allowed us to spend almost eight years together. He sleeps with me and in the middle of the night he raises a hand—he uses his paws as if they were human—and strokes my cheek. When I'm cold, I squeeze him against me and he allows it.

He's also a coward. Outside on the street he's a killer, but at home, if he hears a noise that's alien to his everyday routine, he immediately runs and hides. If, when the doorbell rings, the voice at the door is male, it terrifies him and he slinks under the covers on my bed. More than once, of course, one of the girls has sat on him because they've flopped down on the bed and not seen him. Basically, he has a phobia. Showing his face to men horrifies him. What's more, he's arrogant. The most typical situation would be this: he's left in the morning for his daily run-around and doesn't come back until dawn. I've gone crazy searching for him and I'm desperate, thinking he's been run over by a car ten blocks from the house. When he appears, cool as a cucumber, he stares at me with profound indifference. If he could talk he would say, without a trace of remorse: It's all your fault.

Well, when I'm asked why, out of all the cats that populate the universe, I've chosen the one that causes me the most suffering, I answer: The thing is, it's worth it, believe me. He loves me.

I'd say exactly the same about Vicente.

I was born to a fairly comfortable family, in a decent house—nothing special—in east Santiago, on Calle Bilbao. My father is an economist who always has worked in the financial world. A rather weak character and evasive, but all in all a good man. He married my mother when she was very young and they had two children: my older brother, Nicolás, and me. My mother didn't work and it didn't occur to anyone that she ought to. She slept until midday, she read and

smoked ceaselessly, and in the evenings she would go to the movies.
Every day, I'm not exaggerating. When cable television and video
arrived she stopped going out and watched movies in bed. Early in
my childhood they had to resort to separate bedrooms because of
their incompatible timetables and because my father hated cigarettes
and the TV always being on. During the day, my mother was always
a bit distracted. Enough for me to note her boredom when I told her
stories from my day; it was obvious she was only listening to me out
of a sense of duty. With my brother, however, she seemed more alert,
perhaps he was the only one who could awaken her. Sometimes I
would say to Nicolás that he was like an only child, without realizing
the horrific truth that surrounded my words. She wasn't interested in
clothes or romances or the ins and outs of friendships, which are so
intricate during puberty. I remember, at the age of about seven, the
day I fought with Verónica, a close friend. Naturally, I arrived home
in tears.

This was the conversation:

Mom: What's wrong?

Me: I fought with Verónica.

Mom: About anything important?

Me: She didn't invite me to her birthday party. I thought she was
my friend. I thought she liked me.

Mom: No one likes anyone much, honey, it's better you know
from the start.

Because of her issues with "women's problems," she forgot to
warn me that girls menstruate, and if it weren't for my high school
friends the shock of the blood would have killed me. When I began
to grow and my curves accentuated, she didn't seem to notice. I went
to her room one day, moaning: Mom, my breasts have grown, do
something. She looked at me distantly—a typical look of hers—and
replied: Tell your dad to give you money and buy yourself a bra,
it's quite simple. I told her, through my tears, that I didn't want to
grow, that I didn't want breasts. She burst out laughing. Come on,

Francisca, don't be a child, was her response before she returned to her reading.

She never touched me. Nicolás, yes. Under no circumstances would she take my side in a fight, she never backed me up in front of my brother or cousins. It seemed as though I was never right, which made me feel enormously insecure. Looking back, I should recognize that she simply didn't love me. That does happen, although people don't believe it. There are mothers who just don't love their children.

As the years passed, I developed like any other girl my age. I did the same activities as the others, turning to the outside world more than ever, to my friends, my boyfriends, high school, sports. I conveyed a false indifference that helped in my day-to-day life. I decided that perhaps my mom would love me more if I distinguished myself at something and I decided to be a brilliant student. But she was more interested in Nicolás's studies and only congratulated me on my grades in passing. So then I devoted myself to sports, sure that it would impress her, especially given how sedentary she was. I became one of the best basketball players in high school but I only ever managed to get her to attend one game. As a final attempt, I decided I would learn how to become a perfect housewife. I took a cooking class and at the age of fifteen I was like a pro in the kitchen. I learned how to set the table and decorate it like no one else, yet this only led to exploitation. When we had visitors my mother would ask me to take charge. Sometimes she looked at me with a strange expression. She'd furrow her brow and ask, Who do you take after, Francisca? One day, she finally acknowledged my merits, but with a mocking backhanded compliment. She said: I've always suspected that, deep down, people who are good at everything are good for nothing.

I looked for substitutes, but there wasn't much choice within the family. My mother was an only child, so there were no aunts on her side. My father's sisters were boring, provincial ladies who lived in Antofagasta, I barely knew them, and his sisters-in-law were never anything more than the mothers of my cousins. I was perceptive enough to realize that a teacher is only ever a part-time substitute. So I turned to my imagination. Religion was never important in my family. We were passive Catholics, we went to mass occasionally, we observed the basic rules of the church, but no more than that. The same phenomenon occurred with politics: we supported Pinochet, again passively. We had inherited my grandmother's anti-Communism as something natural, devoid of any mysticism. So, I turned to angels, and pondered at length their androgyny. They were neither men nor women and I needed a mom. So I decided that my angel would be female. I invented her. My angel was a wonderful guardian angel, always available, always fair and wise and, more than that, beautiful. She lived in my bedroom and we only talked at night. I told her about my day, I made the most of the chance to recount all the details that bored my mother, I complained about home and high school. I apologized to her when I behaved badly but I knew that her love would release me of any punishment, so I never lied. I called her Ángela. I got so used to her. Her presence was the most natural thing in the world. Sometimes Nicolás would hear me talking in my room, open the door and ask, Francisca, are you talking to yourself? I, of course, replied that I hadn't opened my mouth, that it was all in his mind. From time to time I left Ángela pieces of paper in my nightstand drawer. That way, in an empty chocolate box, I guarded the sweet words of a loving mother. I wonder what my life would have been like without Ángela. Even today I occasionally turn to her, the way someone else would turn to God. The difference is that Ángela was friendlier than God, whom I've never thought of as particularly amiable.

My mother wasn't an unfriendly woman. She managed to make her distance and distraction seem attractive. She had the strange capacity to make everyone submit to her will so she could do whatever she felt like. She manipulated us as she pleased and always had her way. For example, when she didn't like something, she simply stood up and left. This tended to happen at mealtimes. We would all be sitting at the table and suddenly I would say something, like that my friends' moms went to the basketball games to watch their daughters and she would look at me, drop her fork, throw the napkin on the table, and make a dramatic exit, even though we'd only just started to eat. So my dad, with immense patience, would say to me: Francisca, go and apologize to your mother. Because this happened continually, no one in the house said anything to annoy her. She managed to prevent all of us from ever saying or doing *anything* she didn't like. Anytime I have caught myself, as an adult, doing the same thing, I hatefully recriminate myself mercilessly.

What's more, she was an attractive woman. Quite tall, she had a nice body, rather thick at the waist but with good legs, and her brunet hair was soft and beautiful. She changed her hairstyle according to fashion but she always wore it very short and, despite the cigarettes—she seemed to live in a movie from the fifties, constantly smoking—it had a tremendous luster. Her mouth was the feature I liked least in her. It was narrow, a hard, mean line, as if she had swallowed her lips. To my mind, it was a mouth lacking in generosity. However, her nose was perfectly straight and shapely and her eyes, like her hair, were brown, large, and very lively. They tell me that my fair, pale, slightly washed-out features were inherited from my paternal grandmother, whom I never met.

Speaking of grandmothers, perhaps my mom can't be understood without mention of *her* mother.

My grandmother was a crazy Russian who wanted to be Isadora Duncan but ended up a bankrupt gambler in an unfamiliar and at that time fairly underdeveloped country called Chile. Her parents, wealthy Russians who supported the White Army, fled the revolution and, like many others, settled in Paris, where my grandmother grew up. From a very early age she used money to compensate for the suffering of exile, which in her case, to tell the truth, wasn't all that bad. She soon became a fan of gambling. Casinos were her fascination, the place she felt *at home*. She used a fake ID to appear older, which was very easy, according to her, in those days when poor Russians did a bit of everything to earn a living. When her father died and she received her inheritance—she was no more than nineteen—she left her mother in Paris and went to live in Monaco. She moved into a hotel room a few blocks from a casino and slept by day and played by night. Quite beautiful, with pretty blond hair, a doll's nose, and formidable eyelashes, she was precocious, irreverent and fun, and enjoyed an enviable ability to speak languages as though they were her mother tongue. I have no doubt that she was an intelligent woman but that she wasted that gift. Men weren't very important to her, she saw them as gambling companions more than suitors. A lost addict. And probably frigid too. While she was living in Monaco, when she was already twenty-five, her mother died of tuberculosis. She returned to Paris to bury her; all that mattered to her was being able to convert the house and assets into cold hard cash. She won and lost. After one of the major wins she decided she would buy herself a castle and so she did. She didn't sleep there more than three times before she lost it, gambling again, but she enjoyed the idea of feeling like a princess for a while. Her fortune wasn't destined to last for long. When it ran out, she was about to turn thirty and hadn't even thought of marriage. A Chilean man entered her circle and became fascinated by her, he saw her as the embodiment of the romanticism of the European woman. He was a diplomatic clerk, on a fairly meager salary and rather unworldly, not to mention very young. When he met her, she had a pale, sickly beauty that matched her poverty. Her life hadn't been very healthy, she barely saw the sunlight. Lots of champagne and not enough salad. He decided to look after her and took her on as his mission. When it was time for him to return to Chile, he convinced her to marry him. I suppose my grandmother was left with no choice but to accept. She didn't have a peso and friends are fleeting in the gambling world. Perhaps she thought this was an opportunity for someone to take care of her. Besides, she knew that in a city near Santiago de Chile, by the sea, there was a casino.

During the trip across the Atlantic—according to her tale, she was constantly nauseous and vomiting—she discovered she was pregnant. Such an eventuality had never crossed her mind. She decided she wouldn't be able to bear it, that she would die in labor. She asked my grandfather to take her to live in Viña del Mar. The idiot quit the Ministry of Foreign Affairs and left for Viña, where he found employment in a bank in order to keep this woman, who was as sophisticated as she was fragile. My mother was born next to the Pacific, in a difficult birth and with a parent who didn't know what to do with her. I'm not lying if I say that my grandmother didn't know what a diaper was. They hired a wet nurse, Nanita—she gave her breast to my mother and her own daughter simultaneously. Nanita also raised my mother. Of course, my grandmother returned to gambling, except now she bet less extravagant amounts than in Monaco. She had only her potential good luck, added to whatever she took from my grandfather's wallet, at her disposal. Her daughter was never a relevant factor in her life.

I didn't know her very well. She died of a heart attack when I was ten. I would really like to have gotten to know her, such an unusual, sickly and entertaining woman. Perhaps she would have loved me as I grew up. Because they lived in Viña, we didn't see them much and she gave me unloving kisses, as if she didn't mean them, and dismissed me immediately afterward. She didn't know how to talk to a child. Since I didn't have a paternal grandmother, I grew up believing that this was the way grandmothers were—alien, distant, and not very affectionate. When, as a child, my friends talked about caring grandmas who knitted and baked cakes for them, I was stunned. Grandmothers didn't knit or bake, grandmothers gambled at the casino.

When I visited her in Viña, the greatest attraction was rummaging through her trunk. Dresses from the thirties with long waists, made of chiffon, organdy, muslin; velvet gowns full of tassels; silk negligees with Chinese motifs and others with feather necklines; boas; extremely long necklaces of precious stones; coats made of unknown furs; never-ending shawls like curtains. I wrapped myself in them, sometimes putting on several at once. When I knew I wouldn't be caught, I walked around the house in disguise. The strange thing is that the day I did get caught, instead of being annoyed at me wearing her sheer black organdy dress, she looked at me, almost with pleasure, and said: You could be me.

Three-quarters of my blood is entirely Chilean—that is to say, Spanish and Mapuche. But when I get any eccentric ideas, I tell myself that this is my Russian side, which doesn't bode well. Perhaps that's why I have become the conventional woman I am: everything by the rules, pretty much by the book. No, I'm not entertaining, far from it; if I let down my hair or deviate from convention, where will I end up? Even in bed I'm traditional, no exotic sex or strange games. No. Him on top, me underneath. All a bit boring and predictable. But all safe. She, my grandmother, said it: You *could* be me.

It's funny that Natasha has Russian roots too, as if an invisible force were pushing me toward a denied or lost origin. Of course, coincidences only go so far. My grandmother's family didn't escape from the Nazis but from the Communists, my grandmother wasn't educated at the best of schools in Argentina. But she was Russian. Like my therapist. Like my addict grandmother. Like half of my mother.

Nicolás inherited my grandmother's physical fingerprint, her elegant bone structure, her high cheekbones, her near-white skin, which my mother didn't get. She looked as Latin American as my grandfather. Nicolás resembled her and even had the name of a tsar. He even beat me in that.

Nicolás won right to the very end. He died. It might seem crude to put it like this but there's nothing as romantic, heroic, and beautiful as a premature death, even if it is the result of a stupid illness. To this day I can discern those feelings, somewhere between the frightening pain and shock his departure caused. I often envied him. What if it

had been me who died? Would my mother have loved me when I
was no longer there? I really hated him for dying, even more than
when he was alive, but I've only come to recognize that feeling now,
thanks to Natasha. He was born of a woman's body and was nour-
ished by that body and loved by that body. He was able to live in
paradise, he held it in one hand. I had to create a space in the world
with no primitive memories to save me, with no Eden marked out
in my cells. I was born in occupied territory, doubly occupied, like
Germany after World War II. Nicolás died within that paradise, if
paradise really is being loved by the one who gave birth to you.

My mother's grief, you can imagine, was thunderous. She didn't get
out of bed for a couple of months. She locked the bedroom door and
shuttered the windows, refused to eat. She added a new element to
her life: booze. She slept, smoked, and drank. I don't blame her. Now
that I'm the mother of three girls, I don't blame her. I contrasted my
dad's pain to hers. He managed to keep living. After all, he hadn't
given birth to Nicolás. Giving birth involves the body, the whole
body, and therefore the mind too.

The day when she finally got out of bed, much to our surprise,
she acted as if nothing had happened. Of course, she stole our grief
from us. Her grief was more important than ours. She didn't allow
us to cry. We felt terribly guilty for her pain. She always needed to
be the center of attention. But she seemed to garner strength from
nowhere and returned to her daily life without any apparent traces of
the grief. Then we left the country. A yearlong position opened up at
my father's work at the headquarters in New York. He volunteered,
reasoning that the change would be good for my mom. I missed that
year of high school because the American and Chilean academic
calendars were opposite, but that didn't concern anyone and it was
useful for me because I still learned proper English.

The first warning sign appeared that afternoon at The Plaza Hotel.
We had already settled in New York. There was a small movie theater

in the hotel and we had planned on watching a Woody Allen movie and afterward having tea, right there, in the hotel. She arrived slightly late, after the movie had begun. Mom, I exclaimed, startled, you forgot to change out of your slippers. She looked at her feet and shrugged. It's just too hot to wear shoes, she said, and watched the movie, happy with life. I made up an excuse not to have tea, I wasn't going to subject myself to the embarrassment of going into that lounge with a woman in slippers. The Plaza was The Plaza, after all.

She liked walking through Central Park. One day, a homeless woman sat next to us on a bench. She was accompanied by two dogs, black, skinny, and flea-ridden, just like her. She carried a sign that read: *I'm all alone. My family was kidnapped by E.T.* It made me laugh at first. Since my mother didn't see the humor, I said to her, contritely: Poor woman, how dreadful. Without turning a hair or changing expression, she replied: Dreadful? No. I'm jealous! And then she added, pensively: Have you ever thought about a homeless person's imagination, about how they manage to live? Accustomed to her eccentricities, I didn't think much of the comment. I remember having been struck by the dogs, wondering how the woman fed them, let alone herself.

Apart from the fact that my mom got dressed less and less frequently and sometimes wore pajamas to go and buy bread, the second symptom surfaced a couple of weeks later. My dad and I were waiting at home for her so we could go out for dinner. But she called us and said, Go without me, I'm in the park and it's too hot to walk, I'd prefer just to lie here among the trees. We stayed home and made sandwiches. She returned around two in the morning. My poor father was about to call the police but she acted like nothing was unusual. This happened a couple more times. On the final occasion, she appeared with a brown paper bag in her hand, which contained a blouse and a dress, used and dirty. My dad grabbed them, shouting about where she found them before he threw them in the trash. She responded innocently, as if nothing had happened. I found them in a shopping cart in the park, she explained, why are you taking them from me? True to her nature, to punish him for having thrown out the clothes, she told him she was going away for a few days and left.

Later on came the night when, with no warning, she didn't come home to sleep. Instinct told us *not* to call the police, that she was out somewhere of her own free will. Instead, my dad called the consulate to obtain the details about Vanessa de Michele, who, although her surname sounded Italian, was a Chilean who lived in New York and worked in the movies. The name was totally unfamiliar to me. I insisted to my father that I had the right to know who my mom was spending time with. He finally told me that she was a Chilean who had lived in New York for many years and they'd met at an embassy dinner. My mother had remarked to him that she had found her soul mate. Sometimes they went out together and my mother accompanied Michele when she was filming. Now and then my mother slept at her house. I suspected that my father feared that Vanessa liked women more than men.

Clutching the address provided by the consulate, he set off for the Village, only to learn that Vanessa had moved. My mother returned the following day as if nothing had happened.

My father decided to take her to the doctor. She stubbornly refused: It's this city's fault, darling. I'm not sick in the head. It's just that you can let yourself go in New York. It's a dangerous place.

Let yourself go, that was precisely the phrase. And that was what she did. Sometimes she didn't wash. I began to keep track of how often she washed her hair. Then she stopped washing her clothes. She piled what was dirty on a chair in her room and wore what was clean. When she ran out, she rummaged through the heap on the chair. Of course, I ended up taking them all to be washed but when she saw me coming back with clean clothes, she didn't care at all. I was concerned about her underwear and bras. I think that was the hardest thing to bear, seeing her with dirty underwear. The sides of the bras ended up showing the same sweat stains that could be seen around the collars of her blouses. Sometimes my dad put her in the shower and rinsed her, hair and all. I never did. I wasn't in the habit of seeing her naked and she probably wouldn't have wanted me to start under those circumstances. I watched all this with a mixture of incredulity and fury. I simply didn't understand what the hell was going through her mind. My mom had been swapped but this new version was no better than the old one. When my father used to lean on me a great deal, I reminded him that *he'd* married her, not me, that she was *his* problem. I defended myself, refusing to face the fact that *this* was my mother. She shut herself away in a cave of isolation, her feelings as dirty as her fingernails and underwear.

I missed Nicolás so, so much! Despite the jealousy he caused me in life, I never stopped adoring him. It was as if two different personalities flowed from him: one, my mother's son who made me suffer in spite of himself, and the other, my concerned and loving older brother. His absence ached through my entire body. I struggled to understand life without him, but I cried for him silently, so as not to cause my parents more grief. Yes, I cried for him every day of that time in New York.

The hardest part of my mother's deterioration was when she began to lose all sense of shame. I couldn't stand entering her room and seeing her naked, wearing only her pajama top, sitting with her legs open. I was sixteen. I was a virgin and my entire upbringing had been so, so chaste. She only got dressed to go out. Where are you off to, Mom? For a walk, she would reply and slam the door. My knowledge of life was so confined, I was so young, that I couldn't imagine the situation reverting to normal. Today I think quite angrily about my dad. Why the hell didn't he grab her grubby locks and drag her to a psychiatrist? Why didn't he scour the city for a solution?

The truth is, my dad missed many of these episodes due to his job, and because of his wonderful capacity for denial. I left for my English classes and when they finished I walked and walked, I went into stores, museums, a bookstore, anything so as not to have to go home. Without meaning to, I began to cultivate a series of interests that until then had been unknown. Architecture, for example. On my strolls, contemplating and analyzing buildings became my greatest passion, along with painting. Before New York and MoMA, painting didn't interest me in the slightest. I also read a lot since I could spend hours in Barnes & Noble with a book in my hand without anyone throwing me out. I found the Metropolitan Museum a fascinating way to consolidate my knowledge of history. In short, I was coming close to being a near-perfect woman, all because of my mother. I looked so normal, so annoyingly normal. No one would say I had a crazy mom and a dead brother.

Without saying as much, my father was grateful that I didn't cause him problems. His education had never been particularly comprehensive, he knew numbers but not much else, and he was delighted at my *making the most* of the city. He had a conventional notion of culture. He thought that going to the theater or ballet and keeping up-to-date with the movie listings made you *cultured*. I, on the other hand, learned to believe in the depth of experience: returning ten times to the art gallery near my house to look at that Kandinsky again because I identified with its shapes, on a deep level, in my soul. I didn't care at all whether it was fashionable and I didn't attend the concerts my father timidly suggested. For me music worked better in the solitude of my room than it did live. I learned to hate the theater—and to say so, which is scandalous to some people, as far as I can tell—and to love musicals. I would buy matinee tickets on sale in Times Square for less than half the normal price. I accumulated hours and hours of musicals in my body. With a nonexistent mother and a dad immersed in the world of Wall Street, the city was my refuge.

Unfortunately, just when I began to take an interest in literature, my mom stopped reading. Why don't you read anymore, Mom? What do you mean I don't read, it's all I do at night. She was lying. There were no books on her nightstand, like there were in the house in Santiago. What about those difficult Hungarians you liked, Mom, don't you read them anymore? No, I've read them all.

* * *

Of course, the day came when my dad begged the people at his firm to release him from New York. We went home. I was happy. I was returning to my environment, my high school, my friends, to feeling that there were solid things in my life apart from my parents. My mother resumed—for a while—her previous life and my dad thought that New York really was a dangerous city and that Chile suited her better. But that wasn't the case. Something had come undone inside her and there was no going back, although we didn't realize it then. Several months passed in relative normality as I was turning into a woman with few role models. I invented my personality as I went along and waited eagerly to start college and study architecture. A certain episode from those days particularly sticks out in my memory. My mom was spending the weekend with her sister-in-law, in the country. I had promised to arrive on that Sunday, have lunch with the family, and return to Santiago with her. I was swamped by an essay I had to hand in the next morning and I was running late. At two in the afternoon, feeling guilty, I called my aunt to notify them of my delay. I asked her to pass me to my mom, which she tried to do. Down the line, I could hear her: Francisca who? I don't know any Francisca!

For me that signals a strange new indifference toward the lack of affection from my mom. I didn't care anymore. What a poor thing I was, what naivety, as if you ever stop caring. I wasn't particularly keen on dating, perhaps I cultivated something of an unconscious shyness, but it appealed to me less than it did to my companions. I was a bit colder. I wasn't a natural at sweet-talking. Or perhaps it was much simpler than that. I loved men and could have been a flirt but such was my insecurity, my fear of not being loved, that I stepped back and used distance and frigidity to protect myself.

One Sunday during a long weekend I'd gone to the beach with my friend. I'll never forget returning home that night. My dad was in the living room, alone, sitting on the large couch facing the terrace, with the lights off. I knew it right away: something had happened to my mom. My poor father, he told me we had to talk. Faced with such a statement, I fixed us drinks, a whiskey for him, a Coke for me, and I sat expectantly in front of the sofa, on the corner of a fussy, unstable chair that no one used.

She left.

Those were his first words.

He didn't want to show me the farewell letter. He had his reasons. But she was returning to New York, she didn't know whether she would stay there or carry on to Europe, but she wouldn't be coming back to Chile. She asked that we didn't try to find her.

Did she say goodbye to me in the letter? I asked.

Yes, my dad replied, though I knew intuitively that it was a white lie.

I never saw her again. Not in person, at least. Perhaps that's why I talk about her in the past tense. I had to face that ancestral terror of losing a mother, or rather, of losing my sense of identity. What that meant for me was fairly predictable. Not only was I impossible to love but my own mother fled from me in order to make a life for herself. That, and the terror of turning into her, now that she had disappeared. Even back then I contemplated a subject that later on would become crucial: my own motherhood. I feared, in a very abstract, undefined way, transferring to my own children my hatred of my mother. The fear of repeating my experiences and becoming a mother just like my own.

As I was finishing college, I met Vicente. As I've already mentioned, he was a construction engineer and worked in an office where I was doing work-study. I immediately found him attractive, seductive, and difficult. As children, his siblings called him "Button Face," because all his facial features are concentrated in the center. But even so, he has his charm. I love his thick, shiny black hair, a bush of hair made for my fingers. Freshly combed, it has something of a gangster look, which I love, not to mention the fact that he'll never go bald. He's a bit arrogant, a bit self-centered, slightly evasive, but deep in his eyes I recognized a kindness similar to that of my father. He was the typical macho man who amasses all his hardness in what is visible, reserving his tenderness for intimacy. Very shy and socially inept, he used me as his armor against the outside world, and day and night I felt like I was being thrown to the lions. I don't know why I'm talking in the past tense. He still does it today. But the important thing is that he loved me. Despite turning out to be a bit elusive, as if he were always about to escape, he loved me and still does. In my mind, I wasn't worthy of affection. If the blood of my blood needed to flee from me, why would someone else love me? And yet, it happened. Vicente loved me.

We married as soon as I got my degree. It was the best way to escape. I clung to Vicente like a snail. He loved me, he loved me, my being was worthy of some love. Even now. I'm a good wife. I know how to do so many things that, in spite of myself, I turned out to be a good catch. I get up early, I work, I earn money—Vicente loves that because he's a little bit mean. I look after my daughters whom I adore and to whom I devote all the warmth I have—if I have any—so that they don't go through what I did. I have ended up following the opposite trajectory of my mother. For example, I can't remember my mom cooking. However hard I try to conjure up an image of her doing something in the kitchen, I just can't. That's why it's my favorite space. I have a large table there and a good part of family life takes place around it. I love whiling away the time there, doing laborious things, like the cherries. Both my cat and Vicente are fascinated by cherries. But both have refined palates. They like eating them pitted, cut in half, empty in the middle. During the summer when they're in season, I spend long periods in the kitchen with a small knife I bought for this very purpose. Once my finger is red and wrinkled, I divide the cherries in two and serve each of them their portion.

At times I think I made a mistake by demonstrating how energetic and efficient I am. It's impossible for them not to take advantage of me. On the days when I wake up feeling far from charitable, I see my husband as a cannibal. He feeds off my vitality, like a vampire. Sometimes, when I'm alone, I lower my guard and collapse in exhaustion. I've injected Vicente and the girls with so much enthusiasm that there isn't a drop left for me.

I always thought I would have boys. I considered them significantly easier. With any luck, I would have been able to achieve something similar to Nicolás. With boys I would have been less likely to replicate my mother's behavior toward me. However, I had girls, three girls. Because of them, I made huge efforts to dredge up more recollections of my childhood and adolescence—a time when I was only concerned with myself—to try to understand my mother. Efforts in vain. I always came to the same conclusion: my mom is a monster. I came to adore these extremist views because they gave me clarity, a line to follow, all black and white. But perhaps my daughters think the same of me. I go to great lengths to be a good mother. I'm constantly revising my attitudes, which detracts from the spontaneity, and I will be judged for it in the future, there's no doubt. You always do badly as a mother, if not because of this, then because of that. The guilt will always be there, no matter what.

My father returned to New York. At sixty-five, he looks more like fifty and he can't retire. He married again and to all appearances he's satisfied with his new life. I suppose it's unnecessary to add that his new wife is twenty years younger than him. The last time I went to see him, a few months ago, he had news for me. (Thank God, Vicente couldn't get time off work and I went alone.) Vanessa de Michele, my mother's old friend, had contacted him. She was living in Connecticut and told my dad that she had news of his ex-wife. My father didn't want to hear about it, he just handed me her telephone number.

I called Vanessa and she invited me to her house.

I entered the courtyard of a small building, an old house converted into seven minuscule but delightful apartments. I found a woman sitting on the only stone bench, a red watering can resting at her feet.

She was surrounded by geraniums and creepers, with the radiant white of the house behind her, and even though we were in the heart of the United States it was a very Mediterranean image. She stood up when she saw me and automatically picked up the watering can. She was of medium build but, for some reason, she gave the impression of being a tall woman. Her brown hair was short, you could see the hand of a skilled hairdresser behind it, and in the lock that fell to the right of her face flashes of blond glinted. Her appearance was truly eccentric, to say the least. She was wearing a pale blue nightgown with very faint, tiny, green flowers, a small piece of lace on the bodice and long sleeves rolled to the elbow. Over the gown she wore an apron tied at the back, the kind tinsmiths or leather-workers wear, a masculine apron, black, and with an enormous pocket at the front. Her body was plump and splendid, well built, and I reckoned she was in her late fifties. She was wearing frameless glasses and her eyes—the same color as her hair—were large and expressive. Her mouth seemed small but it enlarged incomprehensibly when it started moving. Her smile was radiant, it completely changed the severity of her appearance, and from her wrinkles I could only assume that she had enjoyed life.

She was the messenger of horror.

Inside the house and holding a coffee, she led me to a darkened room, switched on a projector—it wasn't a DVD player, this was a movie in the true sense—and that typical noise of the movie theaters of my childhood began, as that certain amount of white film spooled across the screen before the subject of the filming appeared. The first image to appear was a grand avenue in New York, it could have been Broadway or Fifth. Pedestrians on the sidewalks, cars on the street, a couple of kids playing, a very tall black vendor with a puny table and something colorful laid out on a cloth, hankies or scarves. Suddenly, a homeless woman standing near a magazine kiosk. The camera zooms in and rests on her: a very thickset figure dressed in black rags, her pants seemed to have been salvaged from an old man's tracksuit and although it was a sunny day, almost summery, she was wrapped up, covered with several vests, some shorter than others, which accentuated her corpulence. Her hair—between white and brown—had turned into thousands of long, tight, unwashed curls shooting out around her head. Rasta, my daughters would say. Her face—which could barely be discerned—was also dark. Everything was dark, even her feet, which were bare. The gaze was unmistakable. The eyes required no close-up to perceive the infinite indifference in them. She begins to lower her pants. She squats and the camera draws in and focuses on an enormous backside, as if thousands of oranges were hiding beneath the skin. My mother urinates in complete tranquility. The image isn't entirely in profile, more like three-quarters to the side. She finishes peeing, she pulls up her black pants as she stands, and begins to walk away as if nothing had happened.

I asked Vanessa to stop the movie. She said: You have to learn, Francisca, that not everyone wants to be saved. I left right away. Why did she do it? What made her show me that movie? Even today I don't know. I cut short my visit to my father and returned to Santiago. I never mentioned what I had seen, not to Vicente, not to anyone. Should I have stayed in New York and tried to contact her? Should I have tried to *save her*? The only sure thing in my life was that I was the most miserable of God's creatures. More miserable than my mother.

Back in Santiago, I walked stealthily along the street, ever alert, ever vigilant, like someone allowing herself the whim of staying silent, of pretending. I behaved like someone who, after the storm, is still sodden, never drying off, who cares for her misery as though it's her only responsibility. Perhaps recognizing the damage my mom has done to herself could signal the beginning of my own cure.

My mind and my moods began to take a hundred and eighty degree turn. On any given night I would stay awake and, without waking Vicente, tiptoe to the desk, turn on my computer, and go to lanchile. com to check offers on flights to New York. I don't know how many reservations I've made so far. But by the light of day, from my office,

I cancel them. I put on CNN and wait just to find out the temperature in New York. The only daily newspaper I read online is the *New York Times*, always expecting to see something related to her. I imagine her in the worst scenarios, the kind that merit a news item, like, for example, that she has set herself on fire in the middle of Fifth Avenue. Or that she has thrown herself from the top of the Empire State Building.

At night, after that dreadful trip to New York, I dreamed, I dreamed at length about that horrible fat rump. I would wake and lock myself in the bathroom to cry in peace. My tears obeyed contradictory rationales, depending on the day. Sometimes I cried because I felt like the most despicable woman in the world for allowing my mother to be a vagabond and not lifting a finger to rescue her. Other nights I cried from rage, from pure hatred, and I couldn't rid myself of it. Hatred is like blood, it's impossible to conceal and it stains everything.

Anyone who thinks that the loss of Nicolás was the reason for this whole story is mistaken. That pain only brought forward something that, sooner or later, with or without the death of her son, would have happened anyway.

Several years have passed since my mother left. I have matured. It would be presumptuous of me to say that I've gotten over it. You don't get over something like this. But I can live with it now. It's no longer destroying me. The fact that sometimes I get cold, sometimes I become paralyzed, sometimes I turn into a distant object devoid of compassion, all seems irrelevant. Because I have done the only important thing I could do. I broke the line of inheritance, I broke the repetition. My daughters are saved.

I carry on with my normal life, with my normal appearance, with my normal family. With my cat, with Vicente.

MANÉ

*M*y name is Mané and I'm just as you see me. I was always the prettiest. I'm five foot eight and a half, which is tall for this country, and I weigh a hundred and thirty pounds. Even today, in spite of my age, I still keep an eye on my weight, although I'm the only one to see my body. I turned seventy-five a couple months ago. There was barely a celebration.

I used to be gorgeous. It's a shame I have to say it in the past tense. No one says "I am gorgeous" and even less "I will be gorgeous." Well, that's all I've got: the past. *Sunset Boulevard*, a movie from the fifties, reminds me of my life. That must be why I find it so moving. Starring Gloria Swanson, it's based on the life of Norma Desmond, a great Hollywood silent-movie actress who starred in dozens of movies, a true diva who had the world at her feet. By the time she'd aged, she wanted to return to acting and seduction but everyone had abandoned her. All the directors and producers who once sang her praises turned their backs on her. She was no use to them anymore, but this was something she refused to accept. They didn't even answer her phone calls. She was rotting, alone and abandoned. Like me.

Ever since I was a little girl I enjoyed dressing up and dancing in front of the mirror. When my parents went out, I tiptoed to my mom's built-in armoire—there were no closets in my house—and pinched her shawls and headscarves. She didn't have many, but I still tried them on every which way, around the waist, on my head, around my ankles. My mom was a seamstress and my dad a construction fore-man, so don't go imagining that those fabrics I played with were des-tined for the Aga Khan's family. The important thing is that I really believed I was Rita Hayworth and my imagination transformed the cheap poplin scraps from the dresses my mom made into oriental silks. Women in those days didn't study, they didn't have the appeal-ing lives they do now. I know it happened in other environments, at other latitudes, but not mine. I was born in the thirties, a great time for women in Europe, the interwar period. Their skirts were shorter, they drank and smoked, they got involved in politics, they breathed deeply as if the world was about to end. *They* did, not provincial girls like me. In Quillota, where I was born, women devoted themselves to the home and only did small paid chores to help with domestic finances. What we did have, though, was education.

In high school, when we put on plays, I always stood out. I liked taking on all the parts, male or female, young or old. When I took to the stage, I forgot all about rural life, which I found asphyxiating. I also won the few beauty pageants there were. I was Quillota Beauty Queen and Miss Quilpué. The principal of the high school was my ally; she noticed that I had the natural disposition to become some-thing more dynamic than a housewife. She was a very perceptive woman, a friend of Amanda Labarca and the suffragettes, all those gutsy old gals to whom we owe so much. So, she sorted out things with my family so I could go to Santiago and study theater under the tutelage of a great director of the period. I lived in an aunt's house and my life changed. Santiago was a lively, fun city, nothing like the drag it is today. It was a pleasure to live here. There were very few cars, lots of trees, mansions in the center, bohemia, theaters, printing houses, poets. The occasional murder reminded us that we were human. I walked alone at night along Calle Brasil, completely unconcerned.

Life back then was very austere. Chile was a poor country, imported goods didn't exist, from jeans to bottles of whiskey, nothing, we were like a socialist state in Eastern Europe. I remember the first time my company traveled out of the country, we went to Cochabamba, in Bolivia. I saw a candy stall at the side of the road and I walked over, thinking about our Ambrosoli and our Serrano or Calaf, the only candy we had in Chile, and to my surprise, there were gums of all flavors and colors, little yellow balls, red hearts, small green triangles, wrappers with English lettering, chocolate bars that looked like Christmas gifts and disposable lighters so magical they seemed unreal. I was left openmouthed. This was my first encounter with what we would come to call globalization. The other day I was at my sister-in-law's house with one of her granddaughters, who wanted to stick some monkeys into a scrapbook but didn't have anything to do it with. I suggested we make wheat paste. She looked at me as if I'd spoken in Aramaic. She didn't know what wheat paste is! I explained how we used to make it with flour and water to stick things down. She replied, Why bother when we can buy glue or a Pritt Stick? That was the Chile I lived in. You thanked your lucky stars if you had enough for a simple radio.

You met all the arty types in the theater world. I frequently bumped into Neruda and de Rokha, and it was the most natural thing in the world if you went to Bosco for a drink in the early hours, or if you had dinner in one of the nearby nightclubs.

One of the regulars at Bosco was a poet with fair hair who had a crafty look, as you might call it. He never fully opened his left eye, and his teeth—although they were starting to yellow from tobacco—were small and perfect. He was always holding a cigarette and I loved looking at his hands, which moved constantly back and forth to his mouth. I asked to be introduced to him. When he stood up to give me his hand I noticed that he was very tall and I liked that immediately. I gave him a look. I began to reject other bars and only went to Bosco because that was where he went. One day I sat down very decidedly at his table, he was scrawling words on a napkin. I remained silent by his side, as muses ought to. When he finished writing, he raised his eyes and read his poem out loud. I thought it was beautiful and

I told him so. He smiled gratefully at me. You're a sweet woman, he told me. I replied, You catch more flies with honey. He laughed. He offered me a beer. The following day I arrived at the same time and sat at the same table as if we had arranged it. Five days passed like that. On the fifth, as I was getting up to leave, he rose with me and walked me along the Alameda. We were about to cross that wide avenue when, out of the blue, he took me by the waist and planted a kiss on my mouth.

I really liked that kiss.

That was Rucio.

I think I fell in love with him because he was taller than me and we looked so good together. We got married after six months. It was almost ridiculous to marry in that environment and at that time but I did it for my family. How else would my poor parents be able to face the family in Quillota if I couldn't show the marriage license? Rucio—meaning blond, that's what everyone called him, unaccustomed as they were in the Chile of that era to seeing a head of hair that wasn't a black helmet—had talent. He composed dozens of poems for me, all of them so lovely, and the only book he managed to publish took my name as the title. Everyone thought it the most natural thing in the world for him to devote himself to praising my beauty, and it didn't surprise me either. I laughed at his craziness. Meanwhile, I was still acting, and things were getting better every day. I was only offered parts for beautiful young women. To make the most of your good looks, Rucio said. Don't you think it might be because I'm not good enough? I asked him. Because despite everything, I was always insecure, like all women. Some of my friends would say to me, You, insecure, when you're that beautiful? I would reply, The one has nothing to do with the other.

Rucio wasn't interested in having children. I, idiot that I am, listened to him. It angers me to see the expression on women's faces when they hear me say I didn't have children because I didn't want to. How dare I challenge the laws of nature, they said without saying as much.

I challenged them because at that time I didn't really mind, because Rucio and the theater were enough, because I lived in the moment and I thought the good fortune would last forever. Nowadays, I regret that, sometimes. Those women who fill their lives with children, planning out their future, they scare me, but let's not beat around the bush. At my age, having or not having children makes all the difference. Back then, art was the only thing that mattered. Rucio wrote and I acted.

We had such a great time! We had so many friends, the nights lasted forever, no one got up early, no one had a normal job, so to speak. On Sundays, we stayed in bed late playing "cute games," as Rucio used to call them. We barely saw the sunlight. It makes me laugh the way younger generations venerate life in the open air. Complete myth! You aren't born and you don't die in the open air, everything important happens indoors.

I came too early for TV. I would have been a hit in the soaps. But by then I had already been cast aside. Because the years were passing. For Rucio too, he couldn't find a publisher and he became frustrated and drank. No one wanted to publish poetry, because it didn't sell. Neruda's success really pissed off his contemporaries, although Rucio was quite a bit younger. But he still loved me, he never had the desire to free himself of me, he cared for me like a little puppy. I remember at that time a virus—or whatever it was—came to Santiago which they called "horse fever." I don't know what it had to do with horses, but I caught it. It was like dying for a few days. Bad flu felt like a tiny scratch compared to this. Rucio didn't leave me alone for a second, he administered my medicines, he made me nourishing soups that I could swallow, he changed the sheets for me when they were soaked with sweat. My memory of that famous fever—the only time I fell ill by his side—is like walking right onto the set of *The Lady of the Camellias*. I, as Marguerite Gautier, allowed myself the luxury of going through my death throes with a man kneeling at my feet, loving me and caring for me.

* * *

My first crow's feet appeared and my eyes had less shine. The work began to thin out. When I didn't have to go to the theater, I stayed in at night with Rucio and his friends, drinking. We lived hand to mouth. We never had much and we made do. But the money was running out. We couldn't make the rent. A friend gave us a loan, which I paid back when I landed a good role. But no matter what, we always scraped up enough for the drink. We were ten cents short of a dollar, and I mean it in both senses, literally and not so literally. Rucio wasn't such a great poet and I wasn't such a great actress.

Finally, the director of the University of Chile Theater decided to bet on my talent, not on my beauty. I was given the part of Blanche in *A Streetcar Named Desire*. I was just at that age when you're no longer young but going out of your way not to show it. Blanche's part is one all good actresses aspire to play. It's a very difficult role. Vivien Leigh did it in the movies, opposite Marlon Brando, remember? It must have been one of Brando's first movies, such, such a good-looking fool, every muscle showing through those tight, sweaty shirts. Women were crazy for him, he had the look of a bad boy. Anyway, let's get back to Blanche, straight off the streetcar. I rehearsed with the fervor you apply to something that you know you're going to lose, like the last few lays of an old man waiting for impotence to strike. I was so bored with—and slightly humiliated by—my recent appearances onstage. Blanche would give me the prestige I never had and no one would have the bad grace to say that I was given my roles for purely aesthetic reasons. I arrived home at night exhausted, having left my soul at the rehearsal. I barely saw Rucio. I couldn't join him on his drunken sprees anymore and I fell asleep the minute I saw my bed. But he didn't complain because he was so proud of me. I remember that time as one that was very precious, energetic.

It was then that I experienced the "full moon effect." That's what I called it. I felt as if I were a large moon, gradually growing and growing, night by night, to reach that complete state, fully luminous, where nothing is too much or too little. I sensed that when this equilibrium ended, I would begin to decrease, to shrink bit by bit until I almost disappeared. In every life there's a full moon. As long as you can recognize it, at least, you can enjoy it and feel crystal clear and complete.

We organized a big party for opening night. I hadn't allowed Rucio to attend the rehearsals. I wanted to surprise him as Blanche arriving in New Orleans, with my dress, hat, and everything. The truth is, although it doesn't sound very modest, I acted wonderfully. The applause brought down the theater and as I waved and received a bunch of roses, I searched in vain for Rucio's face. I imagined the newspaper critics and the headlines, nonsense like: "True talent finally revealed!"; "Rebirth of an actress."

When the play finished and I went to the dressing room, almost faint with emotion, it wasn't Rucio waiting for me but Pancho, his best friend. The expression on his face should have warned me but I was so full of triumph that I didn't see it.

Rucio was dead. He'd been run over crossing the Alameda on his way to the theater. A bus struck him and killed him instantly.

I played Blanche on opening night only. They say that the following day I was in a state of shock, I didn't hear anything, I didn't talk, only my open eyes showed that I wasn't asleep. My eyes were nothing but tears, so clear and watery. I remember very little of the funeral, someone recited a poem next to the grave and it was a bad poem, much worse than Rucio's. A couple of actress friends took pity on me, they heated up soup and made sure I drank it. They took turns staying over for the first few days because my nights were strange. I sat up in bed staring at a fixed point with my eyes wide open and I didn't close them for hours. Anything that entered my stomach came right back up again, I vomited ceaselessly, from the bed to the toilet and from the toilet to the bed. That's what those days were like. I couldn't return to the stage, I couldn't remember a single line, as if the play had never existed. That's as far as the rebirth of the great actress went.

How do you think I survived? With the help of three things: drink, men, and the theater. In that order. I drank like a woman condemned, anything, *pisco*, gin, wine. The important thing was getting to sleep, being dead, that's what it was about. I went to Bosco, I didn't have any money to pay, so Rucio's friends offered to buy me drinks. When all is said and done, no one wants to disrespect a dead man. But after the binges, the next day inevitably would arrive. I opened my eyes and before feeling the headache, the furry mouth, and all the effects of the hangover, I remembered that I had been widowed. No, it can't be, it's a bad dream, I would say to myself and try to get back to sleep. Then, to resist it, I would grab the bottle of red wine. I didn't get up for days on end. Why would I? I didn't shower and tried to sleep, with any luck for the whole day. I went to bed with whoever showed up in front of me. We all bear our burden in our own way, there's no doubt about that. Very often I woke up next to men I had never seen before, I couldn't remember a thing. Some of them were theater folks and managed to get me some little part, so I could eat, no more than that. No one trusted me enough to give me anything important. I took those parts, despite having been Blanche, just to make a few bucks.

It didn't take long before I had to leave the apartment we'd rented in Calle Merced. I couldn't pay for it. Leaving was like saying goodbye to Rucio all over again. I had come to hate Blanche; if it weren't for her, Rucio would be alive, I repeated to myself over and over. Since I didn't have money for an apartment of my own I started looking for a room. I found one in a building on Calle Londres and I moved in with my few items of clothing. At least it had a nice view, it's a very pretty street, down there, in the center of town. But it was freezing, colder than a polar bear's toes. I carried on bringing men to my bed and ended up catching a really nasty infection. The pitcher that goes too often to the well breaks at last. Charo, Rucio's sister, called my parents. When I met her, on my wedding day, she seemed like a conventional person and too cautious for my taste. She wore twinsets and pearls, although they were fake. Not a hair on her head moved. Perhaps that's why I was reluctant to approach her. She always gave me the impression of someone who, for better or worse, was in possession of herself, she owned her own mind. When I was widowed, she must have decided to intervene and take charge of me. My only brother lived in Punta Arenas and was distant and unfamiliar to me, so Charo became my family. She's a good woman, a nurse, hardworking, serious and diligent. She works extreme shifts at the hospital, and you can never tell when she hasn't slept. Her children are my only contact with the younger generations. If it weren't for them I would understand very little of how things are nowadays.

My parents arrived in Santiago, neat and healthy. They both smelled so good. They dragged me out of Calle Londres and took me to Quillota. They put me to bed, *my* bed, which hadn't changed since I was a child. Everything was the same, the hall, the big kitchen, the sense of decency. They looked after me. In the family home I began to recuperate. I stopped drinking, ate properly, and recovered from my infection. But the only job for me in Quillota was working at an uncle's store. I hadn't been an actress to finish up weighing out sugar. The provinces are fatal in a centralized country. It's where there's always something lacking, where everyone and everything is always the same. In the capital you might marry again, my mom suggested hopefully, you're still so pretty. I felt bad saying goodbye to her, so innocent, so modest in her shirtdress, with her clean smell, so far removed from my dark and desperate sides.

I returned to Santiago and my old circles. My dad had given me some of his savings so I could rent a very small apartment. The size didn't matter, my only dream was to have my own bathroom. In the house in Quillota there was only ever one bathroom for the whole family, and although it was always gleaming, I never dared to enter into that state of deep and sensual idleness that a hot bath or a full-length mirror can inspire. So began my years on Calle Vicuña Mackenna. I measure periods of time according to which street I lived on, and the first few were difficult. As long as I insisted on being an actress, I encountered nothing but humiliation. I experienced what it means for a friend to turn you down on the telephone, just like poor Norma Desmond. Men who had begged for my body a few years before now looked through me as if I were invisible, as if I didn't exist. I begged for a small role, as if treading the boards would solve everything. We don't have any parts for someone your age, that was the phrase I heard most during that time. I dyed my hair, I changed my wardrobe, I made myself up like a young woman, but it was no use. Illusion is more dangerous than a monkey brandishing a knife. With all of this as a backdrop, I kept turning over that illusion my mother had mentioned: remarriage. A man wouldn't solve everything but it would help. There were indeed a couple of candidates, although they had me for bed, not for the home. However, when we met at parties or in the theater, they appeared with their wives. The spouses are here, I would say, annoyed, how I hate the spouses!

A husband is a place. A solid place. One of purity. I needed a place of calm.

One night my sister-in-law came to my apartment. She took me out to eat at the nicest restaurant and said, That's enough, Mané, the theater's over, period. There are no movies in our country and TV has only recently started. They're looking for promising young women or character actresses and you are neither. Why not teach acting to others? There's a good academy where a couple of my friends work, I can introduce you. You'd have a permanent income, you'd pay taxes, you could even have a pension.

I listened to her because I had no alternative. I told myself, You have to cut your coat according to your cloth, Mané.

So I taught at the academy. I was a good teacher, I paid taxes—like my sister-in-law told me to—and today I live off my pension. When my parents died we sold the house in Quillota. I shared the proceeds with that stranger-like brother of mine. I put it together with the little bit of money Rucio's parents left me and felt like a queen. I bought my first and only property, a tiny apartment on Calle Santo Domingo, very cute; it has electricity and it's mine. I don't know how many square meters I'm living in, it can't be more than fifty, but it's enough for a small living room, a bedroom, a kitchen like a doll's house, and a *private* bathroom. What more could I want? Sometimes I think that a balcony, even just a small one, would have made me very happy, but it doesn't matter. My expenses are very, very controlled and I breathe easy, I won't die a beggar now, without so much as a dog to bark for me. What's more, it was during that period—the period of serenity, as I call it—that I understood that life had given me an enormous gift. I had been loved, and I, in turn, had loved.

To love and be loved, as the years and my eyes have confirmed, is rare. Many people take it as a given, they believe it's a common currency, that everyone, in some way or another, has experienced it. I venture to claim that it doesn't work that way. I see it as an enormous gift. There are so many people who never know it, it isn't some asset you find on every corner. It's as though you've won the lottery. You become a millionaire. Even if the money runs out, can anyone take away your experience? Can anyone accuse you of having had a run-of-the-mill life? Nothing is run-of-the-mill if you've been a millionaire. Love is a bit like that. Although my Rucio died, although I'll be alone until the end of my days, it doesn't matter, I was transformed by what I felt, that was unshakeable. When I came to understand that, my anxiety disappeared, along with all of its companion habits.

Being old is always feeling tired. It's waking up tired, it's going around all day tired, and it's going to bed tired.

Every morning, when I wake up, I remember who I am and I have to begin to make friends with myself. I wonder why I have been allowed another day of life. Should I be grateful for it? My sister-in-law says that I'm still moving with ease, that only bodies that were once beautiful move that way. It could be true, perhaps she's right, but that beauty, which no longer exists, becomes even more painful.

That's perhaps the worst part: the physical deterioration. The warning sign is the neck. When it begins to move of its own accord, to hang, when you have proper strands of skin extending from one ear to the other, then you no longer have that beauty. It's leaving, it's off. You still see your internal self as young and the fact is that you aren't and the neck is the first thing to give you away. The second giveaway is the lips. They begin to recede, to withdraw, like a couple of defeated animals, and you ask yourself, Who fought with them? Mine have turned into a line, and to think that I had attractive plump lips. They used to kill Rucio. Yes, I know there's Botox nowadays but, come on, you're not going to tell me it looks natural, they look like fish with those protuberant mouths. Old age is measured by the percentage of the body that bears scrutiny. When you want to cover up yourself completely, you're screwed. I remember when I said—about being naked in front of a man—that I would cover my belly but show my tits. When the tits began to droop, I decided that I would only show my legs. Later on I wanted to cover my legs and leave only my arms visible. One day I covered my arms. Done. You don't want to reveal a single part. Then you're old, and there's no point in looking for someone to blame.

Let's talk about deterioration. You're on a bus and you want to look at something that's already behind you. You turn your neck but it's stiff and the muscles are so beat that you can hardly see over your shoulder. I'm talking about getting out of a chair. The body propels itself to stand up, an unconscious, automatic impulse that younger people make several times a day without realizing. I struggle to do it. A deep armchair can be a source of great humiliation; once you sit in it you can't get out. I'm talking about bending down to reach a slipper that's under the bed and not managing. I'm talking about stiff, painful joints. I'm talking about swollen muscles. About seized-up legs, not to mention all of the dark veins appearing on the skin all over my legs. Until I hit my fifties I didn't have a single one. You don't know what happened or when it happened. One morning your legs don't seem to respond like before. I'm talking about never sleeping through the night. I fall asleep early. I can't fight the drowsiness at ten o'clock but by two in the morning my eyes are wide as saucers and I know what's waiting for me in the dark: memories and obsessions.

I don't switch on the light for fear of revealing myself but I reveal myself all the same. I manage to doze off at around five but I wake to go to the bathroom because my bladder can't hold much anymore. An old friend of mine, a famous actress in her day, uses diapers. She smells bad. When I see her I think I'd rather die first. It's so easy to say you want to die but as the years go by you grab hold of each day and you don't let them go for anything. The body has to empty itself of liquids and solids, and sphincters put up with less and less. Today I say "better dead than using diapers" but when the time comes I'll be willing and I'll want to stay alive. What for, I don't know. Why stay alive? Rucio's mom was unable to walk when she died; she broke a hip and never got up again. It was a burden for everyone and her life was junk but there she was, gripping onto it because it was the only thing she had. Any life, bad as it may be, is better than nothing. Better than terror and that frozen fear of death. It's strange that the only certainty life gives us is one we fear so much.

The eyes. I use three different pairs of glasses. For reading, to see in the distance, and to see close up. I mix them up, I lose them, I pick up a pair to read the newspaper and they're the wrong ones, and I go around my fifty square meters twenty times looking for my reading glasses but they don't turn up. In the end they were hanging around my neck. So often, when I'm walking along the street, I can only find the pair that doesn't help me see in the distance. Half of my clumsiness is a result of this. The eyes cease to be part of the face, they're always filtered through glasses, and mine were so beautiful. I can no longer wear makeup, much as I'd like to. I can't really see the contours properly and I'd end up looking like a bad mime. Then there's the problem of teeth. A good dentist is priceless. So you go to a bad one. There's something new every day that you can't eat. I no longer have the teeth for meat, I have very few molars left and one of my front teeth is false. My gums bleed. Very hot or cold things hurt. I should have things done but I can't afford them, so, instead of root canal treatment, I get the molar extracted and that's it. It costs too much money to save the tooth. Sometimes my whole mouth hurts and if I laugh a certain way you can see everything I'm missing.

Old age is laughing less too.

Not to mention the medicine! I take nine pills every day, each for something different—blood pressure, cholesterol, blood sugar, tranquilizer. Need I go on? I look completely normal, but I take nine pills a day for that. My nightstand is shameful, little plastic bottles everywhere. When there are no generic drugs at the pharmacy, I start to panic. I can't pay for the brands.

While I'm on the subject of deterioration I realize that I should mention money. They say that the elderly become miserly. Isn't it more that there are fewer pesos and that's frightening?

A tiny, tiny percentage of people my age live comfortably. I've already told you about my meager pension, which I get from the INP. If I'd gone for the private provision Pinochet invented I'd be begging for money on the street. Artists have never been characterized by their foresight or for thinking about the future; it's perhaps the professional sector that lives most insistently in the present. There are very few who earn money from their art, so no one saves, you live day by day. We read in the paper that such and such a writer or musician has died and always in the most despicable poverty. In other words, if my sister-in-law hadn't forced me to get my act together I don't know what would have become of me. Although I'm no beggar, I can't allow myself any luxuries. That's where the word *luxury* starts to blur. Is it a luxury to have root canal so as not to lose your teeth? When you hear about new medicines, they're only relevant to those who can afford to order them from another country, something I'm not able to do. Even when they finally arrive in Chile I still can't buy them because of the price. Rich folks don't take the same medicines as the poor. We also can't get depressed, that's another luxury. How could we pay for therapy?

I'm here because half of us pay for Natasha's services while the other half doesn't. That's the way she views her profession: the wealthiest pay for the poorest. I don't know how many of you pay what Natasha's services are really worth, but to those who do, I'm so grateful to you. I fall into the category of her pro bono work, a concept she herself taught me.

The other day on TV, a woman was saying how her antidepressants cost sixty thousand pesos for thirty pills. Two bucks a pill. I can feed myself for two months with sixty thousand pesos. Poor women are given an aspirin when they go to see public doctors, trying to explain their symptoms of depression. Strange country, this: according to the statistics, everyone gets depressed, and it's not like we live in Iceland. But those who have money are cured of their depression, the rest aren't. A girl I know, daughter of a television actor, is bipolar. Well, that's not saying much, everyone in the world is bipolar these days, it's become fashionable. But this girl, between psychiatrists, psychologists, and medication, so her father told me, spends several times a minimum wage. What does that same woman who was given aspirin in the doctor's office do if her daughter is bipolar? Nothing, the kid commits suicide. We come back to the same thing: therapy and its medications are a luxury.

Let's identify the luxuries that merit the word, the genuine ones: cosmetic surgery, weight-loss massage, super health foods, trips to the United States to treat difficult cancers, beach houses, bespoke clothing. The thing about food is comical. The healthier it is, the more it costs. A raw Easter Island tuna steak, like they use in Japanese food, pure protein, you know how much it costs per kilo? It's the same as eleven or twelve packets of lentils. A kilo of beef fillet is ten kilos of bread as well as the mortadella to go with it. It goes on and on like that.

So, you have neither money for your health, nor for entertainment, nor leisure. Books are very expensive. I only read if someone lends me one. I get invited to the theater sometimes, but I don't go to the movies anymore, even though I used to love it. A rental is cheaper, but only on days when there's a special discount. I'm condemned to watching whatever's on free television, because I can't afford cable either, and I swallow up those eternal commercials. I know them by heart. I have no car. I never learned to drive. No one had a car in my day—and at my age long bus journeys are too much. Just to go to Quillota, which is nearby, it takes me three and a half hours. So you start to narrow your horizons, not only does everything become complicated and difficult but you start to ask for less and less, aspirations shrink and when the outside world becomes that small, the internal world just goes along with it.

Don't get me started on the weather. When I was young it wasn't an issue, I didn't care what season it was, I dealt with cold and heat without any great bother. Now, like the old English ladies you see in the movies, the weather is everything. I spend the summer months in the city, overheating almost to death, boiling away in my fifty square meters, surrounded by cement. If you don't have friends or children with money, where do you spend the summer at my age? Summer and winter, fall and spring, I see them all through Calle Santo Domingo, with the infernal noise of the buses pounding in my ears. So much for the brand-new public transport system. On my street the same old yellow buses pass by with the same horrendous racket, the only difference is that they've been painted green and white. It's no better during winter. Don't go thinking that my apartment has central heating. The concept doesn't exist in my building. I have a paraffin stove I take with me wherever I go, to the bedroom or living room. The problem is buying paraffin. I suck up to the super so that he brings me a can and I offer him a piece of cake or something like that because I can't give him a tip. Every year I get stingier with the paraffin, because of the can and because of the price. I switch it off at night, so as not to waste money or poison myself, and I throw all my blankets over the bed because, deep down, I'm always a bit chilly. I won't even tell you about the weight of my bed in winter, with all those blankets as well as the socks and the bed jacket, from which I won't be separated. When the temperature drops below zero, I don't get up. Elderly people are always cold, that's just part of old age. When I see movies with women in short-sleeved nightgowns in the middle of winter, I wonder whether they're lying to us or whether there really is some world where you can spend the winter indoors in short sleeves.

I'm getting too domestic. That's what life comes down to: long sleeves or short sleeves, not great events.

Your sense of time also changes. Everything becomes a sigh, a heartbeat. When we talk about someone I say, Yes, I saw him the other day. They ask me when it was, and I realize that "the other day" was more than a year ago. For me a whole year *is* "the other day." You lose any kind of concrete or true relationship with time, if such a thing exists. Or perhaps it's just related to monotony since when nothing ever happens and you don't expect anything, time is a straight line.

Even the city is flat, uninviting, it folds in on itself. It conceals few surprises. Take the other old women who live downtown. Like me, they are all in decline, poor things, with the same rather threadbare but serviceable overcoat, the same short hair with a bit of a perm, the same black, medium-sized purses—neither very big nor very small—the same slightly worn-down black shoes, marked on the sides by bunions. They all tread with the same lack of security, fearful of tripping and of being who they are. The students are all the same too. They have the same long hair, the hooded sweatshirts, the ripped jeans, the Arab scarves round their necks, the backpacks dangling and earphones in their ears. Another niche: the female street vendors. If you go to La Vega, you'll notice that they are all cut from the same cloth. If they're not fat, they are always slightly overweight, they wear tight clothing, with identical dyed and damaged hair, all dark-skinned, with jeans or tracksuits cut to the hip, they talk the same way and they go by the same names, preferably foreign (in my youth names were always Spanish). Then there are the snobs from the *barrio alto* with their SUVs: arrogant on principle, long smooth hair with fair highlights, rather skinny, always making some kind of sound with their hands, bangles, keys, whatever. The purses are enormous branded bags and they wear knee-high or ankle boots, never shoes. Their daughters are given men's names, Dominga, Fernanda, Antonia, Manuela.

Essentially, they're all rats trying to get out of a jam. And I'm first in line.

Santiago doesn't know diversity.

In developed countries, they keep going on about living longer. Why? What's the point? Children today, take a good look, they are born with great-grandparents as the most normal thing in the world. In my day it would have been impossible. If you were lucky you still had a living grandmother and that was it. So, I return to my question. What is this eagerness to keep us around, for heaven's sake? No time, no money, no space, and sometimes not even any desire. You no longer find those large houses where an old person was barely noticed, or the women with the spare time to take care of them. Old age is becoming a big nuisance for the planet. God, I don't want to imagine what it will be like in twenty years. Sometimes I watch a funeral procession on the street and I see what I would call old men, and there they are, burying their mom. She should have died centuries ago!

If we participated in some other culture, like the Asian ones, where the elderly are venerated, well then it would be a whole other ball game!

As for the main characteristic of old age: solitude. If I regret anything, it's not having been more involved in friendships. I had friends but, apart from my sister-in-law, none of them was a soul mate, and I didn't even choose her. I just ended up with her because she was Rucio's sister. Plus, we're not so close that I can unburden myself to her about all my woes. I tended not to trust women, that was very much in vogue in my youth. The other woman was always your potential enemy, and since I was so pretty I seemed to be everyone's enemy. Feminists still hadn't appeared and no one spoke about female solidarity—women's networks and those things. But why complain at this point? If I'd had a close friend she would have died already.

* * *

Accepting old age is the only way out. Whoever doesn't is lost. It's an endless pathetic circle. Perhaps women who have a husband and children find it easier, their surroundings don't allow for deception. But when you're alone, like so many old women in this city, there is a great temptation to close your eyes and pay no heed. Have you seen the movie *What Ever Happened to Baby Jane?* Bette Davis starred alongside Joan Crawford. They were a couple of old sisters who hated each other. In the end one kills the other, but that's not what concerns me. It's Bette Davis's role. She hasn't accepted her age and she dresses and does her hair and makeup like a teenager, sometimes like a little girl. I always remember the blush on her cheeks, two inexplicable red stains. I thought that the day I look like her will be my last. But it wasn't, of course. Your last day is never the one you think.

I'm going to tell you a short story.

About fifteen years ago—I had already turned sixty—I received a letter from Mendoza, Argentina. I looked at the sender and my heart started pounding. It was from a man I had liked a lot, perhaps the one I liked best out of those crazy romances I had after Rucio's death. He said in the letter that a mutual friend had passed through Mendoza and given him my address and that he'd really like to hear from me. I replied straightaway. I told him about my life, slightly embellished, naturally, since paper will accept anything. So began an active and healthy correspondence. He devoted himself to business and his family. According to him his wife was a bore. They had several children. But I have no doubt that he was tired of her. We began to flirt via letter. It's free, the other person can't see you, you can come across as the wonderful woman you were years ago. His letters did me so much good. I started to enjoy life more, looking forward to each new letter. He didn't measure his words, and every response was like getting into bed with him. That was a wonderful time, full of illusion, expectations. I was starting to feel like a *woman* again, probably for the last time. Then he announced that he was coming to Chile and wanted to see me. Shit! He wants to see me? I'm sixty years old, that was the only thing I thought. I ran to the mirror. I looked at myself, trying to see myself with his eyes, and I didn't like what I saw. This was a sexual encounter and I was freaking out. I looked at myself from a distance and the impression was different. Appearance is everything, Rucio always said to me, and I confirmed that if I walked a few steps away from the mirror—under indirect light—and moved gracefully, I could pass for fifty or forty-five. After all, the bastard was the same age as me, it's not like he was a young buck. I started to dance in front of the mirror like I used to do as a child, moving farther and farther away, and from there I had it. But he would see me up close. I spent ten expectant days thinking about how the hell to look young and please this man. The anticipated day arrived; we had arranged to meet that evening in a café. He came up with the meeting spot and I thought it appropriate and cautious on his part so I went along with it. I didn't want to come off as too provocative by offering up my place where the bed was practically in the living room. I tried on *everything* I had in the closet, even the dress I kept after Blanche, which was so long out of fashion that it had come back in. I washed my hair, I brushed it a hundred times, I made up myself like I remembered the makeup artists in the theater doing. The aim was to look good without the effort being noticeable. You can imagine my nerves when I left to go meet him. In truth, I had high expectations for him, not for marriage, let's be clear, I'm just talking about finally having a bit of excitement, an adventure at sixty is like being born again.

Dolled up to the nines, I entered the café and he was already there. I was so relieved. He was talking on the phone, leaning on the counter. I recognized him at once, apart from a double chin and a bit of a belly, he was the same. He saw me, waved me over, and carried on talking. He took a long time, to tell the truth. When he hung up and turned his attention to me, I sensed that now we were so close he was becoming more distant. He seemed worried and focused on something else that had nothing to do with me. I asked him what was wrong and he told me about one of his trucks being blocked at the Cristo Redentor pass. If it was delayed the shipment of fruit would rot.

We sat down and both ordered coffee. He carried on talking about the phone call, problems at the border, and how the merchandise could go to waste. The whole time I was thinking about the bags under my eyes. I lifted my neck to hide the wrinkles and moistened my lips so that they didn't look too thin. None of it was very interesting and we carried on with small talk about Chile, the coalition, the difficulties of trading with Argentina, and snow in the Andes. We drank another coffee and by then we'd more or less caught up. There was no relation between the letters of my former lover and this man in the café. Not the slightest glint of mischief in his eyes, not even a joke or a memory of the old days. At nine I stood up and told him I had dinner plans. You want to go already? he asked me, almost relieved. I made my retreat. He didn't like me. He remembered me from twenty years earlier, that was the woman he had been flirting with in those letters. It was that brutal, simple, crude. We parted the typical Chilean way, see you, yes, see you, let me know when you're back in Chile, yes, I'll let you know. I never heard from him again.

Don't think that I started crying when I got home. No. I took out the makeup box from my theater days and I stood in front of the mirror. I stepped away from the mirror and then closer, paying attention to every tiny detail. I devoted myself to observing. Then I cleaned my face, I set up an indirect light and started making up myself again, from scratch. I began with blush. With great care I took the sable brush and gave my cheeks the first strokes, returned to scrutinizing myself, then the second layer, a bit more observation, and the third. Each layer dropped a couple of years off my appearance. When I looked like a young woman, I continued with the most intense rouge I had, a flash of blood red, and I painted my lips in a heart shape. The shedding of years continued. The blue on the eyes and mascara on the lashes were a piece of cake. The thing that took longest was the hair. I practiced different, younger styles, up, down, until settling for two ponytails at the sides, a couple of pigtails, and I shed yet more years. I raised my skirts and fixed them so that they fell above my knees. Once all this was done, I decided that I was fifteen years younger and I started dancing in front of the mirror. Finally, exhausted, I lay on the bed fully dressed and that's how I fell asleep.

The following day I dug out my makeup removal cream and wiped my face, and decided that I would discard my memory of what happened in the trash along with the cotton wool pad. But something inside me was saying, Nonsense, you don't have to settle for what you have. The following night, with a drink in my hand, I couldn't resist and I began it all again, makeup, dancing in front of the mirror. My Baby Jane was less ridiculous than Bette Davis's. I was prettier than her and did everything with more subtlety. But the phenomenon was the same. It began to happen fairly frequently. I would put on this mask drawn by my own hand, dress in short skirts, dance in front of the mirror, and then throw myself down on the bed, immobile, like a rag doll.

That's how a new Mané was born, an aged and grotesque child spurred on by the growing desire never to be seen again up close and au naturel by a man. I became fanatical. I went over and over what happened when I reconnected with the man from Argentina, fatally wounded, scared that I would never be touched again. When I was dolled up and dancing, only then could I convince myself that I was worthy of being liked by someone. Always that cloudy mirror, in the distance, telling me true lies, suffocating that enormous desire to throw my exhausted head against a crinkled, friendly shirt.

There is one wonderful aspect to old age. No one expects anything of you. It's already too late for many things, for almost everything. Therefore, it's too late to go crazy. To become an alcoholic. To pull a malevolent personality from your sleeve. To invent woes of which you were never victim. If jealousy never tortured you when you were young, it won't now. It's a relief.

If you learned in time how to entertain yourself, you'll keep doing it. Lack of ambition in old age leaves you room for good things and gives you lots, *lots* of freedom.

There are people who devote themselves to memories, they open their trunks, they look one by one at old photographs, they read letters written decades earlier. I don't have a trunk, only a box with a couple of objects stored in it: my marriage certificate, the book that Rucio published, my mom's crystal drinking glasses. Those glasses bring something to mind. My grandmother gave them to my mother. Over time most of them have broken and there are only two left. They are made from a very finely cut sky-blue crystal. My mom adored them and never used them because, according to her, they were too elegant. When she gave them to me, shortly before she died, she warned me to take care of them. So I did. I took so much care that I never used them either. I found them a short while ago. Why the hell did I have them if I didn't use them? It makes no sense to wait for the right moment because it *never* arrives. That moment doesn't exist.

Perhaps the solution is to have a little project every day. If there's no reason for you to get up in the morning it really doesn't matter if you are alive or dead. If I decide to stay in my nightgown and not get dressed or shower, many days would pass before anyone noticed. If you knew how much I discipline myself and demand of my body every morning just to get out of bed. I employ all my strength at that moment and thanks to that I'm able to reach the bathroom, run the bath, inject my fallen body with a bit of vigor. It reminds me of the attributes of the great actresses being disciplined and demanding of themselves. You know why I do it? Why I impose this on myself? Because the day I stop doing it I will stay in bed forever. Forever and ever. If I let myself go, there isn't the strength in the world to get me out of there. Because that is the body's profound desire. Then you can consider me dead.

A while ago an Italian movie came to Chile, which I watched with Charo, *The Best of Youth*. One of the characters really got me thinking. A very typical mom, from any country, it makes no difference whether she was Italian, Spanish, or Chilean. She wasn't much to look at. She taught in a high school and she also cooked and looked after the house and the children, typical middle class. As time goes by the boys grow up and leave home, the parents get old, and eventually she is widowed. Everything makes you think she'll fall apart. To the surprise of the viewers, she decides not to break down. At that point she makes the decision to change her life and *she does it*. She gets up willingly every morning and it would have caught someone's attention if she spent days in her nightgown. Her daughter-in-law and grandson, for a start. When she died they missed her.

Who's going to miss me? Why did I not end up like her? Of course, you freeze in Chile, this isn't Sicily, and I have no real family. This woman's project was her grandson. That was how she avoided the final solitude: the solitude of the skin.

No one touches you. People don't go around touching, and with good reason. Sex is a lost memory. You'd give your life for a hearty embrace, for that unique force that holds you, contains you. Or for that stroke on the hair to help you sleep. Sometimes, I think that's all I'd ask for: a hand on my hair before I fall asleep forever.

JUANA

A year ago I would have started by saying: life is so good!
It was, it really was. There were so many good things,
from a long orgasm to an ice-cold glass of *mote con
huesillo* in the summer. But a year ago, because of Susy, everything
changed. I'm not the same Juana I was beforehand and I want to
bring back the old version.

My problems aren't mine, but they're killing me all the same. I
wonder how it's possible for pain to grip like this when none of its
knots have been tied by me. If you screw it up yourself, fine, you
pay the consequences. But there are problems that appear without
you lifting a finger. Everyone suffers, who doesn't, for God's sake?
So there should be some kind of manual explaining how the hell to
bring back happiness in spite of your troubles.

I might look older, because I'm so tired, but I'm thirty-seven. I'm
a waxer, I work in a beauty salon in Vitacura, near Lo Castillo, in the
barrio alto. That's what Adolfo likes us to call it, a beauty salon, not a
hairdresser's. I think I'm good at my job and I have loyal clients. I'm
single, what a bummer, I'd certainly like to have a man. I don't know
about a husband, but a life companion, yes, or at least a bed companion. I gave birth to my Susy when I was eighteen, an eternity ago, and
she is my gem.

I am a single mother, like my mom, who never married. She had a partner who wasn't my dad, they lived together and everything, but he treated her badly, the son of a bitch, he treated her like shit. From a very early age I learned to defend her and I still do it now, not from men but from illness. I was an only child. I was born on Calle Viel, between Rondizzoni and Avenida Matta, on the eastern side of Parque O'Higgins. It was a friendly, quiet neighborhood. The house—owned by my grandfather—was made of brick, nice and solid. I thought it would last forever. The store on the corner gave us credit, the neighbors came and went as if they owned the place, I walked to school, I could go everywhere in complete tranquility, I played with the other neighborhood kids, very few cars drove past, and when it was hot the women spent all day outside. The nights were silent. My grandmother was a bossy old woman, dry but affectionate in her way. Her hands were like two enameled iron saucepans, always hard and busy. She taught me so many things. Thanks to her I'm a good cook, I can sew, knit, and mend plugs. I don't have much memory of my grandfather, he died when I was young. One day they decided to build a highway. Right there in front of the damn house. Some people were happy. They thought the street would become more important, and they even made plans to set up small businesses that would benefit from traffic going past. Businesses my ass. We were screwed over. Concrete, concrete, and more concrete. The street was filled up with workers, machines, noise. Outcome: the subway and the North-South highway. They isolated us from the rest of the city, we were left with an enormous street, full of iron railings, potholes all over the place, and cars whizzing past. You couldn't stop on our road, it was used only for shooting into the city center, like rockets. The din wouldn't allow us to live. It ended everything, the privacy, the intimacy, we were on show. Ironically, we began to feel alone.

That's progress, you'll say. Is it progress when it happens at the expense of normal people, at the expense of some kid watching each day as her childhood is destroyed, as the landscape she thought was eternal is changing? We had to leave, see ya. I remember the discussions between my mom and grandma about where to go, which neighborhood, whether we'd get benefits, whether a house or apartment. We ended up in Maipú. We were pioneers, at that time it wasn't all built up like it is today. It didn't have the megamalls or the hordes of cars, that all came later. Susy was born in Maipú and when I showed her my old neighborhood she didn't believe that we once lived there in peace.

Houses are very important. Describe your house and I'll tell you who you are. Your world is there. It's what covers you, like a bird's feathers.

I'd like to be rich if for no other reason than to have a really nice house. One of those elegant apartments near the hairdresser's where I work. They have twenty-four-hour concierges, they don't live in fear, they're nice and warm in winter and air-conditioned in summer, with terraces where you can touch the treetops. The rooms are big and light, especially in the older ones, the ones that have been there for twenty or thirty years. It's not that I'm complaining, but I would have liked our house in Maipú to have slightly thicker walls, more insulation, slightly higher ceilings, more light, and a bit more in the way of square meterage. When I'm short on money, I do home visits for waxing and I get to see those houses and I look at them and like them so much. I say to myself, Heck, one day I'll buy a nice house for my mother and for Susy and the three of us will be really cozy and we'll each have our own bedroom. Now we only have two. One is my mom's and the other is for Susy, and I switch from one to the other depending on the circumstances.

I'm very hardworking, I don't turn up my nose at anything. I learned to wax when I was still in high school. I liked doing manicures more than anything, but in general I struggle to concentrate, and I'm not great at things that require fine motor skills. I get so impatient, become frustrated and end up doing a bad job, which makes me want to give up. Growing up, a neighbor of mine ran an underground hairdresser's in her house—I say underground because she didn't pay taxes or have permits, she worked for people in the neighborhood, that was all. I often went and helped her after school. I liked being her assistant. My mom used to tell me that I'd be better off staying at home and studying, but my grandmother disagreed. The girl should have a trade, she said, it's better she knows how to do something well than to carry on studying—she's going to have to work either way. I learned to do everything, haircuts, coloring, fingers and toenails, waxing. I practiced on my family and friends, sometimes I burned them and the poor things didn't even mock me. I think my mom hoped I would stick with school, something technical, and that I'd be the first in my family to go on to higher education. But I was an idiot. Like hell was I going to study. The only thing I wanted to finish was my goddamned secondary education and then, shit, it's bye-bye, let's get to work!

The Ant, that's what my grandma called me, a tireless worker. I was quite happy. Happy, but with one great weakness: men. Because jeez did I like men. Then and now. On the night of my graduation from high school I slept with one of the musicians from the orchestra. A month later it was midsummer and I began to feel bad, dying of heat and nauseous. I went to the drugstore and bought a pregnancy test. I locked myself in the house's only bathroom. Come on, Juana, hurry up, my grandmother shouted through the door. There I was waiting for the goddamn result. Nowadays it only takes about a second. Right in front of my eyes: positive. Shit! *Positive.* Studying wasn't an option now. So many kids screw it up with pregnancy, so many.

Anytime I show up at the salon down in the dumps, my best friend Katy looks at me and says: You're wearing your ass face. Yes, I tell her, what do you expect, that I'm always going about with a smile on my face? They've already gotten used to it. Then, when the clients and Adolfo—my boss—have gone, Katy washes my hair and gives it a blowout to lift my mood. Jennifer makes tea and we sit chatting and smoking and I tell them my troubles and I leave feeling comforted. I don't know how I would have gotten through this hard time without them. The good times too. Women among women know how not to feel alone. Men among men, they don't.

For a long time, my mom worked in an artisan chocolate factory. She and the other women made the chocolates by hand. The chocolate lady, I used to call her. She lived surrounded by warm aromas and pleasing shapes. The molds she used were hearts, clovers, little houses, bottles. Our life together had a nice, sweet, friendly, warm tang. Succulent. I liked the liquefied chocolate before it solidified. It was impossible not to stick my fingers in, it was so fleshy and creamy at the same time, so sensual. Of course, I learned the technique and taught it to Susy as well. We all make chocolates. Her friends—when they still came to the house—liked to have afternoon tea with us because there was always a little plate of chocolates. My mom has retired and now, with her illness, she can't do anything, so I buy the cocoa and when I have time, a lazy Sunday, I take out the molds from the pantry and get to work and she really likes it. She watches me. You might think that after her long working life she would have lost interest in chocolate, but no, she still likes it and looks at me gratefully when I make it.

One night, many years ago, I awoke suddenly, around midnight, and noticed her bedside light still on. At the time we were sharing a bedroom in my grandmother's house. The following day I was in a school play. I had the part of Cinderella's fairy godmother and a classmate had agreed to lend me the costume. At the last moment she told me she'd loaned the dress to someone else and that she wouldn't be able to get it back in time. I was on the verge of tears when I got home, I must have been fourteen or fifteen, and I decided to feign sickness so I wouldn't have to go to school. There was no way I could be in the play without a costume. I went to sleep in a bad mood. Perhaps that's why I woke up. I opened my eyes in the middle of the night, and my mother was sewing in the bed next to mine. She used to get up at six every morning, she left everything prepared and departed for the chocolate factory at seven. But there

she was at midnight, her back was hunched, not just from the act of
sewing but from the weight of life. Her bed was pristine, the bedspread—printed with wide green and yellow flowers—stretched out
with barely a wrinkle, and on the white melamine nightstand stood
the lamp, a modest wooden base with a shade made of wax paper, its
bulb couldn't have been more than forty watts. Next to the lamp, an
untouched tumbler of water, the light passing through the greenish
glass. I remember that glass to this day, it gave the impression of tiny
Pacific waves held prisoner inside it. Her medicines were there too
and a Virgen del Carmen prayer card. She didn't see that I had woken
up. I could watch her to my heart's content without her noticing. Her
concentration was absolute. On her lap rested a very fine, vaporous
blue fabric, a kind of gauze that I recognized as a curtain from my
grandmother's room. My mother was sewing some tacking stitches
and that's when I realized that she had transformed the curtain into
a skirt. Only a fairy godmother could wear a skirt like that, I thought.
Hanging on a chair was the tight blue top I wore in the summer—it
had become the elegant bodice of a fairy gown. As I'd slept, she'd
covered it with sparkles, threads of sequins taken from who knows
where. With her index finger jammed into a thimble and working
only by the light of her dim lamp, her brow furrowed with focus, my
mother was sewing a costume for me. Her gaze insisted on concentration, not complaint, and that was important for my adolescence.
I didn't have next to me a long-suffering mother who sacrificed
herself, but a woman who was doing something for her daughter,
doing it meticulously. I realized for the first time that the veins in
her hands bulged out as small, dark mounds. At what point did my
mom's hands get old? Her hair, badly cut, clung to her neck with no
charm or shine, white hairs sticking out at the parting and mingling
with the coppery, opaque tones that dye had left behind months earlier. There's nothing more vulnerable than a figure working in the
middle of the night who doesn't know she's being observed. I closed
my eyes again, touched, and I fell asleep right away under a mantle
of protection.

One day, two years ago, I returned from work at about seven. I'm never able to make it home before that time. Susy had told me that she was going to be at a friend's house studying for a math test. I had been to the market to get some ham. We never have dinner at night, we just snack when I arrive. I put my keys in the lock, thinking that perhaps my mom would have the water boiling already and the glasses on the table, perhaps the rolls warmed. I opened the door and found my mom sprawled out on the floor, right next to the only couch. Her eyes were closed and drool was dribbling from her open mouth. Next to her slumped body, a couple of number eight knitting needles and a ball of thick olive-green wool were on the floor. The tired veins on her legs looked like plum-colored knotted cords. She was wearing a shirtdress, the kind that fastens at the front with a ribbon around the waist, and several buttons on the skirt had come undone. The dress was cream-colored, viscose, with tiny brown and yellow flowers. I kept seeing those flowers in my dreams for a long time, tiny, brown and yellow.

At the emergency room they mentioned a hemorrhage. The doctor talked about apoplexy. Cerebral infarction. It makes no difference. The important thing is the result. She was left a semi-invalid. The left side, almost paralyzed, the arm and leg, useless, her mouth, twisted forever. That's my mom today. She barely has any words left, perhaps she's said them all and now she's empty, like a pot of tea once the water has grown cold and it's no good anymore. The most active and hardworking woman I know, the one who taught me to be tireless, now spends her days sitting on the couch waiting for something to happen, for someone to arrive, for life to tell her something different from the voices on TV, which I leave on when I go out in the morning so that she doesn't feel alone. How I would have liked to stay by her side, to make her better, to bathe her every day, to wash her hair and tie headscarves for her, to chat, cook for her, cheer her up. But I can't stop working. Like all goddamn pensions in this country, my mom's is useless. Without my wages we'd die of hunger. I see her aging, with more and more hair in some places and less and less in others, and I take the tweezers and get rid of that beard. I always keep her looking nice. But comfortable. No vanities that would cause discomfort. She looks like a doll with the socks I put on her, no pant-yhose anymore—getting into a pair of pantyhose is like packing sausages, even I wear them as little as possible. During the first year of her condition, Susy took care of her a lot. We organized ourselves around our schedules, her for school, me for the hairdresser's, with the shopping, with the cleaning. Between the two of us we sorted it out more or less, although I always felt I was in a hurry, always, always. You can't imagine what I'm like now. I outgrew the word *hurry* a long time ago, there's no word that applies to me anymore.

I have attention deficit disorder. That's what they call it. At least nowadays it can be diagnosed and medicated—before you couldn't even do that. They say it's often hereditary and since my mom doesn't have it—nor does Susy, thank God—I blame it, like so many other things, on my unknown son-of-a-bitch father who left as soon as my mom got pregnant. What is attention deficit? It's like an amplitude of the mind, an extension that echoes. For example, the other day I was flipping through a magazine at work while I was waiting for the wax to heat up and I read some guy's obituary. It said he had been a singer, translator, engineer, jazz trumpeter, dramatist, and opera composer. I thought, this asshole obviously had attention deficit disorder. There are a thousand things I'd like to do, and for which I have a certain skill. For a start, anything related to hairdressing, which means hair-dresser, manicurist, masseuse, reflexologist, colorist. I could also be a wonderful chef or a good dressmaker or dancer or yoga instructor, and if pressed, a painter. I'd succeed at all those things if I devoted myself to them. But, of course, there's no time. I'm too busy earning a living. If I'd been born rich, I would have an obituary like the guy in the magazine.

I was always a bit clumsy, things that were refined or too feminine never worked out well for me. That's why I ended up being a waxer and not a manicurist. If I painted nails, the polish would go over the edges. Sometimes I manage it, but it takes a lot of effort. I've spent my life trying not to be clumsy, clumsy with things related to the body, but also with things related to the mind. I'm quicker than most. At parent-teacher meetings at Susy's high school I would get really bored. People seemed boring and slow to me. I would run through life like the Road Runner, arriving to leave, never to stay. I was always afraid of criticism, they always challenged me—my grandmother, teachers, bosses, friends—because I did or said inappropriate things. I still do. Not so much now because I've been diagnosed and medicated, but whether I like it or not, I'm the same. Despite the medicine, I'm still making thousands of useless movements. If I go to look for my cell phone and I see my glasses, I focus on them and then on the coffee cup I have to take to the kitchen, and of course I can't remember why I got up until I notice the cell phone, but the truth is that to achieve any activity I need to have an empty desert in front of me so that I don't get distracted. Everything distracts me—noises, people, the ideas that pour from my mind. I get more tired than most. I'm irritated by clothing labels rubbing against my body; I rip them out so I can't feel them. Technically, what happens is that I process more stimulants than I can deal with. That's how it was explained to me. It's like never coming into port via a straight line, that's why I get so tired. But it's not all bad news. I'm also more creative and imaginative and surely more original, because I make unusual associations and nice ideas can spring from that. I'm fun sometimes, if anyone can put up with me.

They say that people with attention deficit disorder tend to be very intelligent. Not me. I have my resources but I'm not especially intelligent. I'm completely incapable of immersing myself in a topic without spillage. I'm always interrupting myself. I start speaking about the beauty salon and in a minute I've moved on to Susy or I'm commenting on a customer's outfit or worrying because I haven't paid the gas bill. I can't concentrate on one single subject.

María del Mar is one of my favorite clients. She lives about two blocks away from the salon and comes in regularly. She's a cultured and well-informed woman and I always discuss my issues with her because she also suffers the same problems. She calls it ADD, like they do in America. She takes a Ritalin every day and it propels her through life. She defines the disorder as the inability to select what is urgent. She also says that being a woman is more or less equivalent to suffering from attention deficit disorder. In her words, the range of stimuli we deal with is so high that we can't *prioritize*—she loves that word. So, as she sees it, diapers, the stock exchange, fear of death, all three things are of equal importance, they have the same urgency. When I want to come across as interesting in front of a guy I like, I imitate María del Mar. I'm good at imitating and retaining alien words and I use hers to appear smart.

Over the years I've come to the conclusion that I know a lot of things, but in a very confused way. I think time is different for me. For normal people, time is what it is, in other words, short. For me, it's long. I always think I have a lot of time and I organize myself with that in mind and I live like that, realizing every day that I've done badly, that I didn't make it.

Despite everything, I can't say I wasn't happy. I've been crazy, fierce, and out of control and I've enjoyed it all. If destiny meant for me to suffer, then destiny didn't get its way.

I don't make a big deal about not knowing my father. He was a neighbor from Calle Viel. Not even a neighbor, actually—he was the friend of a neighbor. My mom took a fancy to him because he was good-looking, cheeky, and a good dancer. He was from Concepción and spending his vacation in Santiago. Because my grandfather devoted vacations to his soccer club my poor mother never went on vacation. She was in Santiago dying from the heat and fed up and this neighbor invited her to the parties he held. My father and mother had a nice little fling, according to her, but the day she found out she was pregnant, he returned to Concepción. Son of a bitch. The military coup erupted right after that, he was taken prisoner, and when they released him he went directly to Venezuela. My mom learned those details from her neighbor. Presumably he's still there now. Sometimes I imagine little Venezuelan kids who could be my siblings but, to tell the truth, I don't lose any sleep over it. At most, I'm a bit curious. I've never even looked into his family in Concepción. I had no father. That's why my grandfather was there.

I sometimes learn useless facts from the magazines at the hair-dresser's. For example, the zone of the brain that deals with plea-sure is a cortex with a hard-to-pronounce name. It is activated by whatever the individual likes most. My cortex is activated by sex. I open like a ripe fruit when faced with it. I wonder what it is that makes some women marriage material and others not. I'm old-fash-ioned. I believe in dignity, without question, but that word is rare, it's wrong. What I think is dignified, twenty-five other people would consider stupidity. I believe in male courtship. I don't pursue men, I never take the initiative, I never fight openly for them. I allow them to seduce me. That is until my madness takes over and I lose my temper. But because I know I'm losing what I call *dignity*, I hate and despise myself. That's how it goes for me with men. Almost all of them end up leaving me. Sex for the sake of it doesn't do much for me. If I go to bed with someone I end up falling in love, or at least believing I am. I really envy that male quality of being able to have a good no-strings-attached screw. We end up hooked, like idiots. It's hard for us to get up the next day and expect nothing. Sometimes I feel used. Men never feel that way because even if they are being used they don't realize it and they believe that they're the ones doing the using. My last boyfriend was Greek. He came into the beauty salon for a haircut. My boss, Adolfo, cuts hair for his friends even though the hairdresser's isn't technically unisex. Since Jennifer was busy, I washed Alekos's hair to get ahead. He was captivated. He told Adolfo that he liked my laugh, and my little massages on his scalp, which wasn't included in the price. That afternoon he brought me flowers. He didn't speak Spanish, just a bit of English, which I don't know. We went out to eat, he took me to a really nice restaurant. You tell me how we managed. What does language matter? When two soccer teams play, Uruguay and Holland, for example, neither speaks the other's language. Do they need to? The communication is perfect, from kick to kick there is flawless comprehension of what they are doing together. That's how it was with my Alekos. He left for Greece after two weeks. Bye-bye romance, but it did me a lot of good. I was recharged and happy. Because lack of sex is bad for me. The other day I began to complain in front of Jennifer's sister, Doris is her name. She's a bit older than me and said, As far as I'm concerned, I've closed up down there and my labia have climbed so far up my back that I've got little wings now!

During her final year of high school, Susy spent a long time preparing for a study trip she was going to take with her class. During eleventh grade she studied like she was sick in the head. She studied so much I thought her brain would explode. It was a difficult year because that was when my mom fell ill and Susy's obsession over her schoolwork didn't help much. The thing is, Mom, I want a career, she told me when I asked why she took on so much. They say that eleventh grade is infamous for being stressful and I was concerned that Susy would collapse at any moment. We celebrated the end of that shitty year, which she finished with fairly good grades. It seemed to me that she deserved the study trip in the final year. I scraped together the money and I remember how happy she was when I dropped her at the bus terminal. She was away for a week, in the south. When she came back, a few days later, she did her homework and suddenly she started crying. I asked her what was wrong. She told me that she was afraid of dying. Die, you? I said, taking it lightly. Honey, you're immortal. I hugged her and noticed how she clung to me. That night she climbed into my bed and slept with me. The following day I woke her as usual and as I was making breakfast and preparing something for my mom to eat, I noticed the bags under her eyes. Didn't you sleep well, Susy? I didn't sleep. I watched her but told myself it would pass. When I came back from work that day, my mom gestured with her good hand toward Susy, who was sleeping on the couch. She didn't tend to sleep at seven in the evening and even less in the living room. I woke her and invited her to cook us something tasty. She loves making fritters with dark brown sugar, whereas I struggle with the brown sugar because when I dissolve it in the pan it looks like wax and I can't bear it. I suggested the fritters but she said no, she wasn't hungry, she wanted to keep sleeping. My mom and I exchanged glances. We both sensed that a problem was being presented to us. She slept until the following day. She didn't even notice when I moved her from the couch to her bed and undressed her.

Every morning the alarm goes off at a quarter past six and that signals the official start of the day. I jump out of bed, get into the shower, and I wake Susy at a quarter to seven. When she comes out of the bathroom, breakfast is ready, the water's boiled, the bread toasted, every minute is key in order to leave everything prepared and not arrive late to work. That morning she said to me, in a quiet voice, that she didn't want to go to school. Don't you feel well, sweetie? No, I'm not sick, I just don't want to. That was her response. She wore a sorrowful expression. I told her she could stay home and take care of her grandmother. I left, worried, and thought during the day that I should take her to the doctor. There's an office near the house and the doctor is a great friend of mine, perhaps he would give me an appointment fairly quickly. Was it possible that all that studying had burned her out?

The girls in the beauty salon advised me and gave me a few Alprazolam, to calm her down. The problem is she's too calm, I replied, but they insisted. I called Susy on her cell about three times during the day but she told me not to worry, she was fine. Christ almighty, I thought, between the practically invalid old woman and the depressed kid, why aren't I at home? Why am I obliged to spend all day away, among women's hair, from armpits to legs, waiting for the wax to cool and ripping it right off? I gave Susy the Alprazolam that afternoon, a low dose, and the following day she returned to school but her eyes were still sad. That weekend she didn't want to go out. Susy has lots of friends and they get together and listen to music and dance, basically they mess around, they entertain themselves. But she stayed home and turned off her phone, which was *very* strange because those kids are constantly calling and texting. Giving them a cell is like tying up dogs with sausages, they're always communicating among themselves as if that's what their lives are for. I always wonder what they have to say to each other all the time. They see each other every day.

Susy shut herself away in my house, and she's still there today.

After my mom got sick she was alone during the day until Susy arrived home after school. I bought my mom a prepaid cell phone, I saved my number and the number of the hairdresser's in it and I put it on the small table by the armchair where she spends the day. Every morning I leave it switched on with my number on the screen, ready to connect, she just has to press the key. I did that thinking of the possibility of a future attack, which the doctor warned me about. One day, a year ago, I was mid-wax when my cell rang with my mom's number flashing up. I answered, terrified, I started shouting, Are you OK, Mom?—as if deafness were her problem. In her half language she told me it was Susy. I dropped everything and left. It's such a long way from Vitacura to Maipú, it's like an obstacle course, a mountain riddled with rocks, gullies, and cracks, it's the length of an entire life. I did the last stretch in a taxi. What the hell, I told myself, I might not make it to the end of the month but I'll get home quicker.

It turned out that Susy had left, just like that. According to my mother's labored explanations, she had woken up in a strange mood, as if she were annoyed, no longer showing the sad face we were getting used to. She had shouted a couple times at my mother, she had said things my poor mom didn't understand, she left her without any lunch, she didn't make her bed, nothing. She just left. Four hours had passed and there had been no sign of her.

I called all her friends, I called the high school, nothing. Then I went out to the street. Like a crazy woman, I organized a couple of neighbors to help me search the area. As I ran along those streets the only thing that mattered in my life was Susy. The world shrank until it disappeared and what had seemed important the day before no longer existed. I remember my body, how it ached, every centimeter of skin absorbing the fear. I found her on a side street where cars didn't even go, sitting on the ground at the entrance to a stranger's house and playing with some little balls like a jester. I called her slowly, I wasn't about to frighten her, but she didn't respond. I approached gradually but she avoided me, she stood up and started walking in the opposite direction. When I could finally grab her arm, she shrugged me off violently and ran away.

I set off for the police station.

They brought her back to me.

That same night she was admitted.

I had managed, with great difficulty, to wrap my head around the idea of the first diagnosis: severe depression. I spent two months cradling my sad girl and watching her anguish without being able to lift it from her chest. I had been to her school, talked to her teachers, asked for temporary leave, fought for her not to lose that year of study. I took her to therapy and waited outside for her and until I saw her safe and sound inside the house, slumped next to her grandmother in front of the television, I didn't go out again. I spent nights on end wondering about this illness and its traits. I spoke to as many people as I could, I read all the information I could get my hands on, I asked myself twenty thousand questions about the girl's upbringing, about the quality of my role as mother, about her genes. I managed to get help. María del Mar—that client I told you about—has a psychologist brother and he began to see Susy. He's a saint. He didn't even charge us. The days when she had therapy—twice a week—were the only times she went out. In the same consultation she also visited the psychiatrist who medicated her. Because it was in Providencia, close to the hairdresser's, I took her with me, settled her on the bed next to where I do my waxing, drew the curtain for the privacy of my clients, made her lemon verbena tea, and set her up with a magazine. The girls kept her company if they didn't have much work. Katy tried to make her laugh, Jennifer stroked her hair, and even Adolfo consoled her. Susy was attentive to everything, but calm and passive. Katy said to me, You know what, Juani? Susy is submissive like she's been bitten by a vampire. Sometimes I felt like shouting, to annoy her, to make her disobey me to prove she was alive but I got nothing. She followed me like a lamb, surrendering her life to me because she'd had enough, and the first time she did get annoyed they admitted her and changed her diagnosis.

Bipolar disorder.

Son of a bitch.

I understand that there are four different grades. They don't really know, or still can't agree, which applies to Susy.

When they admitted her I struggled to understand the doctor's fear that Susy might commit suicide. It was like they were talking about another person, in another language. Taking her own life, my Susy? But why? Why?

Every time a siren wails or an ambulance passes I think about the tragedy that exists around that noise, which you take as a given, you almost don't hear it. But someone is suffering intensely, that's what the sound announces and no one pays attention. It could be Susy. Or my mother. I'll never know who each pain belongs to, it'll never appear in the newspaper or on TV but someone's life is marked.

When Mané talked about bipolar disorder, my blood froze, as if she knew my story. Yes, it's true that it has become fashionable, perhaps people weren't diagnosed with that label before. But the real issue that Mané exposed is financial. Susy's first therapy sessions were free, with María del Mar's brother. Then, once we had a diagnosis, she continued with a specialist who now sees her about once a month and medicates her and I pay him with National Health Fund vouchers. But the medicines are impossible. Because there are all kinds of medicines, there are some that are more primitive and therefore cheaper, but they have all kinds of side effects. The best, the most modern, they're expensive, very expensive. I didn't have a hope in hell of getting the money. It occurred to me to ask for a bank loan. They flatly refused with the proof of income I showed them, and the thing is that Adolfo, to help me, had padded the numbers. I was tipped off that if I mortgaged the house in Maipú, they'd give me the loan. But it's in my mother's name. Can you imagine the procedures I had to go through? The number of waxings I had to abandon to go from bank to bank, from notary to notary. But it worked. They gave me the loan. I pay interest every month, I'm going to work up a fortune in interest, but how else could I do it? You have no idea how grateful I am that my grandfather owned his house. If it weren't for that, I would lose Susy. I'll lose her if I don't buy the right medicines, which, besides, have been changed several times. Best not ask what another mom would do if she had nothing to mortgage.

A year has passed since my daughter returned from her study trip. She has left high school. Not that she finished it—she was in the final year—but she had to give it up. She is permanently medicated and she is no longer the docile, sad girl of the first few months, but more like someone who's angry at the world. Sometimes her rebellion is due to her medication, she feels separated from life and blames the chemicals for that separation. She quit therapy, there was no way to convince her. She doesn't leave the house. At this stage she won't even go as far as the corner. Her only relationships are with her grandmother and me. And since her grandmother is sick, I'm her only channel to the world. This humble bosom, her only contact with the outside. She makes token gestures like heating up lunch in the microwave while I'm at work and helping her grandmother eat. But if the bread runs out they remain without bread. One invalid and the other paralyzed. Two cripples. Nice picture. Everything that happens in the house in Maipú depends on me, everything. On top of that, I'm the one who pays. So sometimes I lose patience and I want them to obey me, he who pays the piper calls the tune, right? Well, I run and run to make sure everything's OK. I drag her to the psychiatrist, she never wants to go. I had to talk seriously to Adolfo. When it got to the stage that an appointment with me was harder than getting a ticket for a rock concert, we had to talk. I've been with him for fifteen years and we get on great. He knows I'm good and I know he's paying me as much as he can. So we decided to hire me an assistant for a while but of course that means less cash, although for now it's better than being out of work. All this is temporary, I assure Adolfo, so the doctors assure me. The girl will learn to live with her illness, that's what they tell me. Though she'll always have to take medication.

No, it's not your fault, miss, the doctor insists. It has nothing to do with you or her upbringing. It's genetic. She was born with this inclination. He asked me for details about her father, any hereditary illnesses in the family. I had to call said father. He turned up, did the decent thing, but confessed to having several nutcases on his mother's side.

I was a bit embarrassed to call him. We had no real relationship. He has never been concerned about Susy, at most he takes her out for ice cream once in a while. He's never given me a goddamn peso to help support her. He says that I wanted to have her, she's my problem. But apart from that, he's not a bad person. When I told him why I was calling, he came right away. At least he has that to his credit.

So, life ceased to be life. Someone might ask, Why has it changed so much? Why so much? I ask myself too. There is still light and night, cold and heat, the heart beats, the kidneys function, the lungs breathe, the legs are able to walk. But happiness, where did the happiness go? I can't even remember Susy's laugh. All my attention is focused on caring for her and earning enough to sustain us. Two sick people depend entirely on me but those people are my mother and my daughter. I almost can't call them people, they're more like an extension of me, where I end and they begin. I am them entirely. I don't know, I can't tell anymore, as if the three of us are a whole and I have to work out how to save it. Susy's hands have become soft and moist and I cover them with mine as I watch my mother, immobile in her armchair, with her low pain threshold. She doesn't feel the way

I do, she's already tired of feeling. Bless her, my mother, whose heart doesn't go to pieces every morning.

My emotions are all over the place. I'm exhausted, I've reached a kind of tiredness where it's no longer worth wasting energy on a single gesture. Even just a wave hello, something as basic as that, takes away strength I should conserve for Susy. When I was a girl, near my old neighborhood, there was a shantytown we used to walk through to get to the fair—those shantytowns no longer exist, but it was essentially a heap of poor people living together. I was struck by the women who emerged from under the planks, cardboard, and shreds of fabric that made up their houses, and the filthy children clinging to their skirts. I stared at them because I realized that those women were so beat that speaking to one of the kids was too much effort, they couldn't even open their mouths. They had to economize even on that so as not to collapse in exhaustion. Those women haunt me now, as if I've become one of them.

No, I'm not going to start crying.

Are you asleep, Mom?

No, my love.

If I paint a monkey on the sidewalk in chalk, how long will it take to rub out? Will it rub out one day?

Yes, I suppose so.

How does it rub out?

With the rain.

And if it doesn't rain?

With people treading on it.

Don't go to sleep, please.

I have to work tomorrow.

Don't work anymore.

How will we buy your medicine?

I don't want to take any more medicine. I'm scared, Mom.

That's what my nights are like.

I've always been stupidly sentimental. I know that elegant people hate that, as María del Mar says, it's *such* bad taste to be sentimental. When I occasionally defend myself, she replies: There's a big difference between sentiments, Juani, and sentimentality. Perhaps I lack culture, it could be an issue with my education, I don't know. I'm only telling you so you can imagine how I've become. Always on the verge of tears, damn it, getting emotional at the corniest things, making declarations about my feelings. I can't help it, it comes out of me on its own. All the crap they say about motherhood and the pain of a daughter. Sometimes I think I'm the only one who really knows what that is.

It's good to talk and be heard. Katy listens to me but we're always interrupting each other as we talk. We move from one topic to the next and in the end we don't finish any of them. Before, when I wasn't running around all day, we would sit down with a cigarette and a nice hot cup of tea when the clients had gone and we would devote ourselves to conversation, although everything she said led me onto something else and so the thread would break twenty times. But now I can't let myself be distracted. I met Natasha a short time ago, I'm a bit afraid of her, she's *so* serious. I don't pay either. How could I? I was referred to her by the hospital. Susy's doctor wants me to keep myself together to take charge of my daughter. Therapy has made me smarter, I understand more about everything, but I haven't gotten over anything. I only know that I'm going through a bad time, nothing more. Of course, this is external to me. My pain comes from outside and gets inside me, not like Susy's, which comes from the deepest hollow within her. The poor girl looks as though she's planned every word so as not to say a thing, like a cat. The other day I was alone in my neighbor's kitchen for a while with her cat. Out of nowhere, the bastard had a fit of terror. Its hair spiked up and he ran like he was being chased by the devil, his ears flattened back as if they had been ironed. There was no one in the kitchen, just a window the cat had been looking through. Surprised, I watched this animal spinning around terrified when there was nothing frightening there. Suddenly I got it: the cat was scared of itself.

My Susy.

The doctor assures me that this won't be forever. One day she'll get better and as the song by José Luis Perales goes, a thousand guitar chords will play. Perhaps at that point we'll win the lottery and buy one of those apartments like my clients have. I play every week, every single week, sure that I'll win one day. Then, when I take the bus, I make plans about what we're going to do with the money. The apartment is always the first thing. With central heating, no matter what it costs! Then I imagine traveling by plane. I've never been on a plane, for Christ's sake. How is that possible? Even the lowliest people buy package vacations to Cancún. I imagine myself with Susy, tanning on chaise lounges with colorful drinks in our hands, and a local who will hopefully do delicious things to me at night. Of course there's my mom. Where will I leave her?

I've always dreamed of having green eyes and long legs, the lottery can't give me that. I'm sure that my *whole* life would have been different if I'd been born with green eyes. Keep dreaming, Juani. You can't strike a deal with the lottery, you have to keep buying the ticket on time every week. I'd pay the bank loan, pay off the mortgage, I'd buy all the medicine in the world. I'd buy beautiful clothes, as fine as my clients wear, less acrylic and lots of cotton or silk, and lots of high heels, patent leather, crocodile skin. I love them because when you walk you look straight and tall, as if making a place for yourself in life, secure and sexy, everything I want to be. And some wheels. I'd get my license and my life would change. I could do my waxing at night, come and go with less fear of something happening and me not being there. My time would stretch so much farther. Although my clients who *do* have cars are always cursing the traffic. Santiago has become unbearable, they say, the increase in traffic is a nightmare. Of course, their fear is that lowly people like me will get cars and fill up their streets even more. It makes me laugh the way the snobs complain. They've got so much they complain about everything.

* * *

There are two women close to me who remind me of me. They make me swing like a trapeze artist. I lean toward one, then the other, recognizing an important part of myself in both of them, but learning from them too, when all is said and done. One is Lourdes, a Peruvian immigrant who cleans the hairdresser's, and the other is the client I've already mentioned, María del Mar. There is a desert between the two of them, no, the desert is too small, more like a distant ocean. For a start, one is poor and the other is rich.

Let's begin with Lourdes. One day I asked her when her birthday was and she told me she didn't know. What kind of childhood did you have, woman? I said. One with ten siblings. She was born in the hills, at high altitude. Her father was a porter and spent his life chewing coca leaves to give him strength. Her mother raised the children and tended a small garden to supply them with food. The nearest town was an hour's walk away and the hospital was three. Lourdes's siblings dropped like flies. She wasn't allowed to go to school because she had to help around the house. Men studied but women didn't. You know, indispensable free labor. Nevertheless, they still went very hungry. From the age of three she made bread and cooked corn and washed clothes. Naturally, no one taught her to read or write. Her dad beat the crap out of her every time he came home drunk. Perhaps he raped her too, the son of a bitch, but she didn't tell me that. Her brothers began to paw at her from the age of about twelve, the idiots—that much she did reveal. One day, when she was fifteen, she decided there were two alternatives: throw herself in the nearest river or escape from home. She made the most of a religious festival that took them somewhere beyond the miserable village they lived in and as soon as she got there she went. She simply left. With so many children, it took a while to notice that she'd disappeared. She got into a truck and offered the driver the only thing she had—her body—in exchange for taking her to Lima. Just like that, straight-out. The bastard accepted immediately, he was no fool. Lourdes arrived in the capital, healthy and as relieved as could be. No nostalgia, no regret. She never looked back. At first it was very difficult. How could it not be? She offered her services as a cook in a restaurant in one of the poorest neighborhoods but they had her washing dishes and scrubbing the floor for a year in return for food and lodging, without pay. Lodging is just a word. They let her sleep on a straw mattress in the pantry, among the corn and potatoes. In her desperation, she offered herself to a shit-hole brothel but they wouldn't accept her. They felt she was too young and malnourished and it wasn't worth getting into trouble with the authorities. So she began to take a few customers from the restaurant into the pantry. That was the only cash payment she could get. She relied on that system for a long time. Since she's no idiot, she realized that being illiterate wouldn't get her anywhere and she started studying. One of the guys who ate in the restaurant almost daily brought her materials, starting with the spelling book. I won't say she's exactly scholarly today but Lourdes gets by just fine. Her other obsession was to sort out her teeth. Just as I thought I'd be someone else if I had green eyes, Lourdes decided that with a good set of teeth her whole life would be different. She managed it here in Chile and her teeth are her pride and joy. Though, she still pays the dentist monthly installments. But I'm getting things out of order. I'll return to the restaurant in Lima. Spending so much time watching the chef she couldn't help but learn and now she makes the best ceviche and chili chicken you've ever tried. One day, a client who had grown fond of her gave her the idea of traveling to Tacna with him and trying to cross the border. He explained to her that in Chile she could wash dishes and mop floors, but she would be paid much more. As if we were the United States. How bad must the poverty be in places like Bolivia, Peru, and Ecuador if they want to come to Chile.

Lourdes is an immigrant but she's illegal. She shares a room in the city center with three compatriots, young girls like her. The room is no more than three square meters and they pay eighty bucks a month, with a shared bathroom and the right to cook in the room. They steal the electricity by tapping in to the main grid and several buildings like hers have gone up in flames. So what? She lives in a real hovel but she says she's never had it better. She feels free and she goes out on Saturday nights to chat with other Peruvians. They get together in Calle Catedral, next to Plaza de Armas, and she has a boyfriend and everything. Adolfo pressures her to get her papers and tells her if she doesn't hurry she'll be thrown out. If I had an extra room in my house, I'd let her stay with me. She's sweet and hardworking like no one else, she does everything without kidding around, she never complains. If she were legal she could aspire to cook in a restaurant. I've often heard clients come in desperate because they've been *left without a maid*. That's the great tragedy of their lives. Someone always replies, Get yourself a Peruvian, they're great. I think about Lourdes, but as long as she's here illegally she'll have to keep sweeping and earning peanuts. I don't know what angels of sadness and poverty surrounded her crib at birth, but they've pursued her relentlessly.

I identify with her because, like me, she sees the glass half full before she sees it half empty.

Why am I telling you stories about other people? I'm supposed to be telling you about me. I think that one person's story is always part of other people's stories.

María del Mar is going to turn fifty. She's almost an old woman and she looks young despite how much she smokes and the fact that she doesn't exercise. She was born beautiful, she's blessed, the complete opposite of Lourdes. Her father worked in politics and had family money. With the democracy, he even became an ambassador. Her mom is a historian, one of the first women who went to college, even now she spends half the day reading. Sometimes she comes to the hairdresser's too and I like seeing her. She's going on eighty and happy with life, her hair very white and straight to her shoulders—she doesn't style it like most women her age—and her face is always slightly sunburned. She smokes too! She spends half her time in the country and the rest in Santiago, in a very pretty apartment in Vitacura, near her daughter. How would I have turned out with a mother like her? Not a waxer, perhaps a famous painter? María del Mar's parents were passionate about travel and they took the children with them. The school didn't care, her mom went to the teachers and said, I'm taking María del Mar to Rome, she'll learn a lot more there than in classes so don't mark her down as absent. The teachers didn't dare argue.

She has memories of being a little girl, hanging from her mother's hand in the most beautiful museums in the world. Her mother would tell her, The names of the movements or painters or architects don't matter, what I want is for your eyes to get used to beauty. Aesthetics is María del Mar's number one topic. She studied something like art history and now she teaches at the university, she writes articles in the newspapers, "criticism" she calls it, and she's published a couple of books, really complicated, impossible to read. All with the help of Ritalin, she explains. When I ask her whether she earns money with a job like that she says not much but she has some income from her father's inheritance, so she gets by.

Income. How lucky is she. No one around me earns money without lifting a finger. I always had the impression that something like that could only happen on another planet, or in a fairy tale.

In 1973, the year I was born and when the military took power, María del Mar was a kid entering puberty. Her dad had to leave the country. He was in the Popular Unity Party, deputy or senator or something like that. She still remembers those days like a black cloud darkening everything but unable to decide whether or not to burst. Her parents no longer went out to work. Everyone spoke in hushed tones around her and strange people came and went from her house, people she'd never seen before but who nevertheless seemed closer to her parents than her own family. Without warning, one day they told her they were leaving. She packed her bags in tears, thinking of her friends, her high school, everything that was familiar to her. She didn't want to leave her country. They arrived in Washington, the very capital of imperialism, as she calls it, and a completely different life began overnight, with other people, in another language, with other flavors and another climate. Her mode of rebellion was to refuse to learn English. Of course, it didn't last long because she wanted to make friends with her classmates and a handsome boy who lived next door. She ended up being educated in the best high schools and colleges and today she's grateful for that part of her history.

She visits Washington as often as she can. She tells me what she's seen, what's in the store windows. I feel like I know the house belonging to the friend she stays with, in a neighborhood behind Congress, a long, narrow four-story house. She's always talking about Obama. Obama "happened to her," that's how she lives. She comments on how stunning and contradictory the city is. I quiz her, I ask for details and end up envying the many green spaces in Washington and curse the lack of them in Maipú. She even brought me a book as a gift, a beautiful book with photographs of all the monuments and parks and rivers. The day I go there everything's going to seem familiar.

She fell in love with, and married, an English scientist who was also studying in Washington. They lived in London for four years and she took the opportunity to do a postgraduate degree. That's as far as the marriage went. Realizing that she was young, free, and independent, she decided to return to Chile. She convinced her only brother—the psychologist who sees Susy—to do the same and they settled here, in her words, wanting to take part in the fall of the military and the formation of the new democracy. Then she fell in love again, with a Chilean this time, and she remarried. To cut a long story short, she's now on her third marriage and she says this completely naturally, as if marrying three times was the most normal thing in the world. Each separation, according to her, has been scary and full of suffering. Just the same, she thinks you have to take risks. Without risk, you don't get anywhere, Juani, she tells me every so often. She has two children, one by each Chilean husband, and they and the husbands all adore her. Of course, her children get by just fine, they're diligent and good-looking and neither of them inherited attention deficit disorder.

She loves putting herself down and tells her story as if it were a tragedy, though deep down she knows she's had it good. Her life is so enviable from any point of view that I suppose she does it as a means of apology for her own good fortune. She exaggerates her defects so that you don't notice her talents. For example, she comes into the hairdresser's with a bandaged finger and says, I'm *so* clumsy, I cut myself last night when I was trying to cook, I'm incapable of going into the kitchen without cutting or burning myself. But I know she's a fantastic cook and she's given me some really good recipes. Or she turns up in a hurry for a blowout and says, Shit, I've left my cell phone at home, my head is all over the place, I can't do anything right. But I know she's very organized, it's just because of the attention deficit disorder. She became obsessive in order to function. I'm *disgusting*, just *disgusting*, she says, looking at herself in the mirror, and the only reflection I can see is one of a gorgeous woman, with beautiful thick, abundant blond hair and long, long legs. When I help her off with her boots for her waxing, I touch the leather, it feels like velvet it's so soft and fine. Then I tell myself, she wants me to forgive her, forgive her for being so intelligent, so magnificent, so loved, and on top of that rich. That's why she tells me she's disgusting. But instead of envying her, I love her. She's a generous soul because she knows how privileged she is and, without really knowing how, she wants to share her privileges. Everything around her has something ethereal about it, as if she were wrapped in a celestial tulle that protects her from evil and means that, when it does catch up with her, she turns her back and refuses to play the game.

You'll wonder why the hell I identify with someone like her. The thing is that we have the same expectations for happiness. I've learned that the same experience can be enjoyed by one and suffered by someone else. I think that if my poor mother had been cultured and educated, I could have been like María del Mar. I had to study a speech with Susy by the great liberator Bernardo O'Higgins and I remember it said that only civilization and intelligence can make men sociable, frank, and virtuous. Civilization? Intelligence? Shit!

Poverty is relative. I'm poor next to María del Mar and a millionaire next to Lourdes. I'm a bit of both of them.

I just need to talk about Slim and then I'll finish. Slim's only crimes were having dandruff and being married. More than eleven years ago, on Independence Day, I went to celebrate in Parque O'Higgins. It was one of those events like they used to set up opposite my house when I was a girl, with lots of traditional dancing, empanadas, late-night snacks, and red wine. I'm a really good dancer and I saw a guy in the crowd who couldn't take his eyes off me. He was pretty tall, he seemed to be made of wire, and his limbs moved by themselves as if they were just screwed into his body. His eyes were very black, like the curls of his hair. I liked him, I liked him right away. I was wearing a tight black skirt with a yellow top and yellow shoes. He approached me and said, I want to dance with that happy bumblebee. Afterward he offered me a *pisco* and cola. Suddenly it was two in the morning and I was still dancing with him and my friends had left. At that moment, the whole world seemed empty. I don't know what happened, perhaps my stars aligned, the thing is that I went home with him. The sex was the best gift from heaven. The problem was that after getting a taste of him I found out that the bastard had a wife. He told me the following morning, and it was already too late. That was my Mistake, with a capital *M*. I went home that day thinking it would be good never to see him again. I don't like married men, I never get involved with them. But Slim wasn't just any man.

Although he was a party animal, Slim's was a life of effort and seriousness. He had started out as a taxi driver. Little by little, with loans and savings, he bought his own car. With what he earned he saved to buy another one, while he was still driving someone else's. At the age of thirty-four he owned almost an entire fleet and today he doesn't owe a peso to anyone. He struggled to get on top and he remembers every step of the way. Very boastful of his success, he became an entrepreneur. Even now he always drives one of his taxis, he doesn't stay home looking at what he's earned and he doesn't make others work for him. Perhaps that's why he turned out to be responsible with marriage, which was more a question of hurry than anything else. He got a distant cousin pregnant and the whole family—which is big and meddlesome—fenced him in and pressured him into getting married. He has four kids. Who would have thought it, a big strong man who acted like Rocky but is completely under his family's thumb.

A week after Independence Day, he appeared in his taxi at my job. I thought he hadn't even heard me when I told him where I worked. He invited me to McDonald's and we ate hamburgers and fries. Afterward he took me home, very polite, no mention of sex. I couldn't stop trembling, with disappointment, just on the inside, but still trembling like a fool.

Since my favorite subject has always been men, I've tried to imagine what it would be like to be one of them, genuinely believing that the world starts and finishes with him, feeling that he's the center of the earth, for Christ's sake, even though there are so many of them.

Don't think that Slim was any exception.

He began to court me, gradually, with plenty of respect. Like a big and heavy summer fly, he jumped between my lips and my tongue and even though I flapped about he wouldn't leave. He made himself indispensable. I even fell in love, like a stupid child. When I didn't see him on the weekends that made me sad. I wanted to share my house, my mom, and my daughter with him, watching *Sábado Gigante* on Saturday nights, the walks, the shopping. I thought about the other woman and although I hated her, I felt sorry for her. Slim loved me, God how he loved me. After about three months I told him I didn't want to see him anymore, it made me suffer knowing that he was married and I was single. I felt we were in an unequal relationship. We stopped seeing each other for ten days. That was the first of twenty times we decided to end our story. No need to tell you about our reunion after those ten days. We were worse than starving dogs. He had a room in the garage where he kept his taxis. We turned it into our nest, I even sewed new drapes and bought him a nice quilt. When we'd been seeing each other for a year, I gave him an ultimatum. Either he separated from his wife or nothing. You're a pest, Juani. That's what he said. We were apart for about two months. The son of a bitch didn't dare separate from her and I went back to him.

That was the Mistake. You know how long this story went on? Ten years! Ten goddamn years. When the kids had grown up, when his dad had died, when the kids had left school. I fought with him, no fuss or shame about it, I needed him more than his own wife. I loved him more, it was that simple. But he didn't have the balls to leave her. Too much yelling makes the man docile and submissive. On top of that, his wife got *pregnant*, after we'd been together for five years. That was too much. Then I did lose my patience. Me taking care like an idiot every month and her getting pregnant. Me, unable to have a child of his. Stupid life. That time I did leave him. I tell a lie, I left him for a while, but it was the longest and most painful time. What can I do? Slim would ask me with an innocent face. Convince her to have an abortion, I shouted at him, angry, beside myself. I gave him a week to make a decision. On the agreed day he rang the bell. I greeted him in a singsong voice, knowing that, as if on a violin or guitar, a string had gone out of tune. Of course, you can guess the answer. I died a little bit inside.

What a coward Slim was, my God, he really needed to grow a pair! I, as a client of mine would say, was desolate, desolate.

We spent almost a year apart. I gave him time to see his son born without feeling guilty. When we got back together, I was different. I knew it wasn't going anywhere, that we had no future, that he would never leave the mother of his children. But all the same we were so happy together. We loved each other and we got along just great. I kept watching soccer with him, even taking in the third-division games because Slim was such a fan. Everything seemed the same but my mind was no longer stuck in a movie.

I've read so many articles in magazines devoted to "the other woman." That's what I'd become: the other woman. From the third year, more or less, he began to sleep at my house some nights. Susy went to my mom's room. I never knew what excuse he gave his wife, the taxis I suppose, I didn't ask. I always said to Susy, When you're older, don't even think about getting involved with a married man, don't make the same mistake. Yes, Mom, she would reply, as naturally as if I'd advised her not to drink coffee at night so that it didn't keep her up.

I don't regret a thing. But, ladies, like any good soccer team, I don't give in without a fight. Slim is crying for me. He knows he can't set foot in my house again if he hasn't changed his marital status. Perhaps he'll do it one day, and maybe I won't be here for him. I might meet someone else tomorrow, the way I met the Greek, although with the sorrow I've been carrying with me all this time, with these needles sticking in my chest, I'm not in the best state to meet anyone.

In truth, it's not Slim at all. It's the other things that are going around my head. All the things the doctors tell me about Susy's illness: the change in her self-esteem, the sleep disruption, the irritability, the anguish. That's what they tell me about. Those are the words I've had to learn. That's the way my life is going.

A few days ago a client told me about a tribe of Native Americans who live on a small Arctic island, up there, way, way up there. Around May 10 every year the sun comes up and doesn't go down again until the end of August. The idea has been buzzing around my head: starting a day and not ending it until three months later. Of course, what's a day, you might ask. But I can't get my head around the nightmare of the light. At what point would you spit at the devil to make him leave the house and allow you to sleep once and for all? Always light, at any time, no rest, the white, the illumination, the lack of shade. An almost eternal sun, as if nothing could be hidden. The giant, burning, exhausting day. How the people who live there must dream about night, the restfulness of the dark. I thought about how

I felt defenseless like them, faced with that light that shines without mercy, that accuses, that mistreats.

The son of a bitch.

The night will come. It'll come.

SIMONA

*W*e all have our obsessions. I'm sick of seeing how women give up everything just to keep a man by their side. Men are nothing more than a *symbolic object* and, believe me, we can live without such a token. I agree that this particular symbol has primitive origins and that we can insist on its metaphorical or allegorical value. But I refuse to be an accomplice. It distresses me to witness how women are prepared to bleed to death so as not to be alone. Who decided that the single life is a tragedy?

Let me introduce myself, my name is Simona. My mom was a devotee of Saint Simon. Don't think for a second that she had a fit of lucidity after reading *The Second Sex*. I'm sixty-one, I studied sociology at the Catholic University, I'm left-wing and have spent more than half my life fighting for equal rights for women, out of respect for our diversity. I was involved in some of the first groups to form in this country, debating, analyzing, and publishing on the subject. You could say that was the real birth of Women's Lib in Chile, although some female historian is bound to disagree. Before that, there were women's movements that worked to gradually build up a resolute will, but we were the first to confront and study gender theory. We were practically outcasts. That's how they treated us when we introduced the word *feminism* here. What an ugly word it has become, demonized, misused, worn and hackneyed. It's so basic and simple: to take a risk for a more humane life, in which every woman has the same rights and opportunities as a man. Breaking away from the design of millennia, changing the rules of power. It's a colossal task! We didn't go as far as taking to the streets with our bras in one hand, scissors in the other. We weren't quite that vociferous because we came late to the party, in great part because of the country's economic woes at the time. The world still wasn't globalized and we only learned from North American and European women after they had already advanced their own fights. We read Betty Friedan when *The Feminine Mystique* was already well-thumbed and underlined a thousand times in other continents. We arrived late and by that time we were already under the dictatorship. I don't suppose I need to explain what machismo can be like under a military dictatorship. When I see a young father in a park during office hours, holding his baby and feeding her, I smile and have the urge to whisper in his wife's ear, Tell me, you lucky thing, do you know why it is that you can go to a meeting while your husband takes care of the kid? It's thanks to every woman who fought before you were old enough to know that you needed to fight. It's thanks to your mother who, one March 8, was battered in the street by the dictator's police, to your grandmother who supported the suffragettes, to the North American factory women who refused to work standing up, to Simone de Beauvoir, to Doris Lessing, to Marilyn French, essentially, thanks to thousands and thousands of women.

In English, a language I frequently use to think and work, the Spanish word *historia* can be translated two ways, differentiating between the personal and the collective. *Historia chica*, the "little history," is a story; whereas the larger-scale *historia grande* is called "history." In Spanish, the word *cuento* also means "story."

This is the *cuento* of my life.

I was born into a well-to-do family, large and entertaining, and my childhood was everything a Dickens character would have envied.

Happy childhoods do exist, extremely happy ones, and mine was like that. It made me more or less confident of the world and of myself. I felt, without feeling it, that we owned the universe, or at least the country. My ancestors had played a part in shaping this republic and that heritage was passed from generation to generation. We believed fervently in public service. From my most tender years, I had heard talk of politics and sometimes I accompanied my mother to marches and rallies. For as long as I can remember, there was heated conversation at the dinner table and everyone could express an opinion. This made me a relatively curious, well-informed individual. My family had the virtue of being that way, as long as the subject of religion didn't crop up. Then all common sense and rationality disappeared and real nonsense was spoken. Of course, we went to Catholic school, an American one, that's where my English habit started. Every morning for twelve years I took the trolley, I liked its rhythm and the fact that it was powered by electric cables. The beautiful childhood landscape of my generation. At school, we were what you would call "pious." All of us so pious. We did nothing but pray and go to mass, we celebrated everything, the Month of Mary, Lent. We fasted a lot and took Communion almost every day. All of this diminished my intelligence, I'm sure of it. We were saturated with useless moral scruples. We all wanted to be nuns so as to satisfy that ravenous, exacting God. The Bible caught my attention. I felt very badly toward God. How could he be so chastising and selfish? In the New Testament, the wonderful character of Christ calmed my fears stoked by his father and he comforted my soul.

The rules were infinite. The world didn't exist outside our environment, and our environment was a delight. No blinds can shut out the sunshine from my memories, remembering the warmth of the daily routines. The solidity of those huge kitchens, the wonderful maids who told us stories and plied us with treats, the protection that emanated from the very sound of my father's voice. But the real world was entirely ignored, which makes me wonder about my daughters. Nothing escapes them. Will they be happier? I never met anyone my age who went to public school because I barely knew of the existence of public education. All references and activities related to what surrounded *us*. It was incredible to think there were worlds out there, close by, next to me, in the same city, parallel to mine, that breathed the same air and yet I didn't know, I didn't see them.

We had great respect for outward signs, as if each father had said to each child, You don't just belong to yourself, don't forget that. Wardrobe and language were good examples. We were always, always well dressed. At that time women didn't tend to wear pants. We wore sheer stockings that hooked up to our underwear—a kind of girdle, not at all sexy—and then, to our relief, pantyhose arrived. As an adult, I've never been able to wear sheer stockings, as if they are emblems of prudery and lack of imagination. We were dressed like old women at the age of fifteen, with silk or shantung dresses and tight skirts, full of pleats, with two-piece tweed suits, high heels, court shoes, and backcombed hair. When I see my daughters throw on a couple of rags and mess up their hair to go to a party, I wonder why I was born at the wrong time. I'm never quite sure whether they're in pajamas or fully dressed, they look just the same. I bought my first pair of jeans during my second year of university. I won't go on about what Chile was like at that time. It was a poor country where even some of the richest lived simply.

Language was another indicator of how my world differed from that of so many others. Language simultaneously damned and blessed, never resting, unmasking everything, pinpointing your place in the world, giving you identity, making you show your true colors. Our manner of talking was stiff, *very* stiff. Looking back, I can see that our vocabulary ended up being poor, too many words were omitted for being somewhat suspicious and this left us without names for certain things. For example, *ambo*, meaning a two-piece suit, fell into the category of something that, unlike the more formal three-piece ensemble, wasn't seen as entirely proper in our staid circles and therefore shouldn't be mentioned. But when the day came that you needed to talk about a man's suit where the jacket was distinct from the pants but still matched them, there was no word for it. I remember the first time one of my boyfriends used the word in front of me, I'd already distanced myself from my background and its prejudices years earlier, but I remember how hearing the word made me freeze. I was getting out of bed with him. Had I just been intimate with someone who talked about *ambos*? When I asked him, good-naturedly, not to say it again, he gave me a lesson on the lexical poverty of my social group, on our lack of culture and blah blah blah. What a humorless bastard!

Curse words didn't exist. Sometimes I heard one in my brothers' mouths, fighting among themselves, but never in front of our parents. Or in school, it was a girls' school, unthinkable. Neither my father nor my mother ever said anything inappropriate in front of us, and the same went for the rest of the extended family. I didn't have that eccentric aunt most people do, loose-tongued and foulmouthed. So, when I went to college and began to hear cursing, I had to swallow twenty times and bite my tongue so that no one would notice the horror it caused me. When one of my female classmates referred to sex as "fucking," I almost fainted. I never dreamed that one day it would be one of my favorite everyday words. Fuck this, fucking that, don't give a fuck. I love it. It's perfect for emphasis! One day I was out shopping with my mother on Calle Providencia and she was driving her Volvo. I was in my third year of sociology, so I must have been about twenty. Suddenly, a taxi crashed into us from behind, and the crunch of metal and the sound of my mom's screeching brakes gave us a massive fright. I was thrown forward, hitting my forehead on the glove compartment. At that moment—I was experiencing the schizophrenia of being one person at home and someone else at college—I cried out, "Shit." My mother, in the middle of the crash, instead of getting out to fight with the taxi driver or assess the damage, she leaned over my seat, opened the passenger door, and told me to get out.

Nothing that bore any relation to sex or bodily needs had a name. Neither, of course, did the different genital equipment.

We were so flawless.

* * *

So I was happy as a child, my teenage years were very, very good, I studied a lot, but always had room for parties, friends, and boyfriends. I was quite attractive and daring. I chose the men I wanted and fell in love easily.

Our social lives were played out mainly at home and we only went out to dance at a couple of discos that were approved by our parents, like Las Brujas, in the La Reina neighborhood, which was knocked down a while ago, to the great sorrow of my generation, and Lo Curro, above the city, near the mountains. I should stress that you only went there if a man invited you. There's no way a woman would have gone alone, it would have been as incongruous as showing up on Plaza de Armas in the buff. Those who weren't successful with the opposite sex weren't invited and so never went to those places. The gallant gentleman would pay for everything, we wouldn't even open our purses in jest. At private parties, in the homes of friends, we would let men take us up to dance, and those who were popular gave dances by number—almost like an old-fashioned dance card—and I remember my arrogance when I got to number ten. To think there was some poor bastard who counted the dances one by one, waiting for the tenth, to be able to dance with me. How awful! I always felt bad for the ugly girls, the *wallflowers*, the girls who spent all night in their seats because no one would ask them to dance.

Sex didn't even play a role in our lives. Chastity was the number one guideline in our social lives. The dances were regulated. So many centimeters between you and him, no cheek-to-cheek. The only ones to break those rules were "fresh" girls. Being fresh was the worst thing that could happen to you, nobody married fresh girls. As a couple, you only held hands and after a certain period of time got as far as kissing. What did we do with our lust? The concept didn't exist. When we were a bit older, before leaving school, the kisses became more passionate and we had to hold down the boy's hands to avoid temptation. Somehow, we knew that men still got up to their tricks

but only with women who weren't like us. We accepted this. They
had a right to let off steam. But it never would have occurred to us
not to reach marriage intact. Virginity was *so* important that it managed to tie itself up with muscles and nerves so that it was almost
impossible to free it.

I want to return to language before I continue. Is this a shroud,
a straitjacket? How they coerced us, gagged us. Even today, after all
these years, I'm surprised by how much I'm a victim of my prejudices. Does anyone believe you can ever be free of the education you
received? You can't free yourself, you might rebel, but you can never
be entirely independent.

When I started college, my life changed completely. I found myself
in a world where not everyone was the same. I discovered there were
different people in my country. What a surprise! I started studying
sociology in the hope of understanding something of the world, but
I ended up more confused than ever. We were living through the end
of the sixties, the final years of Frei Montalva's presidency, polariza-
tion in Chile and the whole world. It was difficult to remain right-
wing in that environment. Everything worthwhile was on the other
side: the revolutionary priests, Che, Cohn-Bendit, Miguel Ángel
Solar, the student movement that occupied the Catholic University.
Even today those at the University of Chile, who always looked down
on us, can't stand the idea that the Católica students took the college
before they did. For some reason, back then I didn't quite grasp that
anything related to art was hated by the right. Writers and poets,
musicians and actors, painters and moviemakers were all on the left.
Sexual liberty also appeared to be in their possession. All in all, anything fun or valuable crossed to the other side.

Among this avalanche of doubts and ruptures, many ideas disappeared and others arrived. It was my faith that was most vilified in
the process. It simply disappeared. As Updike would say, *The Holy
Ghost . . . who the hell is that? Some pigeon, that's all . . .*

I changed my religion to politics. I joined the left.

Mine is a very commonplace story. Good-girl rebel abandons social class to join the revolution. I'm a textbook case! Here I am, almost forty years later, realizing how I went from one mold to another, only the contents changed.

Without going on about it too much, I am, to use the language of my profession, one of those who moved from the ethics of conviction to the ethics of responsibility. A difficult transition, that, and I think we did it quite successfully. We didn't stay in a state of adolescence, thank God. It's an environment in which we learn, almost always the hard way, how to grow.

I fell in love with a fellow student who was a few years older than me and an assistant on my course. His name was Juan José and he was my first great love. It took me a long time to make my relationship with him official because, after the rigidity of my former life, it was so nice to go out with several men at once. I discovered, between street demonstrations and wall painting, that sex was fantastic and I didn't want to miss out. If I had gotten married when I left school—to some future businessman or politician, as was the expectation—and remained married to him until today, like many of my classmates, almost all of them, to tell the truth, then, strictly speaking, I only would have known one male body in my life.

Circumstances made the decision for us. Juan José, Juanjo as we called him, was awarded a grant to get a master's at Duke University in North Carolina. We had to get married. Don't even think about starting with any liberal waves, Simona, or they'll take your visa, gringos are very difficult, we were told. That put a stop to any mutterings against marriage from me.

I have good memories of those days. Every day I appreciated the existence of the pill because living off a meager grant, a pregnancy would have made things impossible. I know cases of women who were unable to experience the wonderful lack of worry and educational opportunity afforded by a husband's grant. These same women forced their men to impregnate them to resolve their own deficiencies and fears, without the slightest consideration for their husbands' pursuits. I didn't for a second lose sight of the fact that Juanjo was putting in enormous effort and I was free to use and enjoy my own time. I felt it was a gift and I chose to take some classes, only to discover that I hated linguistics and phonetics. The only thing I liked was reading. The pleasure of reading was about to be snatched away by an excess of analysis, after all, that's what they do to books at college, they analyze them. So I dropped out of the classes and took advantage of the magnificent library to conscientiously devote myself to months of reading, stretched out on the only couch in our apartment. Chile fell to pieces as I flirted with the handsome Mr. Darcy or flung open the doors at Brideshead.

Families were split down the middle, one lot hated the other, agrarian reform intensified, land was lost. We all know the outcome of the whole process that led us to Salvador Allende's death, after having been the first nation in the world to democratically take socialism to power. I'd prefer not to linger on that today. There are pains that doggedly plague us until our final days.

Dictatorship underway, we returned to Duke. This time Juan José would go for his doctorate and I had recently given birth to my first daughter, Lucía. I couldn't even allow myself the luxury of dropping out of classes, as in previous years. All I saw were diapers, feeding bottles, pureed carrots and chard, and hours and hours inside the house, dealing with the North American cold and my increasingly hard heart. Suddenly, I felt as if a crack had opened up in the ground. I returned to Chile with my daughter and that's as far as my marriage went.

I would have to hook up a few more times before I met Octavio, the love of my life. Fucking Octavio. We're both Leo, that says it all. Pure fire on both sides. Rarely have I known a more passionate couple. We adored each other, we loved each other, we fought like a couple from a poor neighborhood of Naples, we screwed a lot, we traveled, we talked, we read the same books, we had an infinitely good time. I wanted him to get me pregnant because of the sheer amount of love I felt, and I did manage, although without much enthusiasm on his part. So my second daughter, Florencia, was born. My saintly mother took care of the girls when I needed her to and that way we managed to keep traveling and maintain our crazy rhythm. I was with him for just over twenty years. How can a relationship fail at our age, after twenty years? It sounds impossible, but that's how it was. Octavio was bad-tempered and a TV addict. No, more of a soccer addict. Or both. Like the set he venerated, he had an ON/OFF switch in his brain and when it was on, Lord have mercy on us.

Of course, it's my fault. Nobody forced me to be his wife. We'd been dating for three months when he invited me to Spain. He had to work for a couple of days and then we would take a week to tour the south. I set off with him fully aware that traveling allows you to discover things that remain hidden during the normal routine of daily life. In this sense, the trip was illuminating. We hired a car and, meandering from village to village, we arrived in Seville. After settling into the hotel we went out for a walk and saw a poster saying that Joan Manuel Serrat was singing in the Maestranza, the city's bullring. I was very excited. We were in the middle of a dictatorship and Serrat couldn't set foot in Chile. We decided to go to the concert that night, no matter what. We ate early and went to our hotel room to rest for a while before going out. Octavio lay on the bed and turned on the television. Manchester United was playing and he became engrossed in the game. After fifteen minutes, I asked him to get up because we had to leave for the Maestranza. He answered with a curt "Wait." I sat on the bed. Every two minutes I looked at the clock. Octavio, we're going to be late. No, don't worry, we'll leave in a minute. Finally, I stood in front of the screen and said, in a firm voice, We have to go. This was the first time I saw how he could change. He turned red, his eyes clouded over, and his mouth contorted into an ugly grimace. Don't block the screen, he shouted. Octavio had never shouted at me.

I just stood there looking at him, incredulous, immobile, as if hypnotized. He repeated himself, only this time it was more threatening. When I came to my senses I left the room immediately and went to the concert, alone. The switch had been flicked on. As I walked, disconcerted, sad and angry, I thought, So this is my new flame? The man I was traveling with had disappeared. I knew I should take the next plane back to Chile. He hadn't just treated me badly, he had broken his promises too. Those two things were enough to end the romance. Today Serrat, tomorrow something else, I now knew him well enough *not to stay.*

He arrived at the concert during the intermission, as if nothing had happened. I didn't take the plane home.

During our relationship, I often told him how crazy I'd been not to go home that day. His response was always the same: Can you imagine what you would have lost? Who in the world would have loved you more than me? Who could have made you happier? The remarkable thing is, put like that, he was right.

The million-dollar question, Why did I fall in love with a lazy man? Because his laziness wasn't permanent, it didn't reveal itself every day, only when that famous switch was turned on. To make things worse, he was fanatical about food. I've never heard so many rules about how things should be just so in that department. With him, *things were never done right.* In the house I grew up in, it was considered impolite to talk about food. Crazy me, from there I took such a leap that I ended up living with someone who had no other topic of conversation. I love eating, but only as much as anything else.

One time, near the end of my pregnancy with Florencia, Octavio was watching the Copa Libertadores, stretched out on the bed totally caught up in the action. I was trying to take a nap next to him but I knew I wouldn't be able to because of the sound of the TV. I got up to look for something to eat in the kitchen and as I walked down the hall I felt a stab of pain and a strange cold sensation between my legs, followed by a spurt of water. When I realized what was happening, I shouted, Octavio, my water broke. No response. He obviously hadn't heard me. I walked with difficulty into the bedroom, leaving a mess in my wake. I shouted again, *My water broke!* Then he looked at me, unable to ignore the spectacle in front of him, enormous legs open and dripping. Do you think he immediately leaped up and looked for the car keys to take me to the clinic? No. He said, Wait a bit, the first half is about to finish. I grabbed the remote control from his hand and threw it against the wall, which at least managed to startle him. The mark remained and fifteen years later, I would look at it when I was annoyed and say to myself, Sorry, honey, but what the hell are you *still* doing with him?

When we were small, I had a dog named Copito. He ate with me, went out with me, slept with me, we were inseparable and I lavished him with all my love. Then—as a good Catholic—I decided one day that Copito should take First Communion, as I had recently. I organized the whole ceremony, I invited some of our cousins, all the maids, my siblings, and our parents. I gave him blessings, as I had been given. I cut up bits of card, I drew angels and cribs on them and on the back I wrote an evangelical phrase, Copito's name, and the date. It was all going great. Then the day before the ceremony, one of my brothers saw me in the garden hitting Copito. He approached, alarmed, to find out what had happened. He doesn't want to say the Lord's Prayer, I told him furiously, I've been teaching him for hours and he doesn't want to pray.

People don't change. We should learn this from the start, without wasting years, pity, or energy trying to force change. If God created a bit of flexibility in the world, it was women who stockpiled it. Men were left with nothing. They never change. Only with Prozac, if you can make them take it.

Speaking of Prozac, medication is an important topic. Men feel ever so virile for being able to overcome problems on their own. *On their own* means without medicine or therapy. They see facing problems without chemistry as a great masculine adventure. Where does such stupidity come from? I've heard men boast about getting over depression *alone*, on their terms. Why don't they understand that chemistry could be their salvation, that one pill a day, one dumb little pill, could draw back the black veil covering the sun? Octavio certainly regarded anything related to therapy and psychotropic drugs with horror.

When I left Octavio, there was *no one* who didn't tell me I was stupid or crazy. I was depressed, in therapy with Natasha and taking my medication. Octavio didn't really understand what was happening to me. To him, connecting with his emotions was something he could do without. He tried to support me but because he didn't understand, his support was immaterial. He thought he should be able to lift me out of my depression by inventing ways to entertain me. He decided we would go to China, the journey would make me better. He didn't quite grasp the effort it took me just to get out of bed. I rented a house at the beach to spend a season away from any pressure, with the promise that he would visit on weekends.

The first Friday night he arrived, full of charm, with a beautiful basket of tasty things I particularly like: pâté, Brie, farmhouse bread, red wine. He told me how much he'd missed me, how empty everything was without me. We ate in the kitchen, very close to one another, and that painful emptiness of my depressed days seemed to alleviate. When we went up to the bedroom, he looked around and asked, very disconcertedly, Where's the TV? There's no TV in the house, I answered. How come you've rented a house with no TV? In my condition, I told him, I find it a relief. But they're showing the Barça–Real Madrid game tonight, he exclaimed. I left Santiago early so I could watch it here. I'm sorry, I replied, slightly concerned that I hadn't warned him, but we can call the girls and ask them to record it for you. The switch went on and he shouted at me for being selfish, of not thinking about him, of mistreating him. I'm the one who's depressed, Octavio, I can barely take care of my own needs. He looked at me like a madman, grabbed the car keys, and left. On the stairs he yelled, I'm never coming back to this house!

I watched him leave and thought how terrifying it was to bear witness to a lucid, intelligent man turning into an idiot in a split second. My depression was a mere tidbit next to the Barcelona game. I felt like that idiot from Steinbeck who, for want of any other skin to stroke, pets dead mice in his pocket.

Sure enough, he didn't return. On the phone, I reminded him of my condition and fragile state and asked him to come and see me. But he didn't. My anger became too great. Two weeks later, when I returned to Santiago, I left him.

I told myself, Never again will I be a receptacle for my husband's trash. Another human being, because he lives with you, because he entered a certain alliance called marriage, believes he can use you as a place to put his scraps, be they his rages, his failures, his frustrations, his fears, his insecurities. I didn't come up with that, I read it in a novel once. The protagonist called herself "her husband's trashcan"—it was definitely written by a woman. That is what almost all of us are or have been. Anyone who hasn't, raise your hand for a round of applause.

Everyone around me, with the best of intentions, reminded me how happy we had been, how much we had loved each other, what good times we'd had. It was all true. But something very deep inside me had been damaged. If I witnessed another of Octavio's tantrums, I would have come undone, breaking into pieces. Or, I would have killed him. I was convinced he would end up in a state of idiocy. How much TV can one brain handle? I knew, to my core, that the price for maintaining this life with him was *compromise*. What dangers that word entails. How far can you compromise without seriously violating your identity, without permanently losing self-respect? I imagined the future. How many more times would his brain switch to ON?

As a committed feminist, it was frightening to realize that my self-esteem was waning. If this can happen to me, I wondered, what happens to other women? This contradiction was bad for me. I felt like I was a sham.

When we met, I gave Octavio a Shelley quote: *Thou Wonder, and thou Beauty, and thou Terror.* When the wonder and beauty diminished, twenty years later, I sent him the quote again, with the last word underlined.

I was alone. At that time I was fifty-seven.

I dismissed the idea of another partner. The market is cruel, as our president Aylwin said, and the kind of men who could emotionally and intellectually be with a woman of fifty-seven tend to choose thirty-seven-year-olds. The truth is, I didn't feel like going back to living life as a couple. I'd already had what I needed to have. When I found myself alone, I began to feel a great relief.

No more soccer on the screen.

No more man lying in bed with a remote control and glassed-over eyes.

No more constant noise from the TV.

No more earplugs to get to sleep.

No more taking my book in search of a place to read because I couldn't do it in my room.

No more competing with teams like Colo-Colo for a little bit of attention.

No more:

"Simona, you buy the wine for tonight because I'm busy, the first half has just started."

"For God's sake, Simona, the Blues are playing, can't you tell the girls to shut up?"

"Listen, Simona, you can take the phone off the hook, nothing's going to happen while I'm watching the game."

"Call this a home? With an empty refrigerator? How is it possible that a man can't find the slightest bit of understanding in his own house?"

"Switch off that light, Simona, please, I can't see the TV with the glare. Go and read someplace else."

I no longer had to take care of another mind, another body, other ambitions, other domesticities—in short, other pains. I felt lighter. Natasha was hugely important in supporting my bold decision. When I think of married women, I wonder how many of them are where they want to be. Sometimes I used to stroll around my neighborhood in Santiago and look at the houses and apartments, thinking about the everyday movements behind the drapes. I wondered, How many of them wish they were somewhere else?

For me, the internal debate was quite clear. Either I resigned myself to cynicism or I left Octavio. Cynicism is a tool many people turn to, especially as we grow older. We tell ourselves we are adults now, we shouldn't think of love as integral. A stain doesn't sully the whole tablecloth, and if the stain is nasty, why not put a vase over it and leave it at that? It's so goddamn simple! Cynicism tends to insinuate itself behind every back like a small snake, tempting, tempting.

But despite the temptations, cynicism didn't seduce me. I'm in the place I chose. We women are so unused to *choosing*, saddled with our dependencies, both financial and emotional.

I did lose a lot. Because if I do the exercise Octavio always asked me to, weighing up the good and the bad in our relationship, the good was *very* good. That's why I stayed with him for so many years. Shit, what happened to our intimacy? We were so, so intimate. I could never be in the same place as him without sensing his presence, there was so much strength and pleasure inside me that I could never stop seeing it. If I got up to fetch a glass of water, I'd interrupt his reading of the newspaper just to touch him, to prove that I always noticed him, that I was grateful to life that he was there. I always touched him. I never let him take for granted our closeness. He appreciated it every day. I never knew anything like the noble way he loved me.

He was never miserly with his love, he never measured it, never calculated it. He loved me entirely and openly and never closed a door, even during the worst moments. He never refused to gently welcome me to his bed if I wanted to get in. He never would have admitted that I might feel insecure about his love, not for a single second.

The relationship was so deep. I could have disappeared beneath it, hidden, protected myself from the whole world, except for him. A thousand times I begged him to do something about his laziness, his addiction, whatever you want to call it, his bad character, which would end up breaking this unique thing we possessed. I begged and begged him, because I knew that sooner or later that same indolence and that same bad temper would make me say goodbye. He paid no attention.

I've lost a lot.

Shakespeare said it all: *Love is merely a madness.*

My friends, especially those who live in a more or less conventional way, used to tell me how pathetic single women are. That there's always one at their table at weddings and the poor things always have high hopes, their desperate eyes revealing the curse of their condition. That they get together to make lists of those in the process of separating or those who have been widowed so they can snatch up a man. That they only meet up with other single women like themselves—go to the movies with them, go out to eat, run errands together on the weekends. Who can fulfill the role of husband? Why can't they go to the movies alone? There's nothing better than watching a movie in silence. I'm no one to judge, but I feel sorry for them. It's so unfair that they live with the permanent feeling of being vacant. When they told me of the *horror* of not having a partner, my mind objected. To hell with the symbolic object, I thought. I'll finally be able to live the way I want. I was even more distressed—still am—by the way that, to get a man, they lower their standards. As each birthday comes around, the standards slip and they resign themselves to men who, in their youth, they wouldn't have looked at twice. Their expectations lower. Equality goes out the window. If you really felt you had a choice, would you have chosen him? So I see wonderful women with real morons.

One of my sisters is married to an important businessman and she spends her time attending "social obligations" that pertain to him. I, being the loner I am, imagine how her night will be as I watch her getting ready in front of the mirror. I think about the obligatory formal conversations awaiting her, the food that will be served late, the hours she has to fill with small talk, about how she's going to feign interest in her dinner companion—and he'll do the same for her—about how many drinks she'll need to tolerate the boredom, how many intelligent comments she'll have to make so they don't think her husband married an idiot, how those heels will make her feet hurt on the way home, the languor with which she'll think of her bed as the woman next to her is describing some incident involving her children. So I say, let's get rid of all these socio-marital obligations! Everyone has enough of their own stuff to deal with, but to take on a partner's too? Accompanying someone else is nice sometimes. Why don't you come with me? I'm by myself. The act of going toward that other person makes sense in itself. I, first subject, am accompanying second subject and the verb *accompany* ties it up beautifully. But when it extends to third parties it makes no sense.

A couple is made up of two independent people, it's not just an amalgam, for God's sake!

I think every human is born with a certain boredom threshold. There's no doubt that some have higher thresholds than others. But I think we need to be on the alert for the moment when we reach the brink. We have a duty to see it in time. If you don't realize it, you can collapse in quite terrible ways. Watch out! Have you already hit your threshold? If so, withdraw, cut, finish. Don't hurt yourself.

Convinced that an excess of optimism is in bad taste, I tried to put things in perspective. I could view the path with low beam or full beam. I made my choice. I must mention that Lucía, my eldest daughter, had now married and Florencia was in England doing a postgraduate degree. In other words, the role of mother wasn't a central one.

In my mind, I no longer pursued *truth* but imagination. I was certain I had already experienced my periods of pure truth; I no longer believed in it or needed it. Yet hunger for imagination grows and grows, it gets bigger with each new day I open my eyes. How strange what I am saying to you sounds. I never thought that truth and imagination could ever be opposites. I don't know whether I truly think that.

Sometimes, like Lewis Carroll, I'd like to know what the flame of a candle is like after the candle is blown out.

I put my house in Santiago up for sale and while the realtor took care of viewings, I toured the Chilean coast in my car. I needed a village, the kind you get in Europe or the United States, where there's life, people, and services during the winter. There are so many small villages on other continents where I'd go at the drop of a hat. We lack these in Chile. All our beauty is hidden in wild places, the most stunning in the world, but still wild. It's difficult to leave the capital and choose somewhere to live sociably in this country. It has to be pretty too, very pretty to tempt me; a second-rate place would horrify me, like my mother and grandmother before me. *That* never leaves you.

I spent a couple of years taking advantage of the privilege of working from home. The organization I do research for doesn't even have an office in Chile, so I can work from anywhere. Going to Santiago once a month to check data and look up a few things in the library is enough for me. I needed an immense horizon, I needed the sea. Minimalism, lightening the load. I suppose a path was marked out for me by that simple and eternal line the horizon gives to the ocean. You accumulate a lot of things in fifty-seven years, from furniture to relationships, from acquaintances who become friends to ornaments on coffee tables. I decided to relinquish it all. As if it were some kind of rite, I cut and bleached my hair so that I wouldn't ever have to dye it again. Then I invited over all my friends and started to give away the thousand things I didn't need, from necklaces to vases. I set aside what I would take to my new life and was fascinated by how little there was. Have you ever thought about all the unnecessary objects that surround you? Bracelets, for example. I love bracelets and every time I see a nice one I buy it. But it turns out I never wear them. I find them uncomfortable. You can't spend long at the computer with those hoops of silver or wood rattling against the table or mouse. All the linen, the whites, as they're known, although it's almost impossible to keep them entirely white. My mom taught me that there are three sets of sheets and three sets of towels, one in use, one in the wash, and the other set clean in the closet. I bought myself a couple of duvets and that's it. Getting into a fluster making beds the old way? No, thanks. Then, my clothes. Those shoes you wear once a year for an elegant dinner. I wouldn't be going to any more dinners like that. A person's social life has an expiration date, like yogurt. But the shoes, the dresses, the accessories ended up in the hands of a couple of friends who never miss a wedding. I put aside some silk, cashmere, and alpaca scarves and shawls, not because of their quality but because I like the feel of them against my body. A couple of dresses for the summer. Just like that, to my delight, the material around me slimmed down considerably.

I bought myself an apartment on the most beautiful beach in Chile.

I didn't want a house, I wasn't up to that anymore. I decided that, as well as a fireplace, I deserved central heating, security, a twenty-four-hour super, someone who would help me up the stairs with groceries and, above all, keep me from having to deal with plumbers and electricians. Never again to deal with a caretaker or gardener. I filled my terrace with plants and I do my own modest gardening. I have immense windows, nothing interrupts my view of the sea. Goodbye security bars. The apartment has two bedrooms with their own bathrooms as well as a small room where I set up my office. Daughters and friends have a place to sleep and the spaces are pleasant and contained. It's all easy there.

I must mention Bungalow Bill. When I moved to the beach, my daughters decided I might get lonely and bought me a dog. Not a little dog, no, a dog that grew and is now enormous and takes up more space in the apartment than me. He's a cream-white Labrador, the color of country butter. To begin with, I didn't attach much importance to him and complained about the responsibility involved in walking him every day and teaching him to behave. But the inevitable happened. He seduced me and now I'm his most devoted admirer. Within the darkness of his eyes, little bits of sadness sometimes appear. *Hey, Bungalow Bill, what did you kill, Bungalow Bill.* No one on this earth loves me as much as he does, and he's a dog. It's pathetic, I know. Because he's been reared in an apartment, with no one but me, he's a very educated animal. I know Labradors are generally naughty as well as playful, but Bungalow Bill wisely decided to make himself comfortable in the reality that befell him and sometimes several hours go by without me knowing anything of his life, nor he of mine. When I want to stay in bed because I can't be bothered getting up and I'm reading some novel I don't want to put down, I call Angélica, a girl from the village who always has her cell phone on, and I ask her to take my place and organize his walks.

The second gift from my daughters was to teach me how to use an iPod. They recorded all my music and I didn't even have to transfer my CDs, or the old cassettes and vinyl. When I'm walking Bungalow Bill, I take my iPod and as he runs I lose myself in the rhythm of Vicentico or Brahms. This device has made a huge contribution to my life. It's good to have young people around so you don't miss out on new things.

Who would have thought it? I bought a very large plasma-screen television and set up a mailbox where I receive all the whims with which Amazon tempts me. As for television series, I have no doubt they play the role novels did in the nineteenth century. I imagine Balzac delivering his weekly chapter, just as the *Mad Men* writers do, while television viewers wait with the same eagerness as the readers of those days. It's the modern-day method of living the fantasy of other lives, to go to far-flung places and put yourself in someone else's shoes. All in all, it's the new form of storytelling. To think that I criticized my husband's addiction so much. But I only watch the series when I have the whole season. I'm unable to keep up with formal television timetables and when I get immersed in them I watch episode after episode, sometimes I stay up all night, as I did with *24*. I don't have the faintest critical sense in front of Jack Bauer—who deep down is a fascist—and no matter what he does, I love him. For some reason, in Santiago I didn't dare stay awake all night. It's strange, the way it works there, merely existing took away my freedom to sleep all morning if I needed to. Because of A, B, or C, there was always something happening about to stop me and if it was still to be done, I was racked with guilt.

I like my new home. I've become contemplative over the years and I give it fantastical connotations depending on the day. Sometimes it's a cave where Eve breast-fed; on other occasions, it's the halls of a Turkish harem, where the concubine, wrapped in silks and fantastic textiles, takes pleasure in the precious independence afforded by the mogul forgetting to choose her. I also think of my house as the austere study of a medieval monk, to which only some apprentices have access and whose shelves of old books cover the walls from the floor to the high ceiling. Of them all, there is one fantasy I particularly like: a Spanish address where a long time ago, in 1799, Goya's *Caprichos* were sold, 1 Calle del Desengaño in Madrid, a perfume and spirits shop.

I take care of myself and I feel it's the first time I have. I don't knead my own bread every morning as Yourcenar did, but I buy it myself. From my own bread to living on my own timetable, everything is in my hands. I go to the harbor and buy the freshest fish, straight out of the sea. I'm already a regular and they'll put aside some hake or sea bass if I'm running late. Angélica, the girl who walks Bungalow Bill, does the cleaning twice a week because I'm tired of vacuuming and washing clothes. She's my only external help and the only trace of how spoiled I have been. In February, I shut up the apartment and go on vacation, like everyone else in the Southern Hemisphere. Don't imagine that I live a stoic or self-sacrificing life, quite the opposite. When I can't be bothered cooking, I eat bread and cheese—my favorite foods, always with a glass of red wine— and think about how the following morning I'll take a stroll along the beach and work off the calories. What's more, I have no need to be a Barbie. I'm sixty-one and no one pays attention to my curves. Sometimes at sunset, I settle down on the terrace with a drink in my hand and do nothing. I just watch. I'll say it again, I have become contemplative. I find inactivity appealing, which is new to me. I've learned to meditate. I do it with great discipline every day and the result is unexpectedly positive. Why did I never learn before?

The mornings are very productive. I wake up energetic and sharp because I've had a good rest. I like mornings. Rain is my favorite weather condition. Its ancient sound is musical to me. It's not that I like getting wet or walking about in it Hollywood-style, but some- thing happens to me when it's cold outside and warm inside behind the big window, languidly wrapped in a throw, hugging Bungalow Bill and watching the waves. I'm never happier than I am then. I look after myself, I wrap up warm while nature does her thing. Perhaps this pleasure has something to do with the feeling that I've beaten the elements. So I feel for all the women who are selling their souls to hold on to their symbolic objects. I feel like shouting at them, Life can be full without a partner, enough already!

I'm not lonely when I'm alone.

I find myself particularly drawn to characters who have an obses- sion, a fixed ideal. There's nothing more potent than that, potent and all-consuming. Perhaps that's the only difference between us all: our fixed ideal.

The precondition for life turning out this way is being able to amuse yourself. Value yourself. Without internal resources, you have nothing. Samuel Beckett wrote something I tend to quote when I'm doubtful of my conduct: *No matter. Try again. Fail Again. Fail better.*

As we already know, defects are heightened with age, especially when they don't have the necessary social control. When you live entirely on your own terms, a life that's almost one hundred percent your choosing, the setting plays a negligible role. My dark parts have become more powerful. I have to live with that. Now that I've opted for this freedom of form, I'd like to liberate my mind too, to be capable of casting doubt on absolutely everything. Allowing my thoughts, not just my body, to go adrift. But I find myself unable to tolerate the doubt. It takes a world of effort to abandon my certainties. Sometimes I see myself as a fool who thinks she knows it all and who, on top of that, tries to lecture about life. I don't want to be that woman.

My worst sin is elitism and only part of it is inherited. I'm not talking about the racism or classism of my ancestors, no. Mine manifests itself due to other reasons, for example, my impatience with limited perspectives and my contempt for middle management. I've never been able to tolerate them or think of them as anything other than dull, mediocre, and generally social climbers. Anything *middle* alienates me, as does middle-class spirit when it shows its most miserable side, full of immediacy, conservatism, and lack of imagination.

The first time I took my daughters to New York, Lucía, who couldn't have been more than fifteen, stood in the middle of Fifth Avenue, looked both ways, and said to me, with complete candor and sincerity, So this is New York? I feel absolutely *chez moi* here! Well, I feel like I'm expelled from *chez moi* when I'm surrounded by tastelessness. This reveals itself in the most trivial everyday things, like broadcast television, reality shows, self-help books, happy hour, group tourism. I find it all an assault. To put it in terms of North American culture, anything with a whiff of redneck or white trash upsets me so much that I hope never to be close to any of its components. I'm not afraid of a certain kind of decadence. I don't find it vulgar like its opposite. Octavio belonged to this country's elite, as did I. There's no getting away from that. I'd rather stay silent for months than get involved in pointless conversations. I've always marveled at the way some people can be friends with anyone, whether stupid, boring, or common. I marvel as I observe them with radical contempt.

Solitude is never radical. It becomes relative, because the presences that accompany me are amazingly solid. They really are. *That* is love, nothing more, nothing less. The strength of these presences. These adorable ghosts who drink tea or an afternoon tipple with you. My daughters, for example. Fucking motherhood, as overrated as it is reviled. How could I be abstract about something as robust as my daughters' lives, even if it hurts? Images of Lucía and Florencia come to me, I observe them closely, fascinated by them, they make me laugh with their expressions and mimicry. I look at their haircuts, their colors, the way they gesture, their shoes, the way they move their necks. I barely blink, as if dazzled. Florencia practices self-control and precision, all her intelligence focused on it, like at breakfast when she spreads jelly on her toast, very gradually, covering the surface only as far as the next bite—the jelly never advances over the whole slice—with extraordinary calm and seriousness. That's her. And Lucía, the tightrope walker, with frivolity in one hand and profound gravity in the other, never allowing either to bolt, simultaneously insecure and emphatically blasé. When she hangs a painting in her new house, hammer in hand, she closes one eye to see it in perspective, always with a touch of extravagance and laughter at the edge of her angelic yet theatrical gaze.

Without them, I wouldn't have the faintest idea of the meaning of love.

I go to Santiago every now and then to do what I need to. I see Natasha, go to the dentist, visit a friend or my extended family, do a bit of window shopping. It's all much the same, I find that it's me who's different. I won't make a trite comparison between the metropolis and a little coastal village. I'll just say that there comes a point when you have to stop pissing about with the traffic and pollution and decide to improve your quality of life. The capital isn't everything, far from it.

On my most recent trip to Santiago I went to the gynecologist for a Pap smear, mammogram, a routine visit. I put my legs up in the stirrups and the doctor—a young man, half Italian, very lovely— placed the gel down below as he watched the monitor up above. After a while, he said, You're great, impeccable. Your ovaries are atrophied but that's typical at your age, nothing to worry about. I returned home thinking, So at my age, you can be *impeccable* and *atrophied* at the same time. Shit!

Personally, I'm a long way from feeling I've narrowed down my life, limited myself and diminished my possibilities. Politics still interest me and every morning, before I start work, I read online newspapers, *El País* and the *New York Times*. I spend ten minutes on the Chilean press, just the headlines, it's too ideological to be good press. My interest in political events is part of my DNA, I can't free myself of it. When I travel, Chile grows in stature. I get emotional when I view it from a distance. We residents of the Third World are sentimental and patriotic. We don't have the sarcasm or distance of the Europeans. Only if we snipped our sense of belonging at the root could we reach their level of cynicism toward *homeland*. Our history is still fragile, short, it could fall from the tree like a branch, so we can't allow ourselves many luxuries.

Once a year, my daughters and I take a long journey, just the three of us. It turns out I don't spend much money in my day-to-day life and I give all my savings to a friend—a financial expert—to move around for me and suddenly I found I had a lot more than I thought. Some of our trips have been very expensive. There won't be anything left to leave them as an inheritance, but we have decided to spend it all on life. Last spring, we rented a little house in Santorini. It's great fun choosing the destination of the next journey. We settle down with a map and the internet and the ideas start to flow. Lucía, who is the biggest fantasist, chooses impossible places. She's trying to convince me we should take the Trans-Siberian Railway, from Moscow to Beijing. I insist that if we do, we'll run out of money.

I'm more than ready to be a grandmother and I hope it happens soon. The problem is that my daughters, like good modern-day women, haven't even thought about it yet. But I sense a tremendous light behind this reality and I watch it with patience and pleasure. Ready, with my body and home open.

Do I miss sex? I don't know, not really.

To be honest, menopause came as a great relief. Whoever said it was a tragedy? Naturally, there were a couple of embarrassments and headaches, some changes in body temperature, but just look at the benefits. No more of those cursed days of bleeding every month, no more contraceptive pills. What enormous liberation.

Sex. What I sometimes miss is a certain intimacy with a man, a way of squeezing a hand, leaning against a safe body, burying my face in a shoulder, typically gestures with thousands of years of learning behind them.

Although Octavio didn't speak to me for more than a year after I left him, he's been to see me a couple of times since then. Like me, he hasn't embarked on another serious relationship, just some barely relevant flings. I think we both feel we'd already had our share of love on this earth and we aren't looking for more. We know it is impossible.

Speaking of which, the other day I wondered, If I die alone in my apartment by the beach, who would tell Octavio of my love for him? He doesn't know. Not him or anyone else because I'm afraid to know it myself.

I never told him. It wasn't possible to tell him. Love doesn't speak. It's always corny, sentimental, slightly loathsome. There's nothing more trite than a spoken admission of love, nothing more throwaway. The image of Octavio, the idea of Octavio grasped me like a hand, digging, boring as far as it could go, there was nothing left underneath. It filled me up. I breathed Octavio, I drank him in.

When we met I told him about Alice in Wonderland, and I said that I wanted to be like that bottle, DRINK ME, and that cake, EAT ME.

Every day of my life, for more than twenty years, I received Octavio like Communion. But he didn't know it.

His job sent him to work in Barcelona. He's been living outside Chile for three years now, but in an email he said that in his retirement, he's on the verge of retiring, he'll come back and buy a house on this beach, so that we can be friends. After everything, he writes, I'm still the father of one of your daughters. In my reply I told him not to threaten me. I remind him of what my aunt Sofía used to say, There are no impregnable fortresses, only fortresses that haven't been sufficiently besieged.

I'll finish by recounting the accusations made against me and what they mean to me.

I'm accused of being antisocial and indifferent toward people, of having renounced the advantages that surrounded me to wash my hands of others. An epitaph for my grave: "Selfish, pure and simple."

I'm accused of refusing duties and conventions, of escaping from the known world because I can't tolerate it. I've also been told I'm a misanthrope, that I hate humans, that I've become a hermit out of vanity, regarding others as unworthy of my presence, that I turn my back on people's affection because the only respect I'm interested in is my own.

I'm accused of being a pedant because I find the world superfluous.

Put like that, I can't deny it. But I could argue that there's an aspiration behind it all: indifference.

I've read a lot during this time by the sea, from Schopenhauer to the Buddhists. I've detached myself from my various possessions, from furniture and clothes to my husband, not to mention the social position I used to occupy, perhaps the hardest to abandon. I'm obsessed with this learning process and meditation helps me focus on the present. I breathe deeply to achieve the greatest liberation I can, which I imagine will always be less than I want. I feel like life is beginning to flow. It flows and I touch it. My fear of death diminishes.

I don't regret being sixty-one. This age has granted me a stillness, a new peace. The past doesn't matter, it's already happened. The future doesn't exist.

I raise my glass to the only truth we really own. The present.

LAYLA

I was born January 30, 1969, the day the Beatles played their last gig on that rooftop in London. My name is Layla. I'm a journalist. I graduated from the University of Chile. Arabic in origin, mine is the second generation in Chile. As an Arab, my life has become suspicious and paranoid, like a Jew's.

I'm an alcoholic. Since this isn't an Alcoholics Anonymous meeting, I feel I'm exempt from the job of supporting others. I'm relieved to be able to unleash myself on you. Natasha won't hold me back. But I'm hesitant to introduce myself with this characterization, immediately reducing everything I am to my alcoholism. It's strange that the tendency in this global world is to accentuate identities, picking the one that most marginalizes you—sexuality, race, disability. I'm struck by the way we all rush to join our particular group, emphasizing what makes us different from everyone else, in order to make us all the same.

Although my mother came over from Palestine at the age of twenty, my paternal grandfather arrived when he was a boy, fleeing the Ottoman Empire. He was put on a boat with a couple of uncles. He set foot in this country without even being able to point it out on a map. He only knew that many compatriots had chosen to emigrate here. They arrived with passports of the Empire, which meant that in Chile they were called "Turks." But that's incorrect, people from Turkey have nothing to do with us. One of the uncles opened a textile store and my grandfather, who hadn't even been to secondary school, was his assistant. My father is an enterprising man who never shies away from work. At the age of twenty, he opened his own fabric store. Today he's a textile entrepreneur with a fine warehouse on Independencia. He complains, of course, about the complete lack of national production. It annoys him to trade only with the Chinese and Koreans, although he knows that if he doesn't he'll be headed for bankruptcy. When he reached the age of starting a family, it didn't even occur to him to look among Chilean women. He ordered a wife from his own land. He married my mother without knowing her.

I was born and raised in an environment of absolute male authority. My mother spoke with an accent until the day she died. She worked in my dad's store her entire life, on the cash desk. Old and tired, she had no hopes of retiring. That's what family businesses are like. One day the numbers began to dance in front of her eyes. She felt like something was pressing on her chest. Within twelve hours she was dead. Like her entire family, during childhood her back had grown accustomed to heavy work. She didn't know how to be sick for more than twelve hours, as if her punishment had been established the day she was born. The only thing that mattered, in those moments at the clinic, was not annoying my dad. She had told me that her parents had one single bed in the entire house. He slept in it; my grandmother on a mattress on the floor. The only thing she did her entire life was work, while he fought the eternal war. He ended up a martyr, he was the hero of his village, and she fell victim to a serious kidney disease. My mother, like her mother before her, had all the children Allah wanted to give her. We are eight siblings. I'm in fifth place. Being fifth of eight is neither here nor there. You almost don't exist. It's the eldest and the youngest who capture their parents' attention. One of my sisters replaced my mother working in the store. I suppose that's why I chose to study journalism, in case anyone tried to appoint me accountant or imports expert. I've always had an aversion to playing by the rules of the house. I imagine my poor mother, an innocent creature uprooted like a plant from Beit Jala, in the West Bank. From her home. From her family. From her country. Removed from the garden with one single, efficient yank by the hand of a skilled gardener. Sent to another continent to the ends of the earth, to be married off to a complete stranger.

I have never envied Arab women for a second. It took years for my mother to dare to walk along the street with her head uncovered. Even though she knew that there was no repression in Chile. At least they weren't religious, my parents. Luckily, I managed to skip both Islamic and Catholic fanaticism. We just believed in a superior being, the name didn't matter. I went to a normal high school. My education, like that of all my siblings, was secular. Perhaps that's why I felt like any other Chilean girl as I grew up. Although I didn't forget my origins. From a very young age, I asked my mother to tell me stories of her land. I learned all the place names and their geography. I was the only one of my siblings who was seriously interested in the subject. When the news showed some Israeli massacre of Palestinian people, I got very angry. They're doing this to us, I would exclaim. My older brother would reply, No, Layla, we are Chilean. Yes, we were Chilean, but we were Palestinian too. I always promised myself that I would get to know that land, my *other* land.

I didn't want to know about fabrics or Arab cuisine. The only thing my mother made me learn was how to make hummus. This may sound arrogant, but mine was delicious, better than anyone else's. I put lots of lemon in it, that's my aunt Danah's secret. When I finished college and was already a professional, I decided to take some time and keep my promise. I was the first of eight siblings to travel to the Middle East. My father's family was no longer in Israel; they lived in Libya. They had first gone to Chatila, a refugee camp. Half the family was killed by Sharon. My mother's side still lives in Beit Jala. Two of my male cousins are Hamas militants, one of them quite a prominent leader. At that time they hadn't yet come to share power with Al-Fatah. They looked after me. Thanks to their contacts, I ended up settling in the Gaza Strip for a good while, in the city of Gaza itself, the kernel of horror.

I was never interested in incidental journalism, or in reporting or working for a newspaper. What interests me is observing a phenomenon. Discovering it, lifting its veil, without the pressure of immediate writing. In my field, someone with my concerns would work in investigative journalism. That was the official reason for my presence in Gaza. I managed to immerse myself in its most unfamiliar aspects, always with a helping hand from one of my cousins or their friends. That's where I began to coexist with pain, and wonder about the value of forgetting, the opposite of what you would suppose. The thing is that living in the midst of this family and these people, I began to view memory as a sickness. My people are sick with it. Palestine. Promised land. Land of tombs. A good memory can become abusive. Remembering everything is equivalent to taking a knife each morning and slicing off different parts of your body. We should organize forgetting. If personal pains have their own rights and their own demands, why not historic pains? Despite understanding it all, I think that forgetting can be a blessing. The final outcome of my wanderings and my reflections was the publication of a book, *Of Orange and Olive Trees*. I'm very proud of having written it. I planted an olive tree in front of my aunt's house in Beit Jala. I had a child. I should be at peace. But, of course, I'm not.

Bodies retain history. In the end, your body is your history because it holds everything. I'll just say that if living in occupied territory is humiliating, dramatic, and unfair, life in the West Bank seems like heaven compared to life in Gaza. If I were forced to choose one single emotion as a synthesis of the rest, I think I'd choose fear. You wake up afraid. You brush your teeth afraid. You eat—if you can find something to eat—afraid. You make love afraid. You go to bed at night afraid. Poverty has no comparison. It's absolute, therefore its consequences, the sickness, the lack of hygiene, the promiscuity, all of that is the order of the day. And as a protagonist: hunger. HUNGER, in capital letters. Either you fight or you die. It's not that everyone has revolutionary blood in their veins that makes them this militant, no, it's just a matter of survival. For me, used to the characteristic order of middle-class Chile, it was very difficult. The only time I could bear it was when, at night, in secret, we got together for a glass of arak, the only alcohol available in the area, a kind of dry brandy that burns your guts. As we drank it, we sensually inhaled from that water pipe, a *narguile*, it's called. Only then did I stop feeling afraid. But I realized, when I returned, that even my concept of death had changed in Gaza. Death becomes just that, death and nothing more.

My prior history with alcohol wasn't alarming. No one drank in my house. I began to do it on teenage nights out, slightly debauched parties, like any young resident of Santiago, with no serious consequences. I only noticed that the more I drank, the better I felt. More potent. More ferocious. Less vulnerable. I'm not a sentimental drunk, no, not for anything. While we're on the subject, I hate sentimentality and everything to do with it.

I hate a great number of things. I love some others. The color black, for example. Everything about me is black. My hair, jet. My eyes, coal. My clothes too. I surround myself with black because it has strength. I also like deep purple, and white, because it's the sum of all colors. But give me something pink and I spit. The same with pale blue. I hate soft stories. Sorry, Simona, but leaving the man of your life because he watches a lot of TV? If she had described perverse impulses, I'd make an effort to understand her. If he had beaten her. My father thought he had every right to hit my mother, and the rest of us. A couple of times, when I was a teenager, I had to miss high school because I couldn't explain a black eye. Was my dad a monster because of that? No, he honestly believed that was how you taught people, period.

* * *

One day, in Palestine, shortly before returning to Chile, I went from Beit Jala to visit a female cousin who lives in Bethlehem. They are neighboring cities, so I walked and hitchhiked to get there. All the villages are very close to one another, the surface area of the country is incredibly small and bears no relation to the magnitude of its problems. My cousin's house was on a small street that had been divided, cut, actually, by the famous wall that Sharon decided to build. Quite literally, the wall ran along the middle of the street, it's not just a manner of speaking. It's gray, built from long slabs of concrete, thin slabs but very, very high. As if the Berlin Wall had never fallen. It follows an irrational route and outrageous things occur in certain places. Like in Bethlehem, for example, where the school my nieces and nephews attended, which was three steps from the house, remained on the other side of the wall.

I'll return to Bethlehem and the day when I visited my cousin. As twilight was approaching, I decided to take a look at the wall from the outskirts of the city. I wanted to see how far you could walk along it before a house or school blocked the path. I walked and walked and I didn't notice that the afternoon was dying and the light was fading. The only thing in my mind was the exact wording I'd use in my investigation to describe the unprecedented route I was taking. I didn't see them in time. They were three Israeli soldiers. They approached me immediately, interrogating me, with an unmistakably suspicious tone. The way they stood on the ground was infinitely arrogant. They spoke to me in Hebrew and I replied in Spanish, saying that I didn't understand. Between the three of them they couldn't have been more than sixty. They were very young, almost fledglings, two of them with very light eyes and skin, Ashkenazi, and the third was darker, probably Sephardic. All three were tall, well fed. Their uniforms, wrinkled but clean. They wore helmets and carried their guns horizontally, ready to shoot. Or at least, that was the impression they gave. I was struck by the aggression I felt toward them. It was even greater than the fear they instilled in me. When they saw that I was making no effort to communicate, they switched to English. They asked me ten questions a second. Who was I? What was I doing there? Where was I from? What was my nationality? Why was I in Israel? When was I leaving? I answered everything fairly coherently. They didn't believe a word. They decided I must be a spy. They looked at my passport and asked where Chile was. They started talking among themselves in Hebrew. They seemed to come to an agreement, which can't have been easy because there was quite a bit of discussion. In the end, two of them grabbed me, one on each arm, and the third, the dark one, walked in front as if to guide them. They took me, quite roughly, to a military outpost a kilometer away. I'll be frank and I don't intend to embellish the fact with adjectives. They raped me. One after the other, once, twice, three times.

I returned to Gaza and stayed there a couple of months. I talked to my cousins. I asked them to accept me as a member of Hamas. They refused. I lacked virulence. I lacked it? My God, I was full of it. But in the end I was a woman. A hindrance, although they didn't say as much. If I had really been like them, wouldn't I have tried to get the names of those three soldiers to go after them and shoot them in cold blood, even if I lost my life in the attempt? Go back to your country, write and raise money for us. That's what they asked of me. In their minds there were no half measures. They are like the desert, burning or freezing, all white or all black. Seasons like fall or spring have no reality. They live immersed in civil rage. It was impossible to *join* them and I knew it. I went home. I didn't dare go back through Tel Aviv, where the airport is. I crossed the Allenby Bridge near Jerusalem and returned through Jordan, that's how I avoided another interrogation. The police in the airport are well known for being tough. They're capable of removing even your soul if they think you're suspicious, or of sending you back. They examine each passenger as if they were planning to blow up Israel. When I finally got on the plane, I knew I was broken. I heard the snap, like the breaking of an arch.

I returned to Chile sure that I had lost all capacity for amazement. Convinced that nothing in the future would surprise me, that no final calm would be possible. In my own eyes, I was as tenacious and abandoned as Gary Cooper in *High Noon*. Still believing in justice.

My method of contraception at that time was an IUD. My monthly cycles were very irregular and I was never alarmed by delays, even if they were long. Any climatic, geographic, or emotional change immediately meant a disturbance. It never occurred to me that the IUD would fail, even though I'd read a thousand times that it happens to a certain percentage of women. When the moment comes, if destiny wants it that way, nothing is invincible. The condom breaks. The pill fails. It's a matter of statistics. When I landed in Chile, I was three months pregnant. I was already over thirty. No one would carry out an abortion for me, no matter what I paid. Everything is serious in Chile, including illegality.

My poor little Ahmed, the spectacle of the family. He was born with green eyes and light skin. I never answered the question of who his father is. At home, they begged me to tell them and I refused.

In Libya I met a great-uncle of mine, an old combatant. A dark man whose deep wrinkles conquered his face and his expression. He wore a white turban on his head, which only signaled the years he had spent in the sun. I talked at length with him about the Six-Day War and the refugee camps. He taught me many things. When he talked about a hospital stay in the Chatila camp, for a nasty infected stomach wound, he sensed my reaction and said to me, very seriously, Pity? We can't afford it.

Ahmed won't be an object of pity to anyone. We can't allow ourselves that.

We spoke in English because it was the only language we shared in common. I wasn't born speaking English like Simona. No one spoke it around me and only barely at school. When I decided to leave for Israel I had to take intensive classes, and make a great effort. The absurd thing is studying a foreign language to communicate with my own family, for whom English is foreign too.

My dad asked me to leave the house. He didn't feel able to raise a bastard. I was already of an age to have left. It was natural to live on my own. The problem was money. I asked if I could stay until I finished writing the book. Pressured by the rest of the family, he agreed. I sold my book and it did well. I supported myself for a while on that success, and I left. Ahmed and I lived in a small apartment on Avenida Peru, near the family home so that my sisters could help take care of him. Sometimes as he slept I sat by his side at night and watched him. That coloring of his. That stain. As I looked at him, I would drink a glass of *pisco* with Coca-Cola, thinking anything could be lacking in my house, apart from that. It's so cheap, as well. Bad *piscos* cost less than a kilo of fruit at the start of the season. After a while, the Coca-Cola became superfluous. The mental whirlwind of my nights only passed with *pisco*. When I went over the top, drinking six glasses instead of three, I felt the epic sensation of being a warrior again. No one could push me around. My strength was unbeatable. I was a fearsome fedayeen. It was always the same, my multiple selves would begin their fight. A fierce competition to establish which would come out on top. My most rational self watched them obstructing one another to win my desire. The self of appetite and addiction sat waiting. It knew it would be victorious in the end. From a certain distance, I watched it and finally gave it a smile. I went to bed feeling that not even an Israeli tank could intimidate me. Then, before I fell asleep, for a few minutes, I felt like a happy woman.

During that time, I earned a living teaching at college, in the School of Journalism, investigative journalism. I was paid peanuts, like all teachers. Traditional colleges believe that you should pay them for the privilege of teaching in their classrooms. The private schools pay slightly better but I had no access to them, and sometimes poverty was preferable to having to face idiotic girls and boys who are only interested in journalism because they think it will get them on TV. I tried to be dignified in my hardship. Generally I don't complain much at all. How can I after seeing true poverty in my parents' native land?

Every night I studied my son's tiny body, so narrow and fragile. I covered him with silence. I never let on to anyone that he came from the seed of the enemy.

The problem is that I know.

When I went to college, I saw that the world was larger than I had suspected. A couple of my classmates belonged to the circle from the *barrio alto*. Through them, and they were good people, I could cast an eye over that strange universe of the rich. Catalina, to whom I was closest, claimed to be leftist. She was a committed activist. To me she was nothing more than a social democrat and I never took her particularly seriously. How could I? She summered on her father's estate. They took a family vacation every year. When she turned twenty they bought her a car and she was the only one in our group with her own wheels. We took all our trips out in her car. She wore designer clothes purchased by her mother. Plus, she was *so* blond. We attended as many events as we were invited to. We never missed a party. We held all our get-togethers in her house. Without quite knowing how, we became inseparable. She was a generous woman, capable of anything to see me happy. Getting me a ticket for some concert, introducing me to all her male friends to see if I liked any of them, inviting me to spend vacations on her ranch. She was also very affectionate, and trusting of life. She never closed her purse. She greeted everyone with a kiss. Everyone was her friend. Fun Catalina. Together, we seemed like a caricature. She was so blond and I was so dark. We shared clothes and studied together for hours on end. Today she works in television and it's going really well for her. She liked going to my house and eating the Arab food. More than anything, she loved dropping in at the store and buying pretty fabric. My mom has a seamstress, she would say. *Having a seamstress.* I found that phrase unusual. A couple of times I accompanied her to get something at an aunt's house or went with her to some cousin's party. I got to know that part of society. If you don't belong to it, there's no way to visualize it. At mealtimes, her parents chatted to me. They were interested in my people and we always ended up talking about the Middle East conflict. They were cultured. Accustomed to that, Catalina loved the chaos that meals in my house entailed. Eight beasts grabbing dishes from one another's hands. There was never any conversation because the background noise was constant uproar, aside from my mom's voice, which was nonexistent.

Catalina had a brother, Rodrigo. Predictably, I fell in love with him. At some time or other we've all fallen in love with our best friend's brother. He was a couple of years older than us. He studied law and seemed to be the most responsible member of the family. At the start of college, when Catalina and I were beginning to make friends, he barely looked at us. He called us squirts. However, as time passed, his view began to change. We had a romance. I was surprised it was kept so secret, but I didn't stop to analyze it. Keeping it hidden filled us with even greater enthusiasm. I fell seriously in love. I would have given my life for that man. In the midst of the ardor, I found out from Catalina that her brother had begun a relationship with some girl from his world. When I confronted him, he told me, very seriously, I have to get married someday, Layla. You know I could never marry you. When I asked him why, the cruelty appeared so unexpectedly. Romance and lust are one thing, he said, marriage is quite another. I can't marry the daughter of an Arab who has a store on Independencia.

This is one of the most classist and racist countries in the world. Whatever happened in Chile for such extremes to exist? I can understand it in societies with monarchies, like in Great Britain. But not us, we've never even had a proper aristocracy. We weren't a viceroyalty, and there weren't even enough indigenous people left after the conquest to justify the fear of being wiped out, like in Peru or

Mexico. The Mapuche didn't get across the River Bío Bío. So, what happened? A Chilean can never look through entirely innocent eyes. His gaze aims at the individual in front of him and before focusing elsewhere, he's gauged that person. Judged. Pigeonholed. Everything has happened at an uncontrollable speed, unconsciously as well. He probably doesn't know what he's doing. But the categories are so profound, so ingrained, that he can't help it. Now, the eyes can stop. This person's appearance has given him all the details he needs. Now their speech. Ten words, twenty. No more are necessary. To the Chilean, the eyes and ears are all it takes to immediately know what needs to be known to establish the differences.

Love of children is a strange quality I lack. It isn't inherent in all human beings, or in all women. It's like faith, either you've got it or you don't. You can't invent it through sheer will. A couple of years ago, I heard a story that has been going round my mind ever since. I ended up telling Natasha. It's about Irena Sendler, a Polish woman who was born in 1910 in the suburbs of Warsaw. She was working as an administrator in some Department of Wellbeing when Hitler occupied Poland. When the Nazis forced half a million Jews into the ghetto, they prohibited the entrance of foods and medical services, even though they were concerned about contagious diseases. For that reason they asked Irena Sendler to control the outbreaks of tuberculosis inside the ghetto. This responsibility meant she could enter and exit without restriction. She made the most of this "privilege" to save children. She spoke to their parents, one by one. She asked them to hand over their little ones so she could take them out of there. It wasn't easy to convince them. Irena doubted any would survive. But the parents clung to various illusions so as not to be separated from their children. Almost all of them gave in eventually, not just because of the possibility of extermination but because of hunger and sickness. In this way, little by little, she took a child every day. She hid them in her rucksack or wrapped in rags beneath her cape. She trained a dog to bark every time a German approached her.

That way, the Nazis heard the dog and not the crying of the child. She got into the back of the ambulance that drove her every day, with her dog and her clandestine cargo, and she crossed the border of the ghetto. She placed each child in a different house with a Christian family who would take care of them. But she didn't want them to lose their true identities. She noted each Jewish name with the new name next to it. She rolled up these scraps of paper inside a glass jar. She buried it under an apple tree by her house.

One day she was stopped by the Gestapo. She was brutally tortured. They beat her with wooden clubs, breaking her limbs. She was declared guilty and they planned her execution. She managed to escape by bribing a guard. She hid and lived in secrecy until the end of the war. Free once more, the first thing she did was go to that apple tree. She dug up the jar filled with the names. Almost all of the parents had been murdered.

During her twilight years living in a retirement home, she was looked after by a fugitive, a Jewish woman she had taken out of the ghetto at the age of six months. Inside a toolbox, with the dog by her side. She died a very short time ago. I heard this story because she was nominated for the Nobel Peace Prize in 2007. Al Gore won.

Prizes don't matter. Irena Sendler gave her life for thousands of children she didn't even know. Jewish children. What if Ahmed's grandmother was one of them?

I suppose that's what you might call love. I'm incapable of feeling it.

I'll try to follow a chronological line, at least from the birth of my son. Of course, my deterioration wasn't immediate. To begin with, I tried to act like any normal mother. I cared for him, fed him, entertained him. But kissing and hugging him was unnatural to me. Only at night was I overwhelmed by love for him, and only if I had had at least five drinks. For God's sake, I wanted to love him. During the day I worked. I earned a living. I moved around the city. But when darkness fell in that tiny room in my apartment, I looked at the glass of *pisco* waiting for me on the table and before I touched it I asked

myself, What are you getting so attached to? I interrogated myself.
The answers I gave were never satisfactory. So in one gulp I drank
down all of the *pisco*, sending all the questions to hell. Reality had
become a frozen and unhappy region I didn't want to inhabit.

The first time I went too far with alcohol and didn't make it to work
the following day, I invented some silly excuse and nothing happened. The third time they viewed it badly at the college and I swore
it would never happen again. But it did. The following semester, they
didn't renew my contract.

Unemployment was the first hard blow.

There were warnings I ignored. Alcoholics ignore *everything*.
There's a period of time between the moment you start drinking regularly and the moment you fall. Sometimes it's a long time, very long.
I know people who have managed to sustain themselves in it for a
very long time. Denial is the element that doesn't help you recover.
Alcoholics always deny being alcoholics, there's no awareness of the
illness. In most cases, someone has to open your eyes. But who?
There are two requirements for doing it, having balls and really loving the other person who has started down the slippery slope.

At the college I had a group of friends, three or four journalists
who also taught. We shared countless things. Work, profession,
visions of the world. When my absences started, they noticed, of
course, because I mattered to them. They wanted to stop me but
didn't know how. In the end, the bravest among them came to my
door. Apollonia, like in *The Godfather*, was very close to me but even
so she must have had to pluck up courage to confront me. She told
me, plain and simple, that I was sick. She told me the truth. What
they thought about me at work. How all my friends were concerned
about me. She spoke about Ahmed. About my lies. She offered me all
the help she could. She made an appointment for me with a psychiatrist who specialized in recovery. Of course, I didn't go. Given my
strong and private character I know it was very difficult for her to do
this. It was a great act of love on her part. She was the first person to

mention the word *alcoholism* to me. I denied it all. I carried on painting her a different picture of reality. I feigned a happiness I didn't feel.
I talked about a functional life I didn't have. Although I didn't say
as much, I was furious with her. Each time, at lunch or some social
gathering, I drank a bit more than I should, I mocked her behind
her back, making fun of her attempts. I lost her. As she said later,
Alcoholics never stop lying, my friendship with Layla is a waste of
time.

I knocked on all the doors. Unemployment was driving me crazy.
The only thing I found was a job writing nonsense for an advertising magazine. At least they paid me enough for the rent. To tell the
truth, it was very cheap. But even so it wasn't enough for me to live.
I began to ask people to lend me money. My family first, my friends
later. To begin with I paid it back punctually. Then I started relaxing,
I just forgot about it. It was impossible for me to take responsibility
for myself. I began to lie a lot, without realizing it. Ahmed survived
thanks to my family. Seven siblings are a blessing. There was always
someone willing to take care of him. My younger sisters used to take
him to the family home and feed him there. Of course, my family
realized that something wasn't right. I remember the first time I
didn't turn up to fetch my son, as I usually did, at six in the evening.
I forgot. I had been in a bar with a couple of colleagues. I met them
in the street and we went drinking. The time passed without me
noticing. When I finally decided to go and get him, my colleagues
ordered more drinks. They were paying. I stayed. I returned home at
dawn completely oblivious to the fact that a son was waiting for me.
When, the following day, quite late because I slept the way you sleep
after a good binge, I arrived at my parents' house, my older brother
was waiting for me. You know what he did? He hit me. He gave me
a good slap. I was the disgrace of the family, so he told me. They had
decided to take Ahmed away from me. I wasn't fit to raise him. I
promised to start again. As if you can ever start again.

Extremely humiliated, I decided to stop drinking. That period
was a nightmare. I played tricks on myself. I swore I would do things

I didn't. I hid bottles. Everything the movies say about alcoholics is true. The problem was how to face motherhood in sobriety. Or rather, how to accept that I had been raped by three soldiers in a country that was both mine, and not mine, and that the product of that was a son. Without alcohol, the movie ran and ran without stopping, the images replaying. Impossible to delete. The physical pain, the rage, the humiliation. All of it interminable, infinite. Those green eyes of my poor little boy, my sad boy, reminding me of the horror. Why didn't I give him up for adoption? It simply didn't occur to me at the time. I was convinced of my ability to face whatever came my way. Later on the family would have forbidden it, they were all in love with him, illegitimate or not. Even my father developed a fondness for him, in spite of himself. He wouldn't say a word to me, but my sisters told me how the little boy was gradually starting to win him over.

But you touch bottom. Almost always, you touch bottom.

I went through a time when I *tried* not to drink although it didn't always work. Sometimes willpower doesn't count for much. Every so often I threw a bit of alcohol into my body and felt radiant. I thought myself intelligent and I forgot my problems with Ahmed. Big mistake, drunks are *always* dumb. In those moments I fantasized about writing another book. I pondered China as a subject. I was sure that some benefactor would fall from heaven to propose it to me. In that mood, I set out for my older brother's house and asked him for money for rehab. He didn't hesitate in handing it over. Very happy, he called my sisters who still lived at home and asked them to arrange for Ahmed to stay there a little longer. I said goodbye and left. An organized addiction, no loose ends. I had money for several bottles of whiskey in my pocket. When they asked for details of the place I would be rehabilitated, I refused to provide them. I judged that I had a right to privacy. The poor things were so tired and nervous about my condition that they didn't even insist, terrified I might change my mind.

I bought lots and lots of bottles of whiskey. Whiskey is the best. I could have gotten several handles of Chivas Regal with the amount of money I had. In the end I decided on Johnnie Walker Red Label, so that it would stretch farther. I made my purchases in different supermarkets and stores. I went with a shopping bag to disguise my merchandise. On one of those trips I was on the bus, sitting next to the window, looking out. The sky was turbid, the color of misery. Then I noticed the person sitting next to me, a woman who looked like me. She was my age. She was concentrating hard, reading a book. Her brown hair was gathered up in a ponytail and she was wearing blue jeans with black boots and a gray top, printed with the Chilean flag. Occasionally she tucked back a lock of hair that was obscuring her vision. She looked through me out the window for a while. Then she took out a pen from her purse and underlined a paragraph. At some point our eyes met and she smiled at me. It was an innocent smile, transparent as water. That smile is still engraved on my mind. I turned her into a symbol of my big lie. She smiled as if saying to me, Here we are, the two of us. Sisters in age, appearance. Both diligent, both intelligent. Both young enough that, above all else, we want to make our lives meaningful. There I was, hiding my bottles of Johnnie Walker in a plastic bag on the bus floor, preparing myself for the alcohol to circulate and burn right to the bottom of my stomach. Sad place, that, the bottom of my stomach. It was that smile, more than any of the sermons and reprimands I'd been given that told me, You're just a good con artist, nothing more than that.

I shut myself in my apartment. I had previously retrieved the key that one of my sisters kept. I wanted to reassure myself. It might occur to them to come get something belonging to Ahmed, or to do a bit of cleaning. My sisters are like that, open and generous. They kept that key in case "something happened to me." Well, I took it back. I was approaching a moment that required no witnesses, the moment of caressing my wound. In all probability, it would stay with me for the rest of my life. But I needed to caress it then, while it was open and bleeding.

And so I did, without mercy.

They found me five days later almost dead. Because I'd taken their key, my siblings forced open the door. The downstairs neighbor had heard strange noises. He rang my doorbell several times and despite the lack of response, he kept hearing noises. Every time I vomited in the bath or every time I fell, I suppose. He called my landlord and she called my family. Presumably I should be grateful to that goddamn neighbor. But I'm not.

They took me to the emergency room. Once the danger had passed, they transferred me to another clinic, a psychiatric one. I was there for a long time, until my addiction disappeared. I worded that badly. Addiction doesn't disappear. I just stopped drinking. Whenever we had to carry out the exercise of imagining something pleasant, I always turned to the image of orange and olive trees. Let's go back there, to that dispirited land which always, always has an orange and a bit of olive oil to offer you.

When I could stand on my own two feet again, I returned to the family home. My apartment had been handed over. My few possessions languished in my dad's warehouse. I began a new life. Arid, difficult, lacking in color, with Ahmed by my side. The poor, sad thing initially rejected me, as if he had completely forgotten about my existence. He would only accept my sisters. Gradually he began to focus on me. Lying in bed, I watched him for hours, until I decided I was grateful for him and grateful that he was born in Chile. I thought everything depended on the place you happened to be born. It's arbitrary. Whole swathes of the earth haven't heard a single explosion in more than fifty years. Others have accumulated all of them. My friend Catalina, the blonde I told you about, doesn't know the sound of a bullet flying through air. The same goes for her father and grandfather. Where would they have been during the coup d'etat? On the beach? When

I saw *Waltz with Bashir* I thought about that Israeli filmmaker who saw with his own eyes the deaths of Sabra and Chatila and had a father and a mother who survived Auschwitz. He can tell the story of what his father and grandfather saw. He carries the pain in his DNA. That's the way my Ahmed could have been born.

I'll come back to those days after the psychiatric clinic. My father, softened by events, offered to put me up. To finance me for as long as necessary. He even offered, advised by one of my aunts, to pay for therapy. Not for sobering up, he told me, sparing with his words, but one that will help you. Help me what? I asked him. That will help you, he repeated, timidly. I didn't fancy therapy. I've never been convinced by the idea of paying for an intimate space. Isn't that what men do with sex? I'm not saying that Natasha fulfills the functions of a whore. But *paying* for someone to listen to you. *Paying* someone to care for you. *Paying* someone to take your side. No, I didn't like the idea. I agreed because I had no alternative. That's the only reason. When I went to the first session, Natasha realized this. A hard nut to crack, she must have thought.

A good while has passed now.

I'm back at the college. I got my old job back after a long conversation with my employers. I try to be the best of teachers so that they believe me, to amend for old atrocities. I feel good there. It's my place. I wasn't made for writing frivolities for some rag. Even less for TV or radio. Mine is the written word. In addition, I teach classes in the afternoon at a private college. They aren't even classes, I direct thesis work. I'm paid decently. I decided I don't want to be so poor. I need to earn more money. My self-esteem needs it too.

I know full well that I will publish that book about China. I've already started writing it. I take notes and read a lot. The time for travel will come. I'm still living at my father's house. I know that's rather embarrassing for someone my age. But worse things have happened in times of crisis. Deep down, no one wants me to go. Not because of me, of course, because of Ahmed. He's like a son to all, son of my father, of my younger sisters, of my older brothers. He's every-one's son, which he enjoys. For my part, it's a great relief to know he's being so well cared for. He goes to a public school and spends whole afternoons in the store with my dad. He plays at helping him with the measuring tape and the rolls of fabric. He looks healthy and handsome. Although he doesn't laugh much. I see him as a human being in spite of me. I ponder his future. I've even opened myself to learning *something* about Judaism. I make an effort, I really do. I think that literature can help me more than any other discipline. I've developed a taste for Amos Oz, for Yehoshua, for David Grossman. All for Ahmed.

I think I've managed to understand something about trauma. About *my* trauma.

When I got drunk, when I harmed myself, I felt that, regardless of my will or initiative, something irrevocable was possessing me. Trauma repeats itself, as if neither destiny nor I could leave it in peace. As if I heard from a distance an irresistible call I couldn't deny myself, inflicting the experience of pain on my body once more. All in spite of myself. I don't know if you understand me. I simply couldn't put the rape and its consequences behind me. Only alcohol allowed an exit from the internal cry of my wound, a cry I couldn't clearly distinguish, the damage repeated constantly on my body. Despite the fact that alcohol damaged my mind, destroying time, myself, the world, the pain returned to the body. Always the body. Like in that sentry hut near Bethlehem.

The surprising thing is that when I began to drink, I *didn't know* that it was *that* precise ghost that would return to haunt me.

When I left Bethlehem and set out for Gaza, I thought I had got-ten away unharmed. Like those people who suffer an accident. They get up from the ground by themselves. They function. They make their police statements. They go home, they lie down in bed under their own steam. But a week later they go into shock. After the fact I kept thinking, I am so strong. It's admirable the way I bounce back from violence.

I congratulated myself on the way that three merciless soldiers weren't able to destroy me.

My shock came when I returned to Chile. When I found out I was pregnant. What struck me then wasn't just the reality of the act of violence itself but the way I was unfamiliar with that reality. I was raped once again when I looked at that pregnancy test. It's incredible the way that, sooner or later, the impact hits you. It doesn't matter how long it's been delayed. I thought naively that I had managed to escape the evil, only to find myself facing it in a subjugating manner. I don't know which was worse, experiencing it at the time or reliving it later.

I was never the same again.

From that precise moment, the story I was creating for myself shattered into pieces. The connections between my past, my present, and what was still to come broke and separated.

I had no other way to cry out my reality, to depict it. It wasn't my voice that took me to the past. No. I didn't alter it. I didn't want to hear it again. It was the voice of my son. Invisible witness and permanent reminder of the trauma. The voice of the wound, of my wound.

Natasha said that only by telling her could I take control of this story. That's what I'm doing today. In order to recover, every survivor needs to be able to take charge of her memories. We need others for that. Today I'm burdening you as witnesses. The load is heavy.

I'm worn out.

LUISA

*M*y name is Luisa.

I come from the south, from a village crossed by the River Itata, in the province of Ñuble. I just want to talk about him, about Carlos. I was raised in the country. I'm the daughter of country folk and if it weren't for Carlos, I would have stayed there. My father was a tenant on a farm. I had lots of brothers and sisters, some of them didn't survive. There are five of us today. In those days in the country, kids died at birth. Not a single woman finished up with as many as she had given birth to. Also, no one knew how to read or write. Things have changed a lot. So many years have passed. I'm old already, sixty-seven.

We lived at the ends of the earth, but then no one in their right mind wanted to live in the center of it, what with everything that went on there. I went to school but I didn't learn much. In winter you couldn't get there because of the mud and the rain and the teacher was absent a lot. They lumped us all together in the same classroom, there were only two, and we were all different ages but they taught us the same stuff. One day the boss asked Ernani, one of the laborers who worked with my dad, whether he spelled his name with an *H*. No, Ernani replied, *H*'s are for rich folks. What would we do with an *H*?

I left school to work. I helped my mother in the orchard and my dad with the animals. Just cows, and a few horses. They all belonged to the boss apart from Tai. He was my dad's, black and handsome Tai was. We also had lots of dragonflies, horseflies, gadflies, they soon got used to me and didn't sting. The snakes there were scrawny and not very long and they didn't do anything. Same goes for the hairy spiders we always found. They made little holes in the ground and crawled inside and my brothers dragged them out from their hideaways and collected them in jars. They were really ugly but they didn't do anything, just like the snakes. The countryside wasn't dangerous. What I liked best was feeling the north wind. I waited and waited for it, and when it arrived I would stand facing into it and I felt like it had come to visit me. When it left, the leaves on the trees were shiny with rain. The house was built next to a shallow stream. The water was crystal clear. There were always lots of dogs in the house there. No one knew where they came from or where they went when they left. Sometimes my mom would complain, saying she didn't have enough food to give them. My favorites were Niño and Batalla. The first was small and light brown, like beaten country eggs and ladyfingers, and had short ears and legs. Batalla, on the other hand, had a long coat with dark brown and orange patches, he almost looked refined. He was tall, too. Batalla really took to me and didn't leave my side in sun or shade. He really loved me. He liked rolling in the soil, he rolled and rolled, stretching out his paws. He turned into a fireball with his orange flashes spinning, as if he were a dog of leisure. I would watch him, dying to join in and roll about too. I often thought I'd like to be a dog, at least Niño and Batalla had a better time of it than us. Sometimes I ran off to the pasture with Batalla and we went to play among the goat's rue, hiding in the stalks. If my dad caught me, he would immediately remove his belt to beat me but Batalla would start to growl. My dad didn't want the dog to bite him so he left, refastening the belt and shouting that if I didn't get back to work, he'd get me next time. Batalla's great allure, and this is why my mom loved him, was that he hunted mice. He had a real sharp eye for mice. The problem was when he caught them he brought them to me as a gift. I never liked mice, I found them disgusting. In the country they were big and fat and Batalla just kept on presenting them to me. Plus he would lick my face and arms with the same tongue he used to get the mice.

When Batalla died I played dead under the chestnut tree. The most beautiful thing about our house was the chestnut tree, a big, old, leafy tree. We did everything beneath that tree, especially in summer. The trough was there and sitting beneath the branches we washed clothes, shelled beans, and husked corn. Then, when Batalla died, I stayed there, eyes shut, for three days. They didn't even send me to work, no one dared speak to me. On the fourth day my mom came out and said, Come on, Luisa, Batalla is in another world, he won't be coming back. I opened my eyes, stood up, and started washing clothes with her.

That's what death was like.

One of my favorite trees was the *maqui*. It's a wild tree that you find all over the Ñuble countryside. It's thin with long branches and dense leaves. Its fruit is a little blue-black berry that stains your mouth and hands. They stain everything. They have a sweet taste. The *maqui* certainly is delicious. What my brothers and sisters and I liked doing was coming home all filthy, all blue, and our mom wouldn't stop scolding us. Our teeth, they looked like slightly blue charcoal. It didn't come off at all when we washed. The stain stayed with us for a long time.

Your maqui-spattered apron, that's how the song goes.

The best thing about the country was the boss's house. We found it mysterious, because it was the only big house and we were forbidden from going there. It was very close to ours so my brothers and sisters and I would spy on it from a hill above the stable where the saddles were kept. Sometimes my dad had to go there to cut the lawn. As a young girl I never saw any other lawn being cut, this was the only one, and he allowed me to tag along. The smell that came from the cut grass was the best smell of the countryside. I liked it so much, almost more than the smell of warm bread or freshly ironed sheets. I'm told that I used to say I wanted to be a gardener when I grew up.

When I was about ten, a church was built in the village, a modest one but it was still a great novelty. Once in a blue moon a priest came, he held mass and baptized and married people and we all took First Communion. He kept up-to-date with everyone, the priest did, and he said he came to save us so we would no longer live in sin. It was so pretty, the church, I liked going there. Carlos didn't like priests. One day he said to me, Luisa, you know, hell doesn't exist. What do you mean hell doesn't exist? I replied. He told me that the Catholic Church invented it to placate poor people, so they'd think there are worse things than this life. I told Carlos, God will punish you for saying these things. He said, I'm already being punished, Luisa, I've been bearing my punishment since the day I was born.

That's the way Carlos spoke and I reprimanded him, but I liked listening to him. He was so independent, as if he didn't care about what he had been taught as a child. I think about what Carlos would have said now, with all the stuff about pedophiles in the church. Carlos would have ranted, priest-basher that he was, of course he would have ranted.

At the age of fifteen I was sent to work in Chillán. One of my sisters had gone before me and she found me the job. A live-in job, cleaning and looking after a couple of young kids. It didn't feel right and I returned to the country. But my dad sent me back and I had to grin and bear it. The owners of the house weren't bad people. They weren't very rich and the place was pretty average. The kids were well mannered and didn't cause many problems but I was always hungry. They kept everything under lock and key, the señora opened the pantry once a day. There were no refrigerators in those days, at least not in Chillán, and anything fresh was bought on a daily basis in the store where they had an account. I didn't deal with cash, never. I'll always remember the señora's bunch of keys; she carried it everywhere. Why so much care? I always wondered. In the country we didn't even know what keys were. I worked for about a year in that house and returned to the country for the summer. I liked being in my own home, although I wasn't allowed to slack off. They always sent me to work in the pasture but I still played with the dogs and climbed trees and ate pears and apples that were really tart. I'd never tasted any others so I liked them. I also ate sour cherries. There was a cluster of cherry trees that my dad claimed had just sprung up. They were acidic and pale. I didn't know there was such a thing as sweet cherries. I only tried them much later in life. I always remember the *boldo* tree at the edge of the pond, and hiding on its branches. The leaves were so green, elegant, so dark and thick and I looked down at the pond, dreaming about how one day I'd have a house like the lady in Chillán and that it would be all mine.

Then the boss lady came, the wife of the owner of the farm. Has Luisa reached working age yet? she asked my mom. Of course, she's big. That's how my mom replied. I was sixteen.

That summer, they took me into their house, to try me. If I worked out, I could then go to the capital. When they spoke about Santiago I imagined a large grid, enormous, with thousands of identical white houses, two stories, with a door in the middle and two windows above. Everyone in the country wanted to get to the capital, like the promised land, Carlos would say. It was more difficult for women, either your boss took you or you didn't go. Men did military service and so they got to leave, we didn't. Everyone on the farm looked at me enviously, the women especially. I understood what it meant. I knew that this was a *privilege*, but I still didn't know that word. I heard it a lot later on, when Carlos was always speaking at meetings about the privilege of the wealthy, and at home he repeated it over and over. I passed the test at the boss's house that summer and I set off for Santiago. What a huge city, I said to myself when I saw those wide streets and so many cars. Good God, I was quite scared. I didn't dare venture out alone. Some Sundays I spent the day shut in my room because I didn't have anyone to go out with. Eventually, one of my brothers, who had left the countryside a short while earlier to do his military service, came to live in the capital and he taught me how to get to his house in the Lo Valledor quarter. Then I had company. It was at his house that the most important thing happened to me. I met Carlos.

Carlos worked in construction. He was a conscientious employee, serious about his job, and the foreman liked him. He was born in Aysén, so he could talk about the real south. He laughed at my south, he found it insignificant. His father was a muleteer and he had lost his mother at a young age. A brother left for Argentina and they never heard from him again. He wasn't a family man, Carlos. He began to court me as soon as we met. Me, with my dark, pretty looks, well filled-out and funny. We were married within a year, just a civil ceremony. I wanted both but Carlos was fixed in his ideas. There was no way he was getting married in a church. God doesn't like happiness, he told me. At first, we rented a room in a house on General Velásquez. I carried on working until I gave birth to Golondrina. When I became pregnant, the boss lady found out immediately. She told me that I could return to work whenever I wanted. With what Carlos earned we were moving forward. In a year, little Carlitos arrived. Today he lives in Sweden. He married an extremely blond Swedish woman, the kind that seems to be straight out of a magazine, and he's an electrician. What I can't forgive him is that he took my Golondrina. He talked and talked about Sweden until she was tempted. They left me alone. I tell myself, if the kids have a right to run their own lives, they aren't going to stay by their mom's side forever. But they left later, much later.

I liked living with Carlos so much that I never mentioned the countryside. I missed it, though. We moved because with two kids we couldn't fit in the room on General Velásquez. I bought myself a rooster and a hen to hear them cluck and crow. The rooster turned out to be undisciplined, or scatterbrained, who knows. He went off at any time of day, not at dawn as I was accustomed to. Back in the south the roosters crow every time a hen lays an egg. The song was a celebration, that's what my dad told me, and when there was lots of singing in the quiet hours of the afternoon, he would prepare himself for the eggs he'd be eating the next morning. In Santiago, I kept the fresh eggs for the kids because Carlos didn't eat them. He said he wasn't going to eat the eggs of a "known hen." Carlos was dumb with all the ideas in his head. I missed the country, especially at night. People think that nights there are really quiet but that's not true. Of course, there are no buses or loud music or horns or kids shouting like you get here but there is an ocean of noise. I can tell all those noises apart, from every bird to the thousands of cicada and cricket songs. They all raise their voices at the same time and mingle together. And the dogs cry at night, they have so many sorrows, dogs do.

That's where we were when Allende was elected, Carlos making buildings and me bringing up the children. The world is going to change, Luisa, Carlos told me again and again. He was so excited. Those years left as quickly as they had arrived, like we were always inside a whirlwind, that's how we all were. Carlos was working so hard with the labor union, the workers' democracy *cordones*, the meetings.

One day he came to look for me during his break and asked me to listen to him. I want to win, Luisa, he said. I fight to win and I know why I'm doing it. I'm doing it because when I was a boy I had no power. I lived with defenseless people and learned that all the evil that surrounded us, and there was a lot of it, was rooted in the abuse of that thing I didn't have. Do you understand, Luisa?

He began to speak about political parties. Don't get involved, Carlos, I told him. What for? He looked very serious and thought about it and didn't tell me a bit of what was going through his mind. He spoke to his comrades, everyone was a comrade. Afterward, I never heard that word again. He loaned me books. He wanted me to understand, to develop myself. You won't have to clean other people's filth again, he promised me. When you go back to work you're going to do something worthwhile. Those days were nice, the thousand days, Carlos called them afterward, after all the horrors.

We were in the south on vacation when seventy-three started. My dad had told me that it was a bad year for wheat.

The sun came down on our heads that September eleventh as the coup erupted.

One night they came for him. They took my Carlos. I was thirty-one and he was thirty-three. It was November, two months after the military coup. We were sleeping and there was a curfew when we heard the knock at the door. They came in shouting and calling for Carlos. They took him in a flash. Let me get dressed, he asked them, but they grabbed him by the arms and just like that they took him. He was still in his pajamas. I started shouting. Don't shout, honey, I'll be back, it's a mistake. That was all he said to me.

Don't shout, honey.

The children woke up. They didn't see him leave, they didn't see the soldiers. The kids didn't see a thing. Dad's gone to the south, I told them the next day, he'll be back soon.

Since September eleventh, since the moment they bombed the presidential palace, Carlos had been very upset. My goodness was he upset. I wondered if he would be strong enough for what was coming. It was a feeling, that's all, never a thought.

The wait began.

We were living in a small house in the Pablo Neruda district by stop seven on the Gran Avenida. It came to be called Bernardo O'Higgins, the Neruda thing ended right away. We were new and didn't really know the neighbors. There was so much hustle and bustle in the days of the Popular Unity Party, we didn't have time for a social life. The following morning I went out to the street. I wanted to meet someone, anyone who could tell me something about what had happened. But no one came near me. No one knew a thing, no one saw anything, as if it was all in my head. My bed was empty, it wasn't just my imagination. I stayed quiet. I thought I had to stay quiet. If I didn't open my mouth, Carlos would come back. The less I spoke, the sooner he'd return.

The days passed. I didn't even go out to buy bread, in case Carlos arrived and I wasn't there. All day shut in the house with young kids, that was something. I felt like I was going to suffocate. I struggled to complete a single errand. One day I left with the kids for Lo Valledor, where my brother lived. I told him everything that had happened. He offered to go to Carlos's work to speak to the foreman. But no one knew anything. Three of the workers in his crew hadn't come back, my brother said. I didn't know his colleagues, Carlos never brought them home. Luisa, my brother said, go to the country, they'll look after you until Carlos comes back. What if he comes back and I'm not there? I replied.

I remembered Carlos telling me, Law and justice aren't the same thing, Luisa. Remember, law *isn't* justice. So, if I listened to Carlos, *what* justice could I turn to?

That's where my torment began.

The first problem was acting as if nothing had happened. The second was getting money. I had two young kids and rent to pay.

Other people got benefits, I had nothing. It made me angry at Carlos, all that labor union nonsense. Why didn't he concern himself with becoming a homeowner? The poor guy must have thought he had his whole life for that. The third problem was learning to live without Carlos. You become a bit stupid when you only live with young kids. I didn't talk to anyone, I didn't know many people at all. I began to miss adult conversation. But gradually I was learning, even if sweat and tears were the price. More tears than sweat, to tell the truth, and I had to wait until the night to cry. Silently, in my bed, on the sly, that's how I learned to cry on the inside.

I missed Carlos. I worried he might be cold. Why didn't they let him get dressed? Those pajamas wouldn't keep him warm. I wanted to hug him. I wanted to do all those things you don't talk about.

I set out to see my old boss, the owner of the farm where my parents lived. Some people might ask why so many poor women work as housemaids. The thing is that the job is part of their lives, a kind of extension. They don't know how to do anything else. It's natural, it's doing what you do every day but being paid for it. Where would someone like me find work? What did I know how to do? Of course, Carlos didn't like me wasting my energy in other people's houses, but I had nowhere else to waste it. The problem was the children. The boss lady would only put up with one. No, not two, Luisa, she said to me. So I went to a neighbor's house, a friendly but quiet woman. She didn't talk much. I liked the fact she wasn't a gossip. When she asked me about my husband I told her he'd gone to the south, and she believed me. We arranged that she would take care of Carlitos for part of my wage. She had a couple of kids too, so she had to stay at home to look after them anyway. So, with Golondrina, I returned to work for my old boss. She behaved so well while I worked. My poor girl. From eight in the morning to six in the evening I cleaned, washed clothes, ironed. Another woman was in charge of the kitchen. During those hours I looked and looked at life in that house. Until then I had never been envious, I didn't know jealousy. The boss was a kind but haughty woman, regal she was, so elegant. She would go out midmorning to "take care of business," as she put it. Who knows what she did. Her husband wasn't in the house very much. He went to the south a lot, to his land. The kids, two boys and two girls, were at college but living in the house. They were so untidy. They left their clothes on the floor. Would it cost them that much to pick them up? Everything on the floor, books, underwear, letters, records, all scattered about. The youngest, Paulina, was my favorite, I'd known her from such a young age, with her pretty little face.

One day she shut herself in her room and there was no getting her to come out. They took her to the doctor. The boss lady came up to me afterward, very serious, and said, This is awful, Luisa, Paulina is depressed. Why is Paulina depressed? I asked. How could I understand? She had everything in life. Her husband hadn't been taken, she had a roof over her head and food, she didn't have two children to raise. On top of that she could go to university. I struggled to understand depression. It struck me as an illness for rich people. Paulina was depressed for a whole winter and she clung to me all day. She wouldn't leave me alone. These pretty young girls, suddenly they're dying of sorrow, there's no understanding why. The boss lady spoke to me, she could hire someone else for the cleaning but I wasn't to leave Paulina's side. So I spent that dark, cold winter in her room, watching TV with her and keeping her company. We were like a couple of ghosts. I don't know which of us was sadder. Sometimes it felt like the shadows were speaking to us. We listened to the rain against the windows. She asked me, Are you sad because of me, Luisa? They allowed me to take Golondrina into the room, she played quietly on the rug. One day Paulina asked me, Do you know why my mom is so worried and letting you take care of me? No, Paulina, I replied, tell me. Because they're scared I'll commit suicide, that's why. What are you talking about, sweetie, for the love of God? I imagined Paulina's future when she grew up, with a career behind her, with a husband who would love her, a husband with a job and money, with her dad's farm for vacations, with another Luisa to clean for her, with pretty, healthy children to look after, with travel, clothes, a nice house. With the whole world in her hands, how could a girl like that talk about suicide? Oh, my Lord, perhaps I hadn't learned a thing about the human race, but nothing made sense to me. What would become of my daughter if Paulina, who had everything, turned out like this? That first winter, the worst one, I survived thanks to Paulina, and my Golondrina stayed warm as I worked. Because when we got back home, the cold began. We had a paraffin stove for the whole house but Carlos had taught me not to sleep with it turned on because that's how fires start. So I switched it off when we went to bed, the two children all wrapped up in my bed, like puffed-up songbirds, and we slept huddled together. We all had enough food, and clothes. My kids were never down-and-outs. But I always had that lie ready on my lips, because every time they asked about their father, I would answer, He's in the south.

Carlos didn't return. Nights and days passed and he didn't come. And the grief inside me never left. Sticky like the afternoon sun, it never left.

One day I asked the boss lady whether she thought that, with the new government, people could disappear. How could you think such a thing, Luisa? she replied. At work I made efforts to find out what was going on. But it seemed that nothing was going on. There in well-heeled Las Condes, nothing was going on. Everyone believed that Carlos was in the south, that he'd left me.

I've learned things now. I've discovered that there are places you can go to ask and seek help. Not everyone was as alone as me. But how could I have known back then?

Christ, how I missed having a family. A mother-in-law to share my suffering, a brother-in-law to find out things, a sister-in-law I could leave the kids with once in a while. A bit of solace. Someone to talk to about Carlos, without it sounding suspicious. On top of that, things were going badly for my brother and he left the capital. He went south to find work in the country. I was left with no one.

Every morning, at a quarter to seven, when I left for work, I left a note on the front door, which I took down in the evening to put it up again the next day. It said: "Carlos, I'm at work. I'll be back at half seven. Luisa." One day the neighbor, the one who looked after Carlitos, asked, What do you reckon, neighbor? How long will you keep pinning up that note? Until he comes back, God willing, I replied. She looked at me with pity.

You know what kills you? The silence. That's what kills you.

Apart from my brother, I never spoke to anyone.

Don't shout, honey.

Years and years of keeping quiet. You grow a kind of knot inside, a tangle, and there's no way to unravel it. Everything grows dark. You tend to allow things that hurt to happen and that's a mistake, it's a way of not learning. It may be hard, but you have to stop and take these things, snare them as if they were a hare in the field, set them traps so you come face-to-face with them, so they don't escape. If what the doctor here wants us to do is talk, I can say from experience that it will do us good. The *doctor*, I call her, I've never been able to use her Christian name. At the start I used to say Miss Natasha but she didn't like it much so I began to call her doctor. I'm subsidized here. I have no money for this. At least I'm not the only one. I'm a bit embarrassed, I don't want to know how much a consultation is worth. But the alternative is going to the doctor's office and being given an aspirin. I don't feel well, doc, I'm suffering. From what? It's my nerves, doc. Everything hurts. I had been admitted to the hospital when a friendly psychologist took pity on me and things began to change. She brought me to see the doctor here, and for the first time, I told this story. For the first time I told someone that my husband was a disappeared detainee. I'd never even said it to myself. But that was later, much later.

The days, months, years passed. From the sky downward, everything became sad. Like a good country woman, I kept my arms folded, that's what we do in the country. I kept waiting for Carlos. I couldn't come to grips with the idea of death. He was alive, in his pajamas, freezing cold, but alive. One day the boss lady told me that the disappeared were in Argentina. Yes, that's right, she told me, they abandoned their wives and left silently, taking advantage of the political situation. I remembered my brother-in-law who crossed the Andes and never came back. But why wouldn't Carlos come back? Carlos loved me. Just the same I was taken for a while by the idea of Argentina. It might just be true. I remembered when Batalla died. It was better to close your eyes for three days lying under the chestnut tree. Anything was better than waiting.

Where are you, darling sweetheart? Where are you that you can't hear me?

In the neighborhood there were posters of Pinochet. People liked him. Or if they didn't like him, they kept quiet. Everyone afraid. Of losing their jobs. Or their lives, of course. Pinochet was like a sickness. Half the country was sick and lived as best as the illness allowed, nothing more. I didn't want my children to be infected, to be screwed over because of their father. I was already screwed enough.

Before the doctor, I visited fortune-tellers, clairvoyants, anyone who might be able to give me some news. One day on the bus, a woman handed me a card that said MIND ALTERER. I went to see her. She told me, From the heavens to the last grain of sand, you're pure sorrow, pure sorrow. You're going to fall ill from sorrow. Can you get sick from grief? I wondered. But what if the suffering begins at the start, just by opening your eyes? I remember when my Golondrina was born. She came out with a screech and a cry, that was the first thing she did when she came into this world. Can you imagine a baby born laughing? What world would he fit into? But the Mind Alterer was right. I had fallen ill and I hadn't realized it. My body always hurt, my whole body, so what difference did it make? And my nerves. But all the same it kept flitting round my mind. I asked for an appointment at the hospital. It took a long time to get one and when I went they found a lump in my left breast. I had cancer. Of course! Do you know what I think? It was the silence and the sorrow that infected my breast.

The cancer came later.

The house.

Such poison.

I kept thinking, if Carlos comes back, he's going to come here, to this house. He won't know how to find me anywhere else. We paid rent, until the day the landlord came to see me. He was an old man who lived in the neighborhood, who also owned the kiosk on the corner. I want to sell the house, he told me. I got scared. No, come on, Don Alberto, what do you mean you want to sell the house? I said. I kicked up such a fuss!

Where will Carlos come back to?

Luisa has no home, sang Violeta Parra. I don't know how that song ever reached my ears. Perhaps I heard it as a girl back in Chillán.

At the Fiesta Nacional
  Luisa has no fire
  No candles and no rags

Luisa has no home
  The military parade
  And if Luisa goes to the park
  Where will she return?

It was September again. I was obsessed by the idea of the house. It was the only thing I could think about. Everyone bought things from Don Alberto's kiosk on the corner of my street: drinks, cigarettes, candy, needles and thread, lottery tickets. But the kiosk was small and had a storeroom behind it. It was no more than four planks but it was a roof. So I said to Don Alberto, Sell me the storeroom and I'll pay you in work. He looked at me as if I were crazy. Work? What work, Miss Luisa? I proposed working in his kiosk every evening from seven o'clock until closing and on the weekends. Very respectfully, he told me no, that this wasn't for him, it didn't suit him. That night I didn't sleep at all and I thought and thought. The next day I called my boss and told her I couldn't work, that I was sick. I grabbed a large cardboard box and wrote, "Luisa has no home." I took the rug from the kitchen floor and settled down in front of the kiosk with my sign and Golondrina in my arms. The neighbors stopped to ask. Everyone in the district learned that I had been left homeless and had nowhere to go. When they asked whether I couldn't rent a house in another quarter I told them no, my children had been born here and I wasn't going to leave. They thought I was being very obstinate. But no one, no one found out that all this hassle was for Carlos. I went three days without moving, sitting on my rug with the sign in my hands. Don Alberto arrived on the fourth day. Christ, Miss Luisa, all the neighbors have been nagging me, asking what are we going to do for you, so I'm going to accept your proposal. I'll give you the storeroom, that's all, but you have to take care of the merchandise for me.

That's how you do business in my neighborhood.

The boss lady got me some wood from the Hogar de Cristo charity and within a month I had a one-room hut. The first night we slept there it smelled of joy, like freshly washed cotton. The vacant lot with all its earth was like a daisy meadow to me. That fall, the rains never came and we looked out every day at what we had planted. I watered the ylang-ylang so that it would be flowering to welcome Carlos. That was the time in my life when I worked hardest. Thank God I was young and had plenty of strength, I went up and down without stopping, at the boss's until six and taking care of the kiosk afterward. The kitchen window of my new house overlooked the street, the same street Carlos had left by and to which he would return.

From my humble fixed-up shack I watched life pass by. I've never liked the cloudy skies of Santiago. They just sit there, they don't announce the rain. What are those skies good for? The kids grew up. Carlitos left school at last and became an apprentice with an electrician at stop ten on the Avenida, until he learned his trade and began to bring money home. Later on he sorted out my papers with Don Alberto and I stopped working so many hours. The house was mine now and I could rest.

The protests came. The plebiscite. Happiness is on the way. The arrival of democracy. The people are winning. I stayed quiet. On TV, I saw the *Rettig Report, Truth and Reconciliation*, in full.

The flag is a painkiller.

But Carlos didn't feature in the report. How would he, Luisa, when you've never declared his disappearance? My brother once asked me this when I went to the country. It was too late for that. My children had grown up well. No one pointed at them on the street. If Carlos wasn't with me, what did it matter whether he appeared on the lists or not? Sometimes I felt I was still at war when everyone else had signed the peace treaty. There was democracy, but I was still alone.

Some days I think that Carlos is talking to me. In what way did you put up a fight, Luisa? he asks. I waited, I reply. I waited for you every day. I never expected this for you, my darling.

You know the worst thing that can happen to a human being? To disappear. Dying is much better than disappearing.

More than thirty years without a man. No one dies from lack of a man. All I know is that I'm tired. I'm tired. I'm so tired.

My cancer was treated, with chemotherapy and all. I had to stop working for a while and the insurance covered me. They removed my breast. There were lots of women in my situation, single, widowed, abandoned, separated, whatever, but all so alone. At visiting time the ward filled up just with women taking care of other women. When Carlitos showed up, everyone joked with him. The good thing was that no one died in there. There was an office I really liked going to, through the Cancer Corporation, where there was a very nice woman who gave me massages. No one had ever touched me apart from Carlos. To begin with I found it embarrassing. Why should anyone else be concerned about me feeling any pleasure in my body? What would they say in the country if they could see me? I wondered. I shed pounds of worries after every session on that massage table. I remember those massages as the good things that have happened to me in life.

I've passed the five-year mark. I'm supposedly fine. The kids didn't want to leave until I was good and healthy. When they left, they took the truth with them in their minds. Because the doctor forced me to tell them how things had been. It was difficult for me and for them, as if they weren't going to forgive me. Eventually Carlitos said: I had a right to know, it's completely different being the son of a disappeared detainee than the son of a good-for-nothing who abandoned us. You should have told us before.

* * *

My story is no more than that. I've told you everything. I'm no good at talking, and I can't think of anything else to say. I don't work as a maid now. I just sit in the kiosk for a few hours and Don Alberto pays me. I get on fine there, I don't tire myself out and I chat with the neighborhood women. The kids send me money. I live in the same house. In the summer I go to visit my family in the country. My mother is still alive, she's just over ninety and is still facing up to life, even though she's become blind. The chestnut and the *boldo* trees and the stream are all still there, everything's the same. There are still dogs all over the place. I have four grandchildren but I don't see them much, once a year at most. How I enjoy them. The kids want me to travel to Sweden but I won't hear of it. How would I ever get in a plane? I'd die of fright. You might say that all the doors have closed on me. I'm sixty-seven. Everything has happened already. But I'm still alive.

I still think about Carlos. In my head, I still walk next to him. I look at the sky because I always look at the sky as I walk and I feel his warmth striding by my side. He is forever young in my mind. He was thirty-three, the age Jesus died. A traveler, that's how I think of Carlos. The return home. As if everything is about that. From the wars onward. I think of Carlos as the traveler who wants to come home, who is exerting his will to do just that but someone is preventing it. All he wants is to come home.

GUADALUPE

y name is Guadalupe and I'm nineteen. I always introduce myself as Lupe. It doesn't seem so virginal, or so Mexican for that matter, because I'm Chilean and not even all that Catholic. Those closest to me call me Lu, as if I were Chinese, and I like that.

My life is complex and sometimes confused and the main reason is that I'm too different from other women.

First: I'm a lesbian. I always have been and I'm not ashamed of it, quite the opposite. Second: my mind works so quickly that I'm not able to understand the quantity of things that pass through it. It's always ahead of me and I trip over my words. Not because I don't know how to speak but because everything inside me is a whirlwind, everything is fast and fleeting. I feel like my grandfather. Sometimes he gets it into his head that he's a writer and lots of words come to him all at once but he can't type properly and the rhythm of his hands doesn't match that of his head. I have a very high IQ, according to the tests I've done, and that exhausts me, but it's not the reason I ended up in therapy. I came to Natasha because my mom forced me to. She made me do it with the idea of analyzing the subject of lesbianism. I really came out of curiosity, but I stayed.

* * *

I left high school last year and I'm studying computer sciences. My secret ambition is to one day end up somewhere like Silicon Valley, designing software and hopefully specializing in creating games. That would be great, my ultimate aspiration. If I manage to get one just right, I could become a millionaire, which wouldn't be too bad at all. Everyone of my generation wants to be rich.

On that subject, I come from a pretty well-to-do family but, as far as I can tell, not traditional. I live in La Dehesa, in a huge house with all the mod cons, but not particularly in good taste. Everything is brand-new, but my grandparents on both sides never left the middle-class areas of Ñuñoa and central Santiago. When I say all the mod cons, I mean that I've never had to share a bedroom or bathroom with anyone. I had my first laptop at fifteen and I was the first in my class to turn up with an iPod. My dad imports machinery parts for a living, and he does well. My mom does nothing, she doesn't even look after the house because she has people to do that for her, two live-in maids who keep everything spotless. She's pretty idle, my mom. I don't know how she doesn't get bored. My dad tells her she should look for a job to entertain herself but she retorts that she's raising the children. There are five of us, too many, to tell the truth. I'm the second. After me there are three kids, the youngest is seven. The oldest is a girl, already married. She got married at twenty, totally crazy, right? Now she's pregnant, which has the whole family shrieking with joy. Her name is Rocío, and despite the fact that we're like chalk and cheese, we get on pretty well. My mom has dyed blond hair and an enormous black SUV and she likes piling us all in it to go to the mall for ice cream and shopping. She always has something to shop for. She's a pretty happy person and fun sometimes. I'm the only shadow in her life, and my shadow is *heavy*, I can assure you of that.

We begin, traditionally, with the idea of the kiss. From childhood tales to TV soap operas, everything touches on it.

During high school, my classmates were always talking about how wonderful kissing was, that fire you felt, those tingles and the million things that happened inside you. But nothing happened to me and however much I kissed I was never able to feel the wonder. Which made me ask myself whether the problem was that I didn't know how to kiss or whether I simply didn't like it.

Through my dad's job, we had to go to Venezuela for a while and I arrived back in Chile turning fourteen and still not knowing what the hell a good kiss was. When I arrived, I had my first official boy-friend, Matías. Things were good with him, relaxed, but I didn't get those incredible crazy feelings my friends did. Until it finally hap-pened. But not with him.

I had a secret friend, Javier, who was quite a bit older than me, and gay. I say secret because my folks would have found it very strange if they'd seen me with him. We had met at a party and we went out all the time. One night we were at another party together, and when the dancing was already underway, after the third shot of tequila, a really good-looking guy appeared arm-in-arm with a girl. They asked us to dance. Javier's eyes popped out of his head, because of the guy. To help him out, I started dancing with the girl, assuming that she was in the same boat as me. We danced for like an hour and she asked me to go to the bathroom with her. She went in and I stayed leaning against the wall waiting for her. Then she opened the door and asked me whether I'm coming in or not. I went in, sat on the bidet and waited, looking at the shower curtain, concentrating hard. Then I heard the water in the washbasin stop running. She had locked the door and I got up to open it so that we could leave together, but she didn't let me. She turned me around and kissed me.

Finally I felt those goddamn tweeting birds, hair on end, the flut-tering, the fireworks, everything!

I got nervous and opened the door, I walked toward a room at the end of the hallway where I found a small, very hippie-style living room with cushions on the floor and fabrics on the walls and a whole load of rather Arab-looking stuff. She followed me. We sat on a giant cushion and I made the most of the opportunity to make up for all those insipid kisses I'd had until then. The funny thing was that at some point I remembered Mati, realized that I was cheating on him, and left the room. I returned to the dance floor and grabbed Javier, and we left.

Javier kept dating the super stud and I saw the girl again several times. Her name is Claudia. Everything was always really cool. I was still in a relationship with Mati, but the truth is that I struggled to resist the urge to kiss her every time I saw her. I was growing increasingly bored with Mati, but I was still fond of him.

One day Matías and I fought over nothing and we broke up. Or rather, we decided to give ourselves some space. For some reason, losing him caused a much greater collapse than I expected. I think that deep down I understood that between me and my relationship with him there was a *line of normality*. He was the reason I didn't just throw myself at Claudia.

With him out of the picture, no one was holding me back.

They were difficult days. My mom had gone with my dad to Buenos Aires and the three kids were with our grandmother. I had felt a bit lonely since my return from Caracas. I had to wait for the end of the semester to go back to high school and I spent long hours doing nothing. The house was ghostly, I don't know where Rocío was, I barely saw her. I picked up my cell phone, searching under C to call my friend Coca, and *boom*, the screen flashes Claudia's number, as if by magic.

She was at my house within the hour. I barely had time to tidy my room, shower, get dressed, and eat something. We stayed in the living room listening to music on my stereo and her Discman, her sitting on the armchair and me lying down, resting my head against her legs. We chatted for a long time. At one point, we kissed. Within ten minutes we were in my bed.

The truth is, I never realized what I was doing. They were my impulses, it was my nature. It was the first time in my life I had *sex*.

I had never been with a man because at fourteen I found it a bit disgusting. But once I awoke that beast inside me, I had no way of stopping it.

The following day I called Mati and told him to forget about "having some space." I didn't need it, we had to end things and that was all.

Claudia was essential for me. Then she got pregnant—all very bi—and the romance ended. She didn't want to be an "official lesbian" until her son grew up, but we're still great friends today.

Relationship over, I tried not to spend too long dwelling on this strange thing that had happened to me. It was an experience, I thought, not a defining moment. Although I found it difficult, I tried to ignore it or to ignore myself. I don't really know how to put it, but sometimes I caught myself playing at "being normal," talking about men the way you do at that age, having crushes on guys on the big screen or TV, partying with my friends like anyone else. I even went out with a couple of guys who liked me for a while but I didn't really like any of them. None of them drove me wild as I thought they might. The strange thing is that I still *expected* to be able to like a man.

About six months after meeting Claudia I went to an art opening for paintings by one of my cousins. We all went as a family. During the cocktail reception, I noticed one of the waitresses passing through the gallery. She was dressed in black and white and she swayed her hips, tray in hand, as she served glasses of red wine. Her femininity and the grace of her movements caught my attention and I watched her for a long time. Later, I went to the restroom and found her there—always in bathrooms! We began chatting, one of those banal conversations girls have in restrooms: what was my name, which high school did I go to, stuff like that. I left and joined my group in front of a painting of an enormous colored horse and concentrated on enjoying myself.

The day after the opening, she was waiting for me after class. I couldn't believe it. She was a stunning girl of nineteen and I was a brat of fourteen and not exactly a beauty queen. She had taken the trouble to find out my schedule and come to look for me. From that day on we were together and with her I was part of my first couple, with all that entails. A girl of fourteen going steady with another of nineteen. At that age, five years is a lot.

Her name was Agustina and people called her Kitty.

Kitty became my reference point in life. With her, things worked so well, I felt safe and was moved by the solidity of our relationship. When I'd hear my mom pissed at my dad over something, moaning behind his back, something inside me was relieved. I don't have to go through that, I told myself. One day, after a long heart-to-heart conversation with Kitty, I arrived home and heard my mom saying to my sister, Men have never listened to women, *never!* I smiled to myself. Kitty listened to me. And I to her. She was my best friend, my confidant, my partner, my girlfriend. She was everything. I had the feeling that finally something was right, as if none of my feelings from before had any independence and therefore were of no use. We were together for three years. We came and went countless times. We fought, we broke up, and the next day we got back together. Meanwhile, when some guy seemed a bit more attractive than the rest, I dated him for a month, just as a screen for my folks, because I didn't want them to find out that their daughter was a lesbian. Of course, when this adventure became more serious, I learned what a *relationship* really meant, the good and the bad of it, the wonders and the difficulties, the way all women learn with their first man.

We had lots of plans for the future. As soon as I turned eighteen we would go to New York together. We would live in Soho, I'd look for a full-time job for a year, doing whatever, so that later on I could finance my studies. She was interested in costume design and was in contact with a couple of young Latino designers, so she more or less knew how to get started, what to do. Sometimes we devoted our-selves to imagining the apartment we would live in, the fabric we'd throw over the couch, the apple-green color we'd paint the kitchen, the coffee machine we would use, how we would split the closet. She

liked clothes much more than I did. Our greatest enemy was the cal-
endar. I looked and looked at it and it seemed eternal. How could
I hurry time, for Christ's sake, how could I make it so that I grew
up now and was free? Kitty was mega-patient. If she had fallen for
someone older, she could already be walking down Fifth Avenue and
not Parque Florestal.

Kitty's parents lived in the south, in Temuco, and rented a small
apartment in Plaza Baquedano for their children so they could study
in Santiago. Her brother was a kind of nerd, a young genius who
studied civil engineering, who never saw or heard anything, always
shut away in his world, absent almost all the time, the ideal room-
mate for us. My schedule was super restricted during the week. My
mom knew exactly how my high school operated and what time
I left. The levels of regimentation that private school pupils in the
barrio alto are subjected to are incredible. All their movements are
controlled. I had to create time for my private life. I had to invent
a *vocation* for myself. There was no other way to see Kitty without
being caught. I decided I wanted to be a writer and that I would join
the most intensive literary workshop, one that gave lessons twice a
week, and, of course, which would be held by some loser writer who
lived downtown. Making it up took me ten minutes. My mom is so
uncultured that I could have given her any name and she would have
believed it. She was happy to see me so interested in something like
that and she proudly told my dad all about it. When she asked me
to show her some of the stuff we did in the workshop, I downloaded
any old text from the internet and gave it to her to read, leaving her
highly impressed. What's more, she paid for the workshop. That
made me feel bad, I felt a bit like a thief. It's not that my folks were
short of money, that wasn't what mattered, it was their credulity. But
I was fully aware that any deception was better than reality itself.

As time went by and I got to know Kitty and her friends better, I
began to realize that she was cheating on me nonstop. Since this was
my first experience, I assumed that relationships between women

were like that, and I kept the infidelity inside as something normal. Even today, I'm permissive in that respect, as long as we can talk about it and there's an explanation. I tend to forgive. But I'm not dumb either and if I find out from someone else, there's no argument, get your things and go.

During the time I was with Kitty I learned a whole load about relationships. I grew a lot, but I was also shitting myself with fear. I felt so alone, insecure, hidden, not accepted. Hiding from the world the affection you feel for someone is very complicated and distressing. I imagine that's why official relationships like boyfriend and girlfriend, engagement and marriage, exist. They must have been invented in order to give the power of feelings the right to exist, to give them a free path to develop and express themselves, as an escape valve, essentially. It makes all the sense in the world to me. Especially during adolescence, when the only, *only* thing that matters is what you feel. You have to crush it so that it doesn't squeeze through the cracks and get noticed. They were years of extreme silence. Loving like that and not being able to tell anyone is harsh. I didn't talk to anyone out of fear. I pretended to everyone and passed myself off as someone who, in reality, I wasn't. I swear, it's one of the worst things that can happen to you. I felt disconnected from everything that was outside my relationship. Alienated, as Natasha would say. At some point I decided that my life wasn't right and I was doubtful of my ability to face it and emerge safe and sound.

You might wonder how homosexuality is assumed. I think it's a long process, gradual, difficult and full of traps. For example, my appearance has always been masculine. Since I was small I've never been able to bear pink ribbons in my hair or full skirts. I've always worn my hair very short. Ever since my mom stopped dressing me and I could choose, I've gone for black as my color and I never liked any "feminine" shades. Just like Layla, no pinks or pale blues. My younger siblings call me "the trucker," which I put down to my way of walking, of smoking. Sometimes, daydreaming, I used to see myself as someone tender, all vaporous, in long, white dresses and my hair blowing softly in the breeze, like a Tolkien elf, beautiful, ethereal, ultrafeminine, like Galadriel, or like Cate Blanchett playing Galadriel, the essence of what you would consider a woman to be. When I saw myself like that, I had the urge to surrender, not to fight the world any longer, to release my defenses, for someone to say to me, Sleep, Lu, sleep, I love you, rest.

By the time I turned seventeen I considered myself an experienced lesbian, wanted by all the girls, although that's not saying much given some of the horrors you see in the gay world of Santiago. Things with Kitty were progressing like a dream and I was increasingly sure that she was the one. Even though we were still hiding ourselves.

Shortly before my birthday, I met her in El Cafetto in Providencia, our usual café, and she told me she'd been offered an internship with a design studio in New York and it could be an opportunity to enhance her studies. She'd be paid enough to survive and, added to what her folks sent her every month, she could pay rent on an apartment and live peacefully. In other words, she was leaving a year earlier than we had planned, *without me.*

The sky fell in on me.

Within a month, she had gone.

A cousin of mine was studying for a master's in Ireland and during the summer vacation I begged and begged for my parents to send me there. They agreed. I left. To make up for things, I took it upon myself to grab any jerk I could get my hands on and I didn't even notice the girls, I hated them. They were all traitors.

Around February, still in Dublin, I received an email from Kitty. She told me about her refurbished apartment in Soho, the coffee machine, the color of the bedspread, how much she remembered me and my desire to live in New York, that the city really was made for me, blah blah blah. At the bottom of the email, a postscript read: "I met a girl called Soledad. She's really pretty and I'm dating her. I told her about us and she has no problem with it, although sometimes she gets annoyed because I talk about you a lot. Doesn't that happen to you too?"

I exploded. I decided not to speak to her again. I replied with an extremely calm email and a month later she replied, telling me that she was already living with the bitch Soledad and that she was *so* happy.

I disconnected from Kitty's life and returned to Chile determined to swear off dating for a long, long time.

I was wrong.

There are many kinds of discrimination in the world, but there are few like we lesbians suffer. Homosexual men have advanced, their reality today is *nothing* like it was twenty or thirty years ago.

The world is more humane, a female president in Chile, an African American in the States, even gay men come close to power. Not us, however. Gay men have reached the point of not just being tolerated but appreciated too. Even the neighborhoods they move to go up in price. The gays have arrived, everything will be nicer, more sophisticated, more elegant. The thing is that gays have such good taste, they take care of their surroundings, bullshit like that. It's only a matter of time before they have a slogan: *Rent a Gay.* They appear in TV series as important and adorable characters. Moms of gay men end up bonding with their partners, they feel protected by this son who will take care of them their entire life—another myth—and although initially they went to shit when they heard about their son's sexual inclinations, they got over it in time and now accept it quite happily. They are the perfect accessory for a social event. But lesbians are hidden, always hidden. I've never heard, in this environment anyway, of a father sitting at the table with his lesbian daughter and her partner in front of his friends. Gay sons can become a trophy, while we are a burden. In Chile, at least. I heard that the French Culture Secretary isn't just gay but that he also wrote a book detailing his sexual adventures. I don't really get politics, but if that's what I did, I'm sure I'd hide it. In the art world, things are a bit more relaxed. But who said lesbians only work in the arts?

I'll continue with my story.

I returned from Dublin prettier than I had been in a long time. Don't think it was by chance. I was older and much more pissed at the world than before. I met Rosario sitting next to me at school, a really *preppy* girl, typical seventeen-year-old brat, uber-feminine and totally hetero. The truth is that I didn't see her as anything special until she began to think I was fascinating and wanted to spend more time with me than any sane person would. We began to go out occasionally, to chat, to sit together at school, and one day we went to a class barbecue and after a good deal of drinking we went on to a party, adding even more alcohol to our systems. That night I slept over at her house and as we lay chatting on her bed, she threw herself on top of me and kissed me.

That's when the shit began!

We were caught.

In an instant, her mom came up, saw us, and I had to tolerate two hours of being talked to at her parents' dining table. Rosario's mom threatened to call my mom to tell her and fear flooded through me. I managed to convince her not to, but I spent two weeks in terror, not knowing whether she would keep her word. Meanwhile, despite everything, we began dating. Rosario never understood the seriousness of the matter and she all but published it on the school notice board. Sooner or later, everyone found out and I ended up sitting in the principal's office. Either I spoke to my parents or they would be told at the meeting the following day.

I arrived home scared to death, knowing that there was no going back. I had to accept "what I had done"—the principal's words—and tell my parents that I liked girls. My mom, who might be frivolous but not stupid, had questioned me about the subject a few times. I suppose it was because of my short hair, my masculine attitude, and my gay friends. They were a clear sign. The truth was you didn't have to be very perceptive to figure out what was going on. But, thank God, I've always been a great one for bluffing so it wasn't too hard to make her believe it when I said I really liked men.

My mom arrived home and I asked whether I could talk to her about something very important. She agreed immediately. I sat opposite her at the dining table, I looked her in the eye and said, Mom, I've been dating a girl from my class.

That's all I remember. Afterward a cloud formed, questions and answers I'm not clear about. But I know that after five or ten minutes my mom began to cry and I decided to get up and go to my room, to shut myself away for a while. I smoked a pack of cigarettes in less time than I thought possible and I waited.

An hour later, the maid came up to see me. She's known me all my life and she gave me a big hug. She looked at me and said, I'll love you just the same, no matter what happens. That phrase has been going round my head all this time and I think it was what gave me the conviction to face what was coming.

My dad was on his way home, summoned by my mom, I assume. I think he always had his suspicions, but he wasn't really concerned about it. Anyway, he arrived and sat in the living room with my mom to wait for me to come down. I went in scared to death. I noticed that my dad had put on a pink-striped shirt that day, and that my mom's face was damp with tears.

I sat on one of the plum-colored armchairs and looked at them with an expression of terror. My dad asked me to explain. I went with a white lie and told them I was bisexual and that I didn't know what was up. The cloud shrouded me again and I can't really remember the conversation. I suppose panic was erasing my memory as I was storing it. At some point, my mom got up and a minute later I heard her backing out the car from the garage. I was left alone with my dad. His first question was whether I had ever slept with a man, to which I answered no. Then whether I had done it with a woman. I said yes. He replied, You don't decide you prefer vanilla if you haven't tried chocolate. I laughed and he joined in. The thing that bothered him most was that I hadn't told him sooner. My dad was quite a bit cooler than I had expected.

I went back up to my room. I closed the door, lay on the bed, and tried to sleep. The following day I set out for school to wait for the outcome of the principal's meeting with my parents. No one asked me whether or not I had told them and the principal never broached the subject with them. They forced me to come out of the closet under threat and it was all a lie. If I hadn't told them, they probably still wouldn't know and I could have avoided all this pain. The principal really screwed me over. But it was the best decision, the only one possible in order to stop lying.

Things with Rosario went from bad to worse. After having been such a big mouth, she was now constantly scared about what was going on. She didn't understand how she could be with a woman when she had always liked men and I think that's why she didn't let me get to the next stage with her. We dated for a month and she treated me badly. Now I understand, it must have been very complicated for her, but back then I blamed her for everything. I hated her with heart and soul and from that moment on I became the Party Monster.

It was a very self-destructive period.

Until then, I used to go out every weekend and I partied hard but without much awareness of what I was doing, deep down. It was just teenage shenanigans. Now I went out to destroy myself. That was my intention. I smoked joints all day. It wasn't the first time, but before I used to smoke to relax, to write or dance. Now it was different. I did it compulsively, almost addictively. I drank every time I went out and although I didn't tend to get drunk, I have a high tolerance, I turned to shit and played whatever games I wanted.

I should mention Johnny, my soul mate, even today. He's gay, of course. At that time he was my partner in crime, binges, games and lies, all of it, cocaine too.

My mom was increasingly concerned about what was happening to me. At school, my grades were despicable, I fell asleep in class or behaved badly, I had no interest in being there. I just wanted to smoke joints and watch TV all day and walk around Santiago or go dancing. Classes tore me apart, as did my classmates, who were a bunch of idiots.

One day, after class, I was chatting with a group of kids a couple of grades below me. One of them asked if I knew where he could get marijuana seeds, because he wanted to plant some. The jerk was sixteen and still in eighth grade, just so you can imagine it, a year younger than me. I told him I had some at home and that I'd give them to him. A week later I remembered and chucked them in my bag. Before I went into class, I passed him a slip of paper with the seeds inside. They were more than a year old, it wasn't likely that anything would grow from them.

A couple days later I discovered why an asshole of sixteen was still in eighth grade. It was a shitty, gray day and I was once again fed up with high school, willing three thirty to come around so I could go hang out on the plaza or at home or who knows where. I remember I spent the entire first hour of classes sending text messages to a friend, cursing at the world.

At the end of that first hour the teacher called me out of the room and sent me to the principal. I didn't know *what* shit I was in now. Mario, that fucking asshole, had given away the seeds. His dad had caught him and he ratted me out in less than a second. Obviously the dad called the school. Three friends of mine had already been expelled for marijuana, one for smoking it, another for selling it, and the third for carrying the seeds. But these weren't illegal, so I thought nothing would happen to me. But they'd been trying for two months to catch me at something. Rosario's mom had launched a smear campaign against me, along with some teachers, on the basis that I was a terrible influence on the poor children.

They threw me out.

I lost my school, which until that moment, as much as I say I hated it, was the only place I felt part of a family. I had to go. Leave all my friends. Start over. They put me in an institute for rich girls who have been chucked out of normal schools. A place of *terror*.

Meanwhile, I had met a woman. I say a woman, not a girl or a chick my age. Her name was Ximena. It was at a fair at Johnny's high school. He was in charge of a coffee stall and I promised to help him. Between the two of us, we served people and sold more cups of coffee than anyone, as well as some little cakes my maid had made. I happily took the money, feeling every bit the entrepreneur. At one point, a play put on by the students began and we all went to watch it, so I closed the stall for a while. But I got bored in the middle of the performance and went outside to smoke a cigarette. As I was finishing it, I saw a really hot lady getting out of a car and I thought she might want a coffee, so I hurried to reach the stall before her. Two hundred pesos isn't much but I was determined that our stall would make the most money. I waited for her to arrive, obviously my seventeen years and my Nike sneakers were much faster than her thirty-seven years and high heels. I don't know what comes over me with heels, but I find them highly attractive, stilettos more than any others. Worn with the right panties, they're a surefire winner. When she arrived she looked at me, surprised there was no one else around, and asked me how long ago the play had started. About twenty minutes, I replied and took the opportunity to offer her a coffee. She told me she had no coins with her so I told her it was on the house. I took a couple of hundred-peso coins from my pocket and put them in the box. She laughed and accepted, charmed. I explained that the play would have an intermission in half an hour and she could go in then, because it wouldn't be a very good idea for her to interrupt. She took heed and stayed talking to me the whole time. She was very animated. She introduced herself and told me that she'd recently separated from her husband, who was a lawyer, and that she had a son in fourth grade. She also told me that she needed a private tutor to teach the kid English. I immediately volunteered, telling her about my time in Dublin. She accepted, charmed again. We exchanged numbers and carried on chatting. She was impressed with me and how easy it was for her to talk to someone twenty years her junior. She laughed at all my stories and I took the opportunity to show my most intelligent and interesting side, since she was extremely attractive.

A week later I started giving the English lessons. Ximena paid me very well. Sometimes I asked her to pay me less because I couldn't charge her for the time I spent chatting to Simón, her son, even less for the time we spent drinking tea and watching *SpongeBob* together. I liked Ximena so much that I never told my mom that I was giving these classes because it made me nervous. What's more, if my mother found out I was earning money, she'd probably stop my allowance and if that happened, it would mean less partying in my life.

Shortly after I was thrown out of school, I went to give Simón his lesson and when I arrived, Ximena opened the door, crying like crazy. When she saw me she blushed and began to apologize. She explained that her ex-husband had been at the house, that everything had turned to shit and that he'd gone out with Simón but she forgot to tell me. She said she'd pay me but I told her not to worry about it. I told her to sit down, and I fetched her a glass of water. I sat next to her and tried to calm her down. We talked for a long time and she ended up embracing me, crying ceaselessly.

I don't really know what happened, but I kissed her.

She got nervous but she hugged me tighter.

From then on I began to arrive early for the lessons and sometimes I left later, after chatting to Ximena. She began to look happier and I, in turn, began to commit to my own affairs a bit more. Sometimes we kissed, sometimes we didn't, we talked more than anything.

One day she invited me to go out, the two of us, as friends, and we went out to eat. She told me it was really complicated because she was starting to like me. I adored her. Don't forget she was thirty-seven, had a son, was recently separated, and who knows how many wild days behind her. But she seemed like a girl. She didn't know how to face this scenario of liking someone of the same sex.

We began to go out more frequently. I slept over at her house a couple of times. I thought, truth be told, that I could stay like this for a long time without getting bored. But by that stage I was getting used to the fact that these things never work out for me. Gradually I became depressed. I continued to go out partying with Johnny almost every weekend. One of those nights I met Lulú, a girl of sixteen, very, very pretty and profoundly sad, which moved me a great deal. I decided that, whatever happened, I would make her smile. I spent the entire night trying to crack her up. We ended up chatting and laughing a lot and I realized how much I liked that feeling.

I love being able to transform someone else, even if for no more than a moment.

The best thing for me is being loved, I suppose everyone's the same. Why the hell do we spend our whole lives seeking love? Why are we capable of doing *anything* for people to love us? Sometimes, when I'm in hetero environments where my inclinations are known, I feel like they look at me, poor things, thinking I'm a charity case. I've caught myself thinking, If compassion means more love, then bring it on, pity me.

It turned out that the same week, Ximena told me that I was making things complicated with Simón and the separation and that she'd prefer we cool things for a while. She didn't want to stop seeing me but she was very confused, we shouldn't close any doors, we could see each other in the future, we would meet again. Being twenty years older than me, she was in over her head and she didn't know how to deal with it.

Devastated again, I didn't go to class for a week, playing truant with my new classmates from the institute and getting up to nothing but trouble. I was always thinking about sex. Sometimes I've even wondered whether lesbianism makes you hornier than heterosexuality. All my lesbian friends think of nothing but sex. An obsession in the middle of the head, as if we've been struck there by an arrow.

When I listen to people like Simona or Mané, I wonder, How can they live without sex? Is it because they're old? What were they like at my age? Perhaps it's just a question of years. All the same, I can't imagine myself in the future not being permanently randy, without a body next to me in bed. The day I lose that, I think I will have lost everything.

Then came Lulú. Bit by bit we began to see each other, relaxed, totally chilled. I really enjoyed her company, being with her was easy and most things were trivial to her. She didn't sweat the small stuff. Everything was simple with her, so it happened fast and we made the most of it.

We were together for a year and a half. We shared our lives and it was the first time I married. There's a myth among lesbians that after the second date you marry. There's even a joke about it: .

"What does a lesbian take to the second date?"

"Her suitcases."

OK, not very funny, but it's typical. That's what happened to me with Lulú. It was so strong that I fought with the entire family to keep this relationship going. We lived together, we traveled together, and I forged strong bonds with her family. Her mom almost became a mom to me too. My own mother was scandalized, she didn't understand how Lulú's mom could tolerate the fact that we slept together under her roof. Once I got sick at Lulú's house and my mom came to see me. When I saw her appear in that house and sit on the chair in that bedroom, I understood that I had won the war, not just a small battle, but the whole war.

That being the case, since everything started so quickly, it ended quickly too. One day we were fantastic together and the next, fighting like cat and dog.

Story over with Lulú, I went back to Ximena. We had a short but intense affair. It was strange to return to her life as if no time had passed. But within two weeks, her ex-husband caught us. Out of the blue he came to get Simón, who was at a friend's house, and I opened the door, in a robe. Chaos again. After that incident, we decided that there were too many risks for her, although I had nothing to lose. I wonder why we always open the door. Why can no one just let the bell ring? People are really stupid, me included. I also wonder about that ex-husband and his set. What must they think homosexuality means? Or bisexuality, in this case? Many scientists say that all humans are bisexual, that sexuality depends on the amount of masculine and feminine hormones in the body, and that often those with the greatest phobia about it are those who fear that part of themselves the most. But returning to Ximena, she thought she might lose custody of her son if her ex-husband found her in bed with me. Is Ximena any less of a mother for being turned on by a woman? Does it put Simón in any danger?

The situation forced me to question myself, to chew things over, like an ever-hungry cow. And to resent myself, of course.

In the midst of the drama, Ximena, very serious, asked me, Lu, have you never thought about capitulating?

I asked her what she meant.

Giving in.

I thought about it for a moment. You might ask, and it would be a valid question, whether, with so many wounds, I wasn't tempted. Not once? You might think I broke. But no.

I never give in, I told her.

Thank God science has made it clear that homosexuality isn't a choice. You're born with it. That has changed things. No one is "guilty," not the parents, not the education system, not you. It isn't an issue of willpower, as was once believed. It's like being born with blue eyes. There they are. Are you going to spend your whole life wearing sunglasses or contact lenses to hide them? Your eyes are your eyes. The trouble is the price you must pay for having them. That's definitely unfair.

I have several aunts and uncles. My dad comes from a large family, and my mom's isn't exactly small either. It's interesting the way they reacted when I came out of the closet. Some were so shocked that they just blocked the subject out, as if it didn't exist. Others decided that it was just "teenage nonsense," that they shouldn't place any importance on it, it would pass. It's a phase, they told my dad.

If I had become a lesbian as an adult, I don't suppose anyone would have gotten involved. But when it happens in adolescence, the *family* factor is fatal. Intolerable. Everyone feels called upon to offer an opinion and everyone feels they have the right to do so. You're trying to establish your identity, and that's enough to absorb all the emotions your body has room for. Imagine what it means, on top of that, to face those around you, the ones you didn't choose. Do you ever have less choice than with aunts and uncles? You waste so much energy on them, on cushioning their blows. Everything would have been easier if it had just been an issue between me, myself, and I. That would have worked out so much better!

But I can assure you of one thing. Promiscuity has a lot to do with exclusion.

Leaving school changed everything. That stage came to an end at the same time as several others. I began to see Natasha. That was an important milestone. Suddenly I had an adult in front of me who was on my side, and that was really new to me. I also went to college, and devoting myself to a subject I was really interested in has made the whirlwind in my mind die down. I don't think so quickly anymore. It's as if my intelligence has settled down, or pushed forward, I don't know how to put it, but it isn't spinning free like before. All the same, Natasha does tests and is regulating my processes. I feel it, I feel it in my body the way it's all stabilized. I'm committed to what I do. Perhaps this is the start of *adulthood*, although the word kind of makes me laugh.

I've been dating an adorable girl for a couple of months. I was *abstinent* for a good while. You should have seen me. Harsh, really harsh, I didn't let anyone in. But Isadora won me over with her sweetness, her interest in music, her patience. She's adorable. It all began at a party and a trip to the bathroom, it's my karma. I resisted as best as I could, which disconcerted her. She thought I didn't like her. But in the end, after a date at the Normandie Arts Movie Theater to see a concert, we ended up in bed. We haven't parted since. I'm not thinking she's the woman of my life. I've been thinking that from Kitty onward. I suppose that's part of growing up too.

To tell the truth, I haven't been this happy in a long time. Between my studies, Natasha, friends, family, and Isadora, life is getting better and better.

Although the anger and all the shit I've dragged along behind me for years reappears on occasion and aggressive Lu never stops bothering me. I think I'm much closer to myself than I have ever been. I know that ghosts, deceptions, fears, mistakes, evils, and excesses will probably pursue me for a long time. For now, I try to bury them in a flowerpot and cross my fingers they won't germinate. As ever, I operate the wrong way around. Most people want what they plant to sprout. Not me. I was born different, as I told you at the start. I have to nurture that difference every day.

ANDREA

I'd like to talk about the desert, just the desert. The Atacama. It's the only thing on my mind. It's the world's most arid desert. When I was a girl I would have said the Sahara was drier, with those eternal, uninterrupted sands that make you think of Moses and Lawrence of Arabia. But it turns out that isn't true. Our desert is the driest of them all. I set off to visit it. It's a wonderful place to leave your bones, if that's the intention. It truly is a great place to die.

I'm Andrea, you probably recognize me from TV.

I always knew I wanted to be a journalist and in the center of things. I began as an intern in the network's press office and within two years I was reporting the news. Later, I got my own program and then I started diversifying. When I was capable of interviewing anyone, from celebrities to the president of the republic, they gave me free rein. Now I'm an integral part of the network's structure and I've discovered that I have a great talent for business, and also for handling power. Things have gone really well for me. I'm pretty famous and I've earned a fair amount of money. Put like that, my life seems fantastic. So why am I here? No idea. Everybody has problems, and being famous doesn't help. I've had to face various difficulties, stage fright, panic attacks, conspiracies, traps, permanent exposure, not to mention a bit of paranoia. There's nothing like fame to make you feel pursued. Occasionally I manage to escape. A couple of years ago I got quite far away, to Thailand, swearing that my future was in Buddhist monasteries and not on the screen. The early rises and fasting were too much for me and I ended up on a beautiful beach on the Indian Ocean, swimming in turquoise waters and buying silks.

After that I still wanted to escape again. Because, apparently, I was angry. I'll say it again. Everything's going well, my work, my health, my family. I don't doubt myself or my talent or my husband's love. Could it be that you doubt your love for him? Natasha might ask me. She loves torturing me, but no, that isn't the question. So, why am I upset? I hadn't even realized I was. One day, after a massage session, Silvia, a divine Argentinean, says to me, Hey, Andrea, you gave me a lot of work today. I had to work on your face like never before and I finally managed to get rid of that frown. What frown? What's she talking about? A few days later I had a photo shoot for a magazine. As soon as the bored-looking young photographer clapped her eyes on me she said, Please, that expression. What expression? I asked, disconcerted. That bad temper, she replied. I wondered again what she meant. A week after that, I accompanied Carola, my daughter, to her high school fair. Afterward she remarked to Fernando, Dad, you should have seen mom's face. She looked furious! What are you talking about? I said. I came to see Natasha and asked her if she thought I was angry. As always, she turned the question around and threw it right back at me.

After that, I shut myself in the sauna to think. It's the only place where I can think. It couldn't be pure coincidence that everyone apart from me could see this anger. A familiar feeling came over me. A yearning to escape. It's misleading to say that the human being exists under one great vital impulse. There are lots of *little impulses* too. In my case, they make themselves known with a huge desire to stop, drop everything, and escape. A tickle begins to run through my body, a bit like a fantasy or an urge, often imprecise, until it turns into the name of a place. I thought about some foreign place, one that, out of pure novelty, would simultaneously suggest enclosure and absolute openness. For the first time in many years I looked at the map of Chile. It's so easy and serene to travel within our own borders. Then I decided that aridity was the answer.

The desert.

At the station, I told them I had a good idea for a new program, which, I should point out, was true, and that I'd be out for a few days. I woke up on the day in question at 6:30 a.m. in my bed in Santiago and by 10:40 I'd landed at Calama airport, where they were expecting me. I found this touching because I was the only passenger and couldn't believe all that effort was just for me. The girl in charge of my welcome looked at me and asked for an autograph. The driver, Rolando, defined himself as "Atacaman." I later understood that this meant declaring oneself to be indigenous. As we glided along through that unfamiliar landscape, nice and safe in the pickup, I thought that coming here alone had been a good idea. I had several things to think about. How strange to see an indifferent landscape, one that doesn't modify itself because of our presence. My eyes wouldn't give it credit. I saw hills that looked like giant eggplants, others that were a creamy coffee color like immense scoops of chocolate ice, the sand rippling like an ocean heavy with waves. The sky is a pristine blue, a blue that's pretty much unseen to urban eyes, shining, sharp, blinding.

Just over an hour away from Calama, we arrived at the Alto Atacama—that's the name of the hotel. Hills surround the small enclave on all four sides. In the center of those hills stands a low construction the color of mud, the same mud the ancients used for building. The hotel maintains the coloring in order to camouflage itself, so as not to clash with the desert.

The manager was waiting for me at the hotel door. Right from the start, I felt welcomed. Cordiality impregnated the air.

My room was very pretty, decorated with dark tobacco colors, which are present everywhere in the Atacaman adobe that the indigenous people used from the very start of their history. There was also a private terrace furnished with concrete beds and air mattresses from where I could watch the sunset, or the dawn, and its design allowed you to see nothing but hills and desert. No neighbors, no television. Not a glimpse of my face on the screen. I found the austere lines elegant. I put my computer in the closet, doubtful of how much use it would get. I placed my books on the nightstand. I get so little reading done in Santiago. I unpacked my case and by one in the afternoon I was in the dining room for a delicious lunch of quinoa, sea bass, and fruit. I was exhausted after waking up so early so then I took a nap. There wasn't a single noise around me. For me, that silence was like chlorophyll to plants or music to a dancer. Within that silence I could connect with myself. That's one of my problems. I don't connect with myself, however much I try. At times I simply have no idea who I am. I only know the Andrea I see on the screen and as long as that Andrea is doing fine, nothing else seems to matter. I end up believing that that woman is real, the only one who exists inside me. The silence of the desert would allow me to get closer to the true me.

After that glorious nap, I went to the spa, which is a luxury to me. In the middle of the sauna, a copper expert from Chuquicamata—I thought there would only be foreign guests who can afford expensive hotels—became ecstatic when he realized who I was. He shouted to his friends in the hot tub, Hey, guess who's here! It was like a slap in the face. I shut myself in the steam room and didn't come out again. When they left, I lay down outside, in a robe and with wet hair, in the middle of nothing to watch the sunset. I didn't know how to react to the solitude.

I'm perfectly happy, I told myself. That was probably a lie but I said it just the same. Then I thought, Shit, how long has it been since I last uttered those words? Not since the last time I was in the countryside, at Consuelo's parents' house. She's my best friend. We've known each other since we were girls, we went to the same school, and we've accompanied each other through every step of life. She calls me "the diva" and doesn't take me particularly seriously. She isn't impressed when she sees me on the cover of a magazine but she refuses to come with me to buy groceries in Jumbo. She can't stand people's excitement. Neither can I. I hardly ever go to the supermarket. I didn't want to tell Consuelo my new plans, she would have insisted we talk about it and I'm not ready. Anyway, she's managed to get used to this woman I am, who lives from intensity to intensity and doesn't scare easily. I imagined her observing this desert landscape. She would define it as *powerful*, that's the adjective she would have used. I would have replied, It's a void, an enormous void.

At dawn, I woke with a start. I opened the drapes and the landscape had transformed. The mountain had teeth, each cut sculpted by water from the Andes during the winter, and beneath them were bands of color like an elegant taffeta gown, reds, purples, browns, blues. The hills had dressed up for me. It was five in the morning and I found myself in the desert. Far away in the city, in my city, the day had not yet arrived. I remembered that trite saying about how you don't make the journey but the journey makes you, or unmakes you, and I thought of that journey as a disappearance.

I was on vacation from real life. I suppose we all hate "real life" and we know how it overwhelms us if we don't take it in small doses.

I slept for twelve hours.

I should mention that my sleep is usually aided by medication. Once I fall asleep I'm like a teenager, but I struggle to get there in the first place. There are too many things flitting around my head when I'm finally left in peace. If I don't take something, I can reach four in the morning with my obsessive thoughts. I confess that my ratings are one of those things, the main one. I rely on pills, but because I hate them I keep coming up with combinations that aren't addictive, whether it's a relaxant in the afternoon or a tranquilizer at night. I play with the doses, I reduce them and take a quarter of one pill and

half of another, that's how I manage them. I'm the classic self-medi-
cating woman.

I put on a sweatshirt over my pajamas and went to the dining room
like that. I don't think I would have done such a thing in Santiago.
I don't go out to the street if I'm not presentable. My awareness of
being a public figure is such that my appearance has become a kind
of fixation. I'm always grateful for having been born with a relatively
pretty face. I wouldn't have the career I have if I had been plain or
ugly. Pure talent isn't enough, it's never enough.

Breakfasting in pajamas in a public place was a new experience.
On the subject of breakfast, there was no room service in the hotel.
The boy who served me at the table kindly offered to bring me something if I liked, but I didn't want any special treatment. If everyone
else ate standing up, I would too. I had a terrible boiled egg. I burned
my fingers and it didn't fill me up at all. I should have ordered the
omelet. When I saw the sliced bread I was grateful for being alone. I
imagined Fernando complaining about it. He doesn't consider sliced
bread to be bread at all, although it's baked right here every morning.

Husbands, in general, tend to complain a lot, much more than
women.

They were kind enough to set up a table, chair, and extension cord
on my terrace so that I could work during the day. This was a proper
hotel, which was strange, those that are luxurious and sophisticated
almost never are.

Work is always my excuse for existing. But I came to the desert to
think, or to remember. I've caught myself correcting my memories.
I have many I don't like, so I correct them. That's what I was doing
until I went to the spa. The previous day I had caught sight of a massage room and, not one to waste time, I booked myself in immediately. It was rather expensive. Once again I told myself, It doesn't
matter, you don't have to explain to anyone. Yu was waiting for me,
a young woman from China with magic hands and a great deal of

strength. An hour of total relaxation with quality lotions, candles, and very subtle music. At some point I realized that only very occasionally do I live in ways that reflect my income. In general, spending makes me feel guilty. But I love money, I find it sexy. Fernando is always attentive to containing my outbursts. But I *can* allow myself this, I *can* stay in one of the most expensive hotels in the country and treat myself to an hour of massage. The only question is why don't I do it more often. What the hell happens to women with money when they've earned it themselves? Why do we feel so guilty?

I wasn't born rich. My father was a reporter on the crime beat and my mother a housewife. During my childhood, we never had enough money to get to the end of the month. My mother sold eggs and cheese from house to house to pay for me to go to college. She always wanted her daughter to "be someone," for me not to follow her example of living in insignificance and obscurity as she and my grandmother did. They say that everything is repeated, that everything happens again generation after generation, grandmothers, mothers, daughters, a never-ending line. Until someone breaks it, gives it that strong blow that stops the repetition.

I had a delicious salmon sandwich and a *pisco sour* next to the fireplace where a couple of guidebooks told me about the wonders of the local landscape. I didn't want to leave the hotel. It was as though I was stuck to the floor, it had bewitched me. Reading on the terrace was so lovely, as was napping. When I went out to walk and saw my silhouette on the sand I felt that mine was an invasive shadow, that it would cause all that was unpolluted to disappear.

As I watched my adobe room and its fascinating dark tobacco color, I thought how I'd like to live in a hotel. I've always thought that. Hotels make me feel free. I've often fantasized about the idea of making them my home, as many people in Europe did between the wars.

I also wondered how many hotels I've slept in during my life. I know that there are women who have never slept in one. I struggle to understand the distribution of wealth. I have stayed in some of the world's most beautiful hotels. I travel with curiosity, in the hope of finding serenity somewhere. Perhaps that's the essence of the matter. If not, why else travel? I'm forty-three and I have very few places left to visit, perhaps the Blue City in Rajasthan, India, the new republic of Montenegro, or Kangaroo Island in Australia. But until recently I didn't know that this place in the Atacama existed, which proves how incomplete my knowledge of the world is. I wouldn't like to have died without seeing it.

In this small notebook, I wrote down the hotel menus every day. An example of dinner: salmon tartare, chili chicken, crème brûlée. Why did I bother? I don't know, I suppose it was to make the experience concrete, so that nothing slipped through my hands, as if what I ingested could keep me forever in the desert. I started toying with the idea that I could abandon my existence, even Fernando. I don't know whether it's exhaustion or just a way of establishing and confirming my independence.

I was the only person who was by herself in the entire hotel. I liked being alone. It's hard to admit it, but I'm kind of fed up with Fernando, I'm kind of fed up with the kids.

There, I've said it.

I couldn't stop looking, the landscape was taking control of me. I thought about Israel, about Jordan. The desert is always biblical. Hours watching, just watching. As hyperactive as I am, I amazed myself with my capacity for contemplation. Even the birds caught my attention. The hills behind the hotel seemed, at a certain time of day, like enormous wounds, living, deep, as if season after season, year after year, someone was picking at the scab.

I observed the other guests too, trying to understand who they were.

Other people's lives make me curious. But the real problem, actually, is the curiosity that I produce in people. How strange it is to be famous. I won't deny that it brings many benefits. You do what you want and others tend to respect that, as if fame gives you permission. All the doors are opened for you. You're paid more than you deserve. You don't need to connect with anyone, you can view everyone else as if through a dark veil, myopically, not bothering about clarity.

I don't have many qualities apart from my on-screen talent, but I do recognize the virtue of not being particularly vain. As much as I value my success, I'm far from dazzled by its results. In India, I bought a wooden chest, quite large, with metal inlays on the outside and the smell of sandalwood inside. It's where all the mementos of my fame will end up, the photos, magazines, videos, DVDs, awards, prizes. They accumulate without me paying the slightest bit of attention. I never intended to become famous, I didn't plan it, I just aspired to do things well. Suddenly it happened. I became a mainstay of Chilean television. I soon realized that what truly interested me was power. That took longer to acquire, that was more difficult. Everything is in that chest, in case my children ever want to see it. But that won't happen. If it doesn't interest me, why would it interest them?

The fact that I never open the chest doesn't mean I'm not thorough in my work—I am, very much so. I remember everything I've had to overcome to reach where I am today, from stage fright in the early days, which, no matter the time of month, made me menstruate every time I had to appear on screen to all-night rehearsals and recordings, terrified of not being good enough. The difference between a fan and a professional is that when things go badly, the first loses calm and the second keeps it. I maintain my precision. As they say, talent is an attribute of responsibility.

It's strange that the word that best defines my life is *success*. Sorrows, pains, uncertainty, everything is covered by the sheen of those seven letters. Chileans hate other people's success and although they admire my face, many of them detest me. As if the Andes were going to crush us. We're such a narrow country, we don't all fit on one same strip of earth. It's the narrowness that makes us mean, always fearful of falling into the water or of being pinned against the mountain if we make room for someone else.

* * *

One day I arrived in the dining room for breakfast and saw that the tables were empty, even the coffee had been removed. The time had changed, so I'd been told, it was already 10:30 a.m. How was I supposed to know? I wouldn't have noticed a coup d'etat. Disconnected, but isolated at the same time, I felt protected.

I wanted to get to work, just to immerse myself in the feeling that nothing else matters, that if work's going well, nothing can touch me. Of course it's a lie, but the truth is I live like that for a few hours and it does me good. As Margaret Atwood says: "When everything's going fine, I feel like a songbird."

The way we defend ourselves with work. Without it, there's such a great fear of being exposed, being laid bare.

Lying in a deck chair next to one of the six elegant swimming pools, I thought about the contradiction I had plunged into. I told myself, I've been overtaken by the life I lead, by the continual demand, by the ratings, by the excellence I have to maintain so as not to be replaced, by the success, by the money, by such a large house. I wanted to have less on my hands. I remembered my son, Sebastián, who, when he heard that same speech one dinnertime, said to me, Mom, what you want is to be a hippie.

Be a hippie? I remembered when Consuelo and I were really young and we wore clothes from India and tied bracelets around our ankles and we didn't have a peso. We were happy. I sent an email to Consuelo telling her about what Sebastián had said. She replied with a quote from James Joyce: "We can't change reality. Let us change the subject." I told her not to get intellectual, but Fernando thought she was spot-on. When I left for the airport on my way to the desert, Sebastián asked me, Mom, are you going to change the subject in a luxury hotel?

Hippie, me? I looked again at the depth of those beautiful pools spreading out among the cacti and the stones and I wondered exactly what I was aspiring to if I ended up lying in *this* deck chair, at *these* swimming pools, in *this* hotel.

There wasn't a soul in sight. It gave the impression that I was the only human being for miles and miles around. The full moon peeked above the hills, and I noticed the existence of two animals, guests like me. I saw the llama and guanaco through a fence, wandering through the open space of their pen. I went to look at them up close. To someone from another country they might appear to be the same species. The llama looked at me with the saddest eyes I've ever seen. The fence between us prevented me from touching it. We looked at each other for a long time. I thought it might start crying. What would a llama be sad about, surrounded by such beauty, cared for, fed? Or is that never enough?

When I left, the guanaco moved its neck with a touch of resentment. What about me? Aren't I alone too?

I went for dinner in the dining room and was approached by three women, they'd been watching me for days, trying to leave me be, although in the end they couldn't contain themselves. You should always be grateful for the existence of fans. But not when you're hidden from the world in the middle of the desert. Fame has turned me into someone vulnerable.

I remembered that movie, *Swimming Pool*, where Charlotte Rampling was a writer and she would get off a train if someone so much as addressed a word to her or recognized her. I should have been born English and dared to be as neurotic and unbearable as Rampling's character.

Had I by any chance forgotten the anger that had led me there?

The desert calls on you to disconnect from society's time. It's a place to unzip, to empty yourself, to lose all references and get nowhere. I would imagine that this *nothing* can give rise to any kind of creation, like art. Don't they say that we rely on art so that the truth doesn't destroy us? The desert is a precise reflection for everyone. For everyone.

I booked a Thai massage. The masseur was a good-looking, affectionate boy. He could be friends with my son, I thought. His massage was sensational and reminded me of my stay in Thailand. Walking alone through the spa between the dry heat, the humidity, and the nice warm water of the hot tub, I said to myself, Hippie, me?

I didn't do any of the touristy things. I was surrounded by stunning sights. It doesn't matter, I told myself, I'll see them one day. I watched the tour groups arrive in the afternoon, exhausted, lugging their rucksacks, water bottles, sun cream, and parkas. Thanks to their excursions, I could enjoy the place as if it were there just for me. I was the only fool not to sign up for the trips.

When I see groups of people, the only thing I wish for is not to have to get to know them. The thing is that my Santiago life is saturated, different people at all times. There's no event I'm not invited to, and although I pick and choose what to accept and what to turn down, it still overwhelms me. What's more, I've never liked crowds, carnivals, festivals, all that supposedly joyful bustle.

The last time I was in Buenos Aires, I bought a newspaper and sat in a café to read it. There was a flyer stuck between the pages, rectangular and on extremely white paper. It announced: PSYCHOLOGISTS— UNIVERSITY OF BUENOS AIRES. The following list appeared beneath the headline:

Phobias
Stress
Depression
Addictions
Personal crises
Panic attacks
Couples therapy
Learning difficulties

I was speechless. Has emotional illness become so commonplace? Are Argentineans even more neurotic than us? No, they recognize neurosis, which is quite different. I skimmed the list again to see which category I fell under and realized, with a shock, that I fitted into at least three.

One day in the desert, I decided to break my habit and go into the village, a couple of miles from the hotel. This was San Pedro de Atacama, which appears so often in tourist guides. I enjoyed talking to the drivers, perhaps the only people who didn't seem to know me. I was surprised to see those high-plains faces here in Chile, speaking our Spanish with an accent. I've only ever seen them in Peru or Bolivia.

In San Pedro everything is brown and the buildings are low. Some old women were dancing to music blaring in the plaza in front of the town hall. They wore that expression of profound indifference or distance that village women adopt when they dance. I went straight to the famous church, which I've seen a thousand times in photos. In 1550-something, the Spanish celebrated their first masses there. In Chile, we aren't accustomed to such old buildings of our own. The roof is made of adobe and in the center of the altar is La Purísima, the Virgin Mary, before the angel visited her.

I headed for an enormous artisan market and then, indecisive, looked for lunch. I landed in a cheap snack bar, where I had vegetable lasagna and where everyone stared at me. Thankfully, no one came up to speak to me.

On the way out of the restaurant, I received a call from Consuelo. It was lucky because there was very little network coverage in the hotel. It had been so many days since I last spoke to her. I sat under one of the large trees in the plaza and we chatted as if we were back in our childhood bedrooms. I told her about the beauty of the place and its surroundings. How lovely, she said. Get wrinkly in style.

The sun was ferocious, burning.

* * *

Back in the hotel room, inspiration struck. San Pedro had revitalized me, and I set to work. I was putting together something interesting, the basic idea of which was pretty original. The words flew, the ideas came together on their own.

I went out for a stroll around the pools. Eventually, another lone woman appeared, I was no longer the only one. She was Chinese. I felt rather sorry for her solitude in a country so far from her own.

The altitude was beginning to bother me. I was always short of breath.

One afternoon I saw animals from my terrace. Lying on the airbed with my eyes closed, I suddenly heard a bleat. Then there were two and then three, in unison. I rose and right in front of me a couple of cows and lots and lots of sheep were walking past with their shepherd. I spent a long time watching them. They all had babies. Apart from the llama and the guanaco, they were the only animals I saw.

I try to imagine myself without Fernando and although independence is tempting, I end up giving priority to my huge desire to be *intimate* with someone, the need to have an accomplice in the midst of hostility. The world of success is the most hostile of all environments. I need the possibility of sharing. You need balls to go without that. A dish of sea urchins eaten alone, is it as pleasurable? Or the color of the stones in Petra. What does it look like? If not to your partner, where do you go when you question yourself, when you feel the world is against you? To whom do you entrust the balance of a bank account or the fact that your own mother and daughter sometimes annoy you? With whom can you listen to a Beethoven concert in silence? I'd never thought of Fernando as my "symbolic object," as Simona put it, but I'll admit how much his image protects me from the world. In my core, if there were no figure of a husband to stand in front of me, I'd feel like I'd been thrown to the lions in the middle of the Colosseum.

A husband is a place.

Perhaps a husband is a prologue, an illustrated annex.

I told Consuelo on the phone that I wrote down the menus every day in my notebook.

I live on a diet. That isn't just a manner of speaking, I'm always on a diet. I've tried them all. The problem is that I love eating. I like sweets the most. Life without a good pastry makes no sense. But extra weight and the screen are incompatible. Public exposure is the number one enemy of pleasures. As the years go by, the pleasures vary. Now, the thing that gives me the greatest pleasure is food. Sex has moved to another plane, which sometimes pains me.

You get the impression that all relationships nowadays are defined in terms of sexuality, apart from mine. I don't even have the time to be unfaithful.

I'm afraid that, with time, you stop loving people. In youth, part of being young is overflowing with affection, playing for it a hundred percent, stretching it to the max. You dish it out left and right, innocently and unselectively. As the years pass, we begin to fine-tune and as a result, to discard. As for me, my gaze has become more suspicious, more judgmental and those same eyes look at others with greater mistrust. People are stupider than they look, more annoying, some more arrogant, others more envious, loyalty is never absolute. Growing older means being more aware of the defects. You begin to get bored. I'm afraid I love less and less. Sometimes I think that's one of the reasons old people are so often alone. You think it's because no one loves them, but perhaps they're alone because they don't love anyone anymore.

I barely hold a conversation if I don't have an objective. I don't have time for idle chitchat.

If I made a list today of all the objects of my affection, I suspect that as the years go by, the list would do nothing but shorten.

The nights in the desert were the most silent of all nights, mute, as if a layer of silence lay above another and another and then another, like a Napoleon cake. I've known silence before, at Consuelo's country house. When the day ended, the noise ended too and the night came, not with noise but with sound. It was a long sound. I spent hours and hours unraveling it, the singing, the howls, the bellows, the sighs, the barks, the wind. It was the sum of enormous yearning. The false silence of the country reminds me of the desert. There are those who truly believe that the night falls silent, never suspecting the chaos that begins with the darkness.

When the passion ends, the attention you pay to what's inside you weakens. Poor Fernando, how tiresome for him, this wife who is always busy. I no longer know what love is. I circle it a thousand times and land in the same place from where I start. In the Atacama, I thought the moment had come to tell myself the truth. At the same time, the altitude was increasingly making itself felt. But it was absurd. The altitude affects you when you arrive, not after so many days. The girl who made up my room brought me tea from some unknown plant. Sometimes we talked. I don't feel Chilean or Argentinean or Bolivian, she told me, I'm Atacaman. She told me her father had seen the records of the church in San Pedro, those the Spaniards collected, and that her family went back to the mid-eighteenth century. The Spanish documented everything, absolutely everything, she said, every baptism, every marriage, every death, every earthquake.

I definitely like the Atacamans. I don't like those who now call themselves winners. People who fail majestically, are they losers? I think about those who were young in the middle of the twentieth century, the reviled century. How they'll miss its epic quality.

My heart began to play tricks on me, the palpitations increased and at times I confused altitude with anguish. I'm not a teenager anymore, I told myself, my body has a right to be exhausted. It's the slippery slope. What doubt can there be? I'm on the verge of growing old. In any case, more than anguish, what I felt was melancholy. That's what the ancients called that sadness. Surely, they were referring to the simple depression of our times, but the name is more evocative. Melancholy. I think Freud linked it to grief directed at oneself instead of the absentee. When it started getting dark, I looked at the hills and a long sadness came over me, like a purple mourning shroud.

Fernando loves me but he no longer wants me.

Couples who argue tend to have good sex. If you think about it, it isn't so strange, both things derive from passion. In my case, only the fights remain. When the passion ends, the allure changes, the attention to what's inside you changes. No more gales to blow it all away. No more sex.

Sex is like the net protecting the tightrope walker. It's there to contain the fall. If the net didn't exist, I don't suppose tightrope walking would either. So, when for some reason the net has been removed, how do you protect yourself? You can do all the acrobatics you want up high, you can risk great big somersaults and fears and disagreements, because you know the net is waiting for you and will catch you. It's part of the game, it's the law of the game. But one day the net isn't there. The tightrope walker, trapped by his own habits, insists on doing acrobatics anyway. He's tempted by the void. He lowers the height of the rope so as to run fewer risks, to allow himself to fall. Of course, he does fall and is injured. Nothing's holding him now.

Like the net, the libido waits, always prepared, expectant, never at peace. It cancels out any past mistreatment, any fear.

Sex stems the flow. The explosion, the fight, the harming gesture, there's room for it all within the relationship because sooner or later the couple will turn to sex, which will heal all wounds, or at the very least will show signs of healing them. When sex disappears, those wounds remain on the surface of the skin. They won't close.

Fernando was sick, a simple flu, and I left him alone in our bedroom and went to sleep in Carola's room for a few days as she was on vacation. Her room leads to a hallway at the end of which is the door to our suite, which in turn has a second hallway that goes into

our bedroom. It was two in the morning and a strange insomnia
had taken hold of me. I tossed and turned in bed without achieving
anything. So I got up thinking that if I clung to Fernando's body sleep
would come. I walked to our bedroom and I heard some strange
noises coming from inside. I paused, listening to the stifled sighs,
moans, small choked cries. Sex. I moved forward. From the end of
the hall I could make out in the darkness the light of the television
screen opposite the bed. A couple was making love the way they only
do in pornography. I stood in the threshold, frozen. I saw Fernando
pleasuring himself. I slowly returned to my daughter's room, my
heart racing. In a few minutes the anguish had turned to iciness,
then into a soft, sticky substance, and my own self looked back at me
numb, disgusted.

I felt like a leper.

I thought for a few days that not mentioning this scene in front of
Fernando meant respecting his intimacy. A lie. The affront, and that
alone, was the reason for my discretion.

In the Atacama, at a certain point in the afternoon, the sand trans-
forms into soft undulations as if the desert were a parted head of
hair. I think about my failure to live through harmonious movement,
like that of the desert.

Or any movement that isn't mine.

I've talked about narcissism with Natasha, I'm not ignoring it.

I've tried to understand which part of me I leave under the spotlights, what price I pay. I live the pain of having loved and no longer
loving. Believe me, I did experience love and it left me. I'm unable to
change that. I'm talented, powerful, but I can't love again. I desired
and now I no longer do.

I've had offers to make my career international. If I accept this
new contract, and I really want to accept it, I'd have to live abroad.
So far, Fernando and the kids haven't been willing to come with me.
Their lives and activities are in Chile and they don't plan to sacrifice

them for me. Worst of all, and I've only said this to Natasha, is that, in my gut, I don't even know if I care.

I've talked about the advantages of fame. But fame is addictive. It's returning to your dressing room to remove your makeup and not recognizing your gaze or the shape of your mouth in the mirror because you only know and like yourself under the spotlights. It's the permanent terror of being overtaken by someone better than you. It's thinking about ratings twenty-four hours a day. It's studying, studying and always being up-to-date, even though the hours of sleep and pleasure lessen until they almost disappear. It's working without rest. It's disconnecting from everything so as not to lose focus for a single second. It's conquering whoever's next to you if they get in your way. It's being capable of selling out your own mother if required.

That's what it is.

What is this exercise we're doing, Natasha? I wonder whether we have it in us to become spectators of ourselves. Perhaps we take advantage of a select audience to invent ourselves to a certain extent, or to silence what we hate most. In real life there are very few conversations that interest me. I leave all that on the set. If I'm with a friend, I ask her what time she has breakfast, or how long it takes her to get to the office every morning. How much she spends in the supermarket. That's why when I was in the desert I told Consuelo what I had eaten that day. That stuff matters, the small actions in daily life.

The desert revealed itself to me like an illusion. You would assume that a saturated mind goes to the desert to empty itself. When I tried to empty mine, I fell into the trap. My palpitations and arrhythmia weren't caused by the altitude.

I can't breathe, I explained to Fernando on the phone. Come back, he replied.

They installed an oxygen cylinder until they saw I was breathing relatively normally. I left at dawn, another escape. Still on the plane, my heart was beating too fast. When I reached Santiago and opened the door to my house, I gripped onto it. Before entering, I cried and cried like a child. There was no force that could separate me from my front door.

For now, I'm still in my crystal tower, with the light and the sun on my face, waiting for life to say what it has to say. The important thing is that, when life comes to look for me, wherever I am, it won't find me beaten.

ANA ROSA

*M*y late mother, may God keep her in his Holy Kingdom, had a favorite phrase, which was that she had an *insubstantial* daughter, quite impressive given her rather limited vocabulary. I've wondered how she came across that word. She loved saying it and looking down on me at the same time. I've always been looked down on by almost everyone, so she didn't exactly have an original point of view, the poor thing. She wasn't original in anything and that's the legacy she left me, along with a couple of other things that I do appreciate, like my excellent diction and good manners. I never curse, I wouldn't know how. She also left to me a love and fear of God and something else I hope to remember.

Honesty is something on which I pride myself and I admire in others. I should tell you that I'm terrified of opening my mouth because I don't think I have much to say and I wonder what would have become of me if I hadn't been born into the bosom of the most religious family in the entire district of La Florida. Everything that happened in that semidetached house could be heard by the neighbors. We believed that praying a rosary a day and respecting your elders would not just bring your own salvation but salvation for the world as well, which means that my mother was right. I'm entirely insubstantial.

I was always taught to respect my neighbors. That was drummed into me to such an extent that I often trust more in the way I was raised than I do in my own reflection. Some people say I live in the last century and I never talk about what has just happened but about what happened before that, which is apparently an unforgivable flaw. As far as I'm concerned, the world is too big for me, which is why in the end I just walk on by. This is no place for the timid. I wonder why Natasha invited me here today. When I came in and looked at all of you I thought, Here are Natasha's favorites, and for a minute I said, Yeah, Ana Rosa, you're one of them.

I'm Ana Rosa.

I'm thirty-one.

I live in the southern part of La Florida, in the same house my parents lived in, which we inherited with the mortgage paid. I live with a younger brother whom I've taken care of since the Lord decided to take my parents. The two of them went together and today they'll be enjoying the divine presence somewhere kinder than this earth, call it heaven or eternal life, whatever you want.

I attended the high school closest to my house and later, because I didn't have the grades to go to college, I enrolled in a professional institute to study advertising, which is the same as not studying anything. My life seems as though it came from a Protestant mold rather than a Catholic one. It's been nothing but work, discipline, aversion to pleasure, waiting for the next life to be happy because happiness doesn't exist among humans but next to the angels and archangels and the privileged souls of the beyond. I never married nor do I think I could because I've never been keen on that kind of love. What's more, you can see that I'm not particularly attractive. There isn't much about me that would catch the eye of the opposite sex. I don't know how to dress, I have no imagination or money. I own four suits, that's all I have, and I wear them in turn every day of the week. One is blue, another dark gray, and the other two are brown and burgundy. I have a blouse in the same shade for each one. That way I don't have to think every morning about what to put on because that would distress me, I know them from memory and so I don't waste time because there are never enough minutes before I fly off to catch the bus and the subway after getting my brother completely ready. I make sure that he's woken up and had breakfast and showered because I'm sure that if I didn't supervise him he'd stay asleep and spend the day playing in front of the screen instead of going to class. I would have given my life to have pretty eyes. Mouse eyes, my grandpa used to say. After all, the eyes are everything, any beauty or unsightliness is born in them and the only thing for which I ever reproach the Lord is having given me these insignificant, dull little eyes surrounded by near-invisible, tiny brown lashes, like all my countrymen. In the street I seek out pretty eyes. The truth is that I don't always find them. I sit for a while on the benches on Paseo Ahumada to look at women's eyes and imagine how they live and what they think and what matters to them and what doesn't. I'm struck by their outfits and the way they always pick a smaller size when they can't get the right one during sales, never bigger. Everything's so tight and you can always see the bulges and when it becomes fashionable to show the hips, there they all go baring their skin, whether it suits them or not. I have to make an effort to be tolerant.

I work as a secretary in a department store in the city center. I'd read in the newspaper that they needed salespeople, but at the interview I told the supervisor about my shyness and my inability to face customers. I described my excellent spelling, a great quality among my generation, which doesn't know how to write or compose, dropping H's and accents, commas and exclamation points, question marks and ellipses, placing articles incorrectly, if they remember them at all. I requested an opportunity to do secretarial work, which surprised the interviewer because no one interviews for a job in order to ask for another one. In the end, that in itself worked in my favor and even though I had the dignity not to explain to him how pressing

it was for me to earn a living and that the education of a future cit-
izen depended entirely on my capabilities, he sensed my urgency
and promised to call me as soon as a situation became vacant for
this type of work. Two months later I settled into the office on the
fourth floor with a computer in front of me. That was five years ago,
when the Transantiago transport system didn't exist and life was
much more comfortable. Now, every morning, I have to take a bus
to the subway station to get onto line four, the blue line, and change
at Vicente Valdés to get to line five as far as Baquedano and from
there a third transfer to line one to get to the University of Chile
station. I don't want to complain, especially given the unemployment
during these times of crisis. I feel privileged to have a job and when
it's a tight squeeze on the subway I offer that suffering to God every
morning and arrive with minimal delays and erase from my mind
the woes of the city's public transport. Until the afternoon, when I
do it all again at rush hour and the only thing that can distract me is
thinking about which sins, whose sins, I mean, I'll devote this journey to. I alternate depending on what I've seen on TV. It could be
the sins of the Chechens or the Iranians or the North Americans for
going to war with Iraq. On more than a few occasions, I've done it
for different Chileans whose divine grace has been snatched away
from them, which I think it imperative to restore. Natasha finds this
entertaining and sometimes when I arrive for my appointment she
asks to whom I have dedicated the troubles of the day or week and I
tell her in full detail.

Returning to my job, the people around me are quite friendly. The
supervisor is a bossy man who goes around uttering odd phrases as
he walks between our desks: "Too much money, not enough life";
"Don't worry, be busy." He never gives orders but *suggestions*, never
an instruction but a *recommendation*, and in the end he bosses like
crazy. If he catches you wasting time he gives you one of those looks
that makes you forget everything you know. But all in all he's a good
guy and I, without being obsequious, pay attention to everything he

says. So I keep my job and I'm making a living and I feel like a winner at the end of the month when I get my paycheck.

It was my father who taught me to read and write properly because he was an elementary school teacher with great educational skills. Although we always lived modestly, he left us an inheritance of spelling, grammar, and reading knowledge, not to mention the house. My sister and I had a lack of interest to begin with, but later learned to appreciate these skills. When we both turned twelve he gave us the Spanish Royal Academy dictionary in two hardcover volumes. I keep them like a sacred object next to the Bible. To this day, I still devote fifteen minutes a day to studying that dictionary. That way I can make sure that the main word in my vocabulary isn't something coarse like *huevón*, as it is for three-quarters of the population. It also helps me not to feel dumb for watching so much TV. When I've made dinner and my brother has gone to bed, I love tuning in to the national programs. I don't have cable and the thought doesn't excite me because I find a Chilean reality show more entertaining than a movie. I've become a showbiz expert. I know everything about who's dating whom, the fights between some, the names of the models, everything, basically. That's how I relax, but always *after* my fifteen minutes with the dictionary. Yesterday, for example, I studied the key word of my life. "*Insubstantial*: adjective. Of little or no substance." Since I was on the subject, I had to turn to the word *substance* and the definition was so long, I was forced to extend the fifteen minutes and I thought it was worth memorizing: "*Substance*: noun. Physical material from which something is made or which has discrete existence." These seemed like rather loose words to me and I didn't know how to interpret them in a way that my dead mother, poor thing, would have approved of.

Once I heard a story I liked and I retained it, thinking that stories in books can suddenly leap off the page and become true. This one takes place in the past, it could have been in India or somewhere like that. There was a village custom that when a couple got married, the groom had to show everyone the bloodied sheet after the wedding night to confirm his new wife's virginity. I know that's nothing new and we've all heard it many times before but in this story she wasn't a virgin. When he finds out that same night, seeing that she doesn't bleed, not only does he *not* reject her or expose her but he asks no questions. He takes a knife that's in the fruit bowl next to the bed and cuts his hand and spills his blood on the sheet. I really liked this story and I wonder whether, among all the men I work with or those who stand on the corner of the plaza near my house listening to music at full blast and smoking marijuana, whether there's one— just one—with that kind of nobility, even though nowadays no one cares a dime about virginity.

I was very happy until the age of eight. The figure who contributed most to that happiness of mine was my maternal grandfather, who had always lived with us. He had been widowed rather young so I never knew my grandmother, who they say was a great woman and whose heart stopped beating without warning as she was baking a cake for my mom's birthday. After that my mom became rather bitter, at least that's what my dad believed. Returning to my grand- mother, she wasn't a Russian gambler with organdy dresses and she didn't sleep on the floor next to the bed of a Palestinian war hero, she was simply mortal, without an entertaining life to relate. She devoted herself to caring for her children and her husband. She never worked outside the home and I've heard that she was a "prude," that's what my grandpa called her. He said it one day when his tongue got a bit loose and then I understood why my mom had memories of my grandfather going out alone at night with his friends, before he was even widowed. Back then, living it up was part of life and men were unfaithful on principle and deep, deep down women acted as accom- plices. I find it very inappropriate to imagine my grandparents' sex life but forced to do it I think that she, like me—and that's why I'm bringing her into the equation—disliked sex. That's why my grandpa looked for it elsewhere, like any proud man would. Apparently this wasn't particularly unusual. I mean, women hating sex, back then there were no magazines that dealt with the subject or psychologists who considered it a kind of illness. No one got involved and if sex was a duty, you fulfilled it and that was it, but with any luck as infrequently as possible. Returning to my grandpa, he was the light of my childhood. My parents worked hard, as I've already told you, my dad at the school and my mom for city hall. She was a government employee all her life and she never missed work. City hall was her life and she always did what she had to, first with the military and later with the elected mayors. If God hadn't taken her to his Holy Kingdom she would have spent her retirement there. She left early in the morning and arrived home after six and her daughters—me, the eldest, and my sister who came after me, who is now married—we had to take care of ourselves and our grandpa. He was already retired from the national railroads and was the only person who was always at home. That's why I say that he was the light of my childhood. When I arrived home from school he helped me with my homework and then took me out for a stroll and bought me ice cream and introduced me to his neighborhood friends. He prayed with me at night because I was his favorite and he saw a bit of himself in me. He taught me to fly kites and make paper boats and paint with brushes when my siblings only used colored pencils. He knew how to tell really long, fun stories and at night it was him who got me to sleep, not my mom. I preferred him because his stories were better and he had more patience. My dad never minded living with his father-in-law—on the contrary, I think he liked it because they got on well and loved playing cards and talking about soccer and drinking beer and they had the same taste in food. Every time my mom cooked blood sausage or stewed pig trotters, they were so grateful.

Although he no longer worked, my grandpa got up early every morning and waited for the bathroom because he was the only one who wasn't in a hurry. He put on talc like a baby and dressed in a tie and an old gray suit from his time as a railroad employee, with a white shirt he changed every three days. On Sundays he wore his blue suit for mass. He only used that suit for mass and for weddings, funerals, and baptisms. At what point did Sunday suits disappear? They've been replaced by tracksuits, jeans, and shorts, which look bad on anyone with short legs and rounded calves. Nowadays you don't see anyone wearing a suit to mass and tracksuits are horrible. No man looks good in a tracksuit apart from a soccer coach like Pellegrini. Returning to my childhood, I don't know why my grandpa wore a tie or what he did in the mornings because I was at school and didn't see him. But he had lunch with us every day, he heated up the food that my mom prepared the night before and then he would take a nap. He never skipped his nap. I clung to him to feel warm and loved.

Although our house was very small, it was my parents' pride and joy because they owned it, a feat they managed to achieve with a teachers' subsidy. The mortgage was the most sacred of all the bills they paid each month. Anything could be overdue, electricity, gas, water, the grocer's bill, but never the mortgage. I learned from a very young age to value the effort involved in owning your own house, especially if it had two bedrooms. This was perfect until my brother was born, a kind of mistake by my parents. I have a hunch that he wasn't planned because he came twelve years after me and eleven years after my sister. Life was already organized and suddenly, boom, another member of the family arrived and there was no room for him so he slept for a long time in the same bed as my grandpa because there was nowhere to put another bed and the living room was too small for a sofa bed. My mom, in her words, would have died before committing the disrespect of leaving her father without a bedroom. The second bedroom was the master, until my parents got tired of sleeping with my sister and me and moved us to sleep with our grandpa. Him in one bed and my sister and me in another, but I think now, looking back, that it made no difference where we slept because the walls were like paper and you could hear everything. Every single one of my dad's snores was audible from my bed and I suppose that the marriage worked because my sister and I slept heavily like the two healthy girls we were. We slept like logs or to use my mom's expression, We slept the sleep of the righteous.

The most important thing in the house was the curio cabinet in the living room. My mom used to look at her reflection in its glass. Natasha laughs every time I describe it and tell her in detail about that cabinet full of tiny painted plaster and ceramic figurines of angels, cats, shepherdesses, and clowns. Today, every time I clean them, I think about what that proliferation of unnecessary objects must mean and what function they fulfill. I suspect they serve to hide our own insignificance and I think that one day I'm going to throw them on the floor and break them one by one because whenever I feel dumb those figurines come to my mind. I don't know why. Of course, in such a pious family, there was also a lot of religious imagery. We had crucifixes, prints of the Holy Virgin, pictures of various saints, some made of embossed brass. You were welcomed at the front door by the Sacred Heart, Jesus with his bloody crown, cut to shreds. I never entirely understood that image. I usually remind myself several times a day how much he suffered for us. There were two small tables, one on either side of the only couch in the living room, and they were covered with statuettes, or "sculptures" as my mom preferred to call them, like the cross at the moment of his death or a blessing at the Mount of Olives. The Mount was a small plaster hill that started to crack one day and my mom got upset. I used some tempera like the kind we had at school and painted the parts that were flaking in green and brown, so that it couldn't be noticed. Every time I hear someone talking about Israel, I think about the brown and green of the Mount of Olives. I preferred the Virgins because they were so different from each other, when, after all, you would have thought that she was the same person. How could there be so many different ones, the Virgin of Carmen, of Lourdes, of Fátima, of Luján? All the Virgins watched us going about our daily business and I thought we lived under their protection and that nothing bad could happen to us. The only thing I didn't like about that abundance of sacred figures was cleaning them. Do it lovingly, honey, *lovingly*, understand, my mom would say. When it was my turn I did make an effort, using a damp cloth to get into every fold of the Virgin's tunics and Jesus's fingers, so that the grime wouldn't get stuck there. This was difficult because Santiago is a dusty city. Everything gets covered in dust, who knows why, and I wonder what other cities must be like.

Until the age of eight, my sister, Alicia, and I had the same class schedule. We went to and from school together and since it was only at the corner we were accustomed to walking from a young age. Something happened that year and my sister had an extra class and she began coming home after me. So I returned before Alicia and my grandpa waited for me and told me I was all his and that we had plenty of time to do things before Alicia arrived.

I turned eight. That day sticks in my poor mind as one of the last bright memories, very bright, because as a child you can't see or sense the clouds. What is there is there and everything was clear that first of March, centuries and centuries ago. I returned from school and saw the cake on the table and the little oranges and colored gumdrops and the wafer biscuits and the small egg sandwiches and my aunts and my cousins. I don't know why they made such a fuss, but even though it was during the week the celebration was tremendous. Even now I can remember all the presents I received. The best and most important was from my grandpa. I don't know where he found the money, but he bought me a Barbie house. What more could I dream of at that time? A pink plastic house with rooms and beds, all for Barbie, who was, I don't have to tell you, my favorite toy. I still have them and now that I have a bed that's too wide for me, I sit them at the headboard even though I have to take them off every night and put them back in the morning. My mom asked me to thank God for such kindness and to say an Ave Maria before opening it. The grown-ups started drinking beer and punch, because there was always red wine with peaches for birthdays and also hot wine with orange peel and cinnamon. As the children played with the Barbie house, my dad and grandpa got a bit tipsy and when everyone had left they were still in the party mood, drinking and having fun and my mom wore that disapproving face we all knew so well. They both went to bed and Alicia and I were asleep when my grandpa entered the room and woke me, just me. Come on, birthday girl, he said and took me out of bed to sleep with him, as we did every day at nap time. But this time it was at night. He wanted to keep celebrating me.

God decreed so many things that are incomprehensible to me. I'm not complaining, but sometimes I wonder why he loaded his dice over this trivial and modest poor soul. I've gone in circles so many times, like a word that's lost its letters. I know why he didn't load the dice for Alicia. How could I not know, when it was me who protected her? She was only a year younger, but in some part of my tiny head I decided that I was the only one who could look out for her. God didn't punish me for my arrogance because today Alicia is happy and married, like everyone else, and she has two kids. When my parents died she got over that old-fashioned attitude we all had and started to be herself. She is still a Catholic and she loves God and fulfills each of his commandments, which makes me think that there's no need to be as fussy as my mom for God to love you. I always felt that God wasn't close to me like he was to other people, or at least to the other members of my family. This made me wonder about the reason why and the reason brought me back to myself. There was something dirty in me that scared God and even though he was used to all the frightening things here on earth, he still kept a certain distance from me. Sometimes I thought that whoever was assigned my case in heaven had gone on strike and chucked the casebook.

During high school, they laughed at me sometimes. It wasn't offensive mockery but my classmates didn't understand why I didn't go with guys like they did. Some of them were really, really forward and there were even teenage pregnancies in my grade and they spoke about kissing with tongues when we were still really young. I used to say, God will punish you, and they'd kill themselves laughing, as if the fear of God was something very, very old-fashioned that had nothing whatsoever to do with them. I never had close friends, because until today I've never seen the sense. I firmly believe in shame and modesty and I wonder why there are people who feel the need to parade naked in front of others when the only truth is that every human being is a small island. You can build bridges, but you'll always be an island and everything else is a lie.

After I turned eight, during the nights I started to curl up into a little ball and overnight my hands became two living beings, independent of me, which squeezed each other constantly and rubbed each other and never rested and covered me with red marks, rough, ugly, and painful. Life began to change and I told myself that it was what God required of me and that my main duty was to make my grandfather happy. I owed him so much that I would do anything he asked. One day, however, it occurred to me to complain to my mom. She looked at me with a sour face and her only comment was to say "How illuminating," with an expression in her eyes which I remember today as stern and mean. They were half closed as if she had dirt in them, as if she were avoiding the dust or the light. It was a sign of anger, so much accumulated anger. But what can we do? Family is sacred because it's our identity. Even if it's a prison, it's still our identity. When I walk to the bus stop every morning, I see slabs and slabs of cracked, monotonous concrete, always the same as I move my feet along the sidewalk and that look on my mom's face comes to mind. The cracked cement is just like her eyes and I think that if I'd had other eyes, perhaps my footsteps toward the bus every morning could be different. As well as that look, she had a tiny body like mine. She was skinny, as if she had never flowered, dry and skinny, her limbs always slightly squeezed and turned inward. Grandpa used to call her a mouse, all mice in this family. Very illuminating. Very illuminating, my mom would say to me, pecking around me like a hen. For a whole week, every time I passed by her she said that and nothing else. Why utter a word, then?

I felt as if my voice had been forgotten in some dark hole. Anytime my mother didn't like something, she got sick, sick for real with visible symptoms. Her illnesses could be seen and she got flu or acute diarrhea or a high fever. If we made her angry and the fever came, it was our fault and our aunts told us so. Alicia and I would be terrified. Alicia dared to start dating when she was about twelve and my mom almost died, as if she had been committing the sin herself instead of her daughter. She developed a nasty allergy, which meant she had to miss a morning of work to go to the hospital. She never missed work. Alicia could do nothing but get rid of the boyfriend so that the allergy cleared up and peace returned and then everyone felt sanctified because the girl had seen sense and my grandpa made me pray double every night or at nap time.

In my memory, there is a long, long period of life during which I can only remember bodies, my body, my mom's, Alicia's, my grandpa's. Just bodies, because the mind refuses to involve itself in memories of the soul, flighty like a cat. The mind is, it does its own thing and plays with me and blocks my memory as it pleases. Aggressors are placed on the same level as victims. Everything becomes complicated and hard to remember, just short, fleeting images. I fix on those I have, even though they aren't many. I have so few because it's hard to clearly make out the everyday, normal world, while it's easy to remember the strange. I'm sure that the thing that blinds the eyes most is what's familiar and that's why I wandered without seeing through the days and the months and the years. You can get stuck in blindness for a long time because you end up not seeing what's familiar.

Natasha and I have worked a lot on memories from that time and what I can remember is thanks to her. When I began therapy I had a black hole in my head. As time passed, at the age of nine, ten, every time I washed my hair I came away with clumps in my hand. Until I was eight I had worn it short and in very cute curls, and suddenly it began to lie straight, increasingly straight. It became so fine that it was almost sparse. Every time I looked at the sideboard in the living room, opposite the display cabinet I mentioned, heavy and static, I thought how resigned that piece of furniture looked. It felt like the sideboard and I were the same thing, even though it weighed more than me.

One day, I decided to attend a free seminar being held two minutes from my workplace. I wanted to cultivate my mind and take advantage of working in the center of the city. I learned that in ancient China the popular understanding of the human body was that it is made of two different elements. *Po* was thick and material and *hun* was vaporous and ethereal. It was believed that the confluence of the two produced life and that death came when both elements, or souls, dispersed. Apparently *hun*, being lighter, I suppose, liked to separate from the body and generally did so when people were asleep and that was how dreams were produced. When the final moment came, this element was the first thing to leave and for that reason, when someone began to die, his children had to go up to the attic or rooftop to call the *hun* souls and ask them to return and only if this failed would real death come. When I learned of this, I thought a lot about that poor son or daughter calling out to ethereal souls. I imagined how it would feel not to succeed and whether you would be blamed for the death, for not having brought back the *hun*, and if you blamed yourself and whether you would believe that the punishment for your inability to save your father would strike you suddenly and whether you would have to live with it forever. I thought about all that when I imagined that son or daughter chasing souls.

It was July, a Friday in the middle of the month, during a particularly cold winter when I was fifteen. Ever since then I've been a fan of winters because I feel that they're real, not like summer, which flies by and seems fun and flirtatious, but isn't, because the sun is always in a hurry and leaves everyone wanting more. Winter doesn't aim to console but, nevertheless, I feel some consolation because you curl up and protect yourself and observe and reflect and I think it's only during that season that you can truly think. During that winter when I was fifteen so many things finished for me.

My parents didn't like moving around a lot and no one in the house even went beyond the corner. We weren't travelers in my family, so much so that I've never crossed the border and I barely know the cities of our own country. Any given point on a map is amazing to me. After a lot of commotion and preparation, my folks decided to travel to Linares to visit my dad's godmother, whom he hadn't seen for years. They would stay there for the weekend and had arranged it all with my grandpa. They allowed me to go out on the Friday so that on the Saturday and Sunday I would take care of my younger brother who was only a baby and that was why I was at a friend's house on Friday afternoon watching TV. Right before the news I said to my friend, It's going to rain, and suddenly there was a news bulletin. The screen showed an accident on the highway and a bus that had rolled over because the driver had fallen asleep. I carried on playing with my friend because nothing terrible that happened on the TV bore any relation to me. But when I heard that the bus had been heading for Linares, a kind of tickling sensation entered my stomach and then turned into something frozen as if I'd been injected. Without saying a word, I left my friend's house and I ran home in the cold. I remember the overcast sky, as if it were announcing a storm, and I could barely breathe, still frozen and defeated, with a fear the size of a house hovering above my head. My parents managed to stay alive for a few hours, but they died at the hospital in Linares. Today I imagine the *po* of ancient China, happy with its viscous, material elements among the blood and chaos, and I wasn't there to shout for the *hun* to come back. I couldn't climb up to a rooftop to call on those evil, abandoning souls. I couldn't chase them or force them to return. I couldn't help my parents and I felt that it wasn't God who was defeating me but something I couldn't stop in time. As if that wasn't bad enough, I found out about my parents from the TV news. No one should find out about a personal tragedy that way, and even less so when they're fifteen and dependent and a girl and unprepared.

I'm thirty-one now. I've lived more than half my life as an orphan, but that moment when I ran home from my friend's house, the overcast sky and the toys we were playing with and the sound of the television pursue me as if they were scared I might forget. As if the glutinous substance of rotten flesh could be forgotten, because that's the image that came out the following day in the press. A photograph of trapped bodies with their blood and guts all mixed up. People in this country like accidents, it's incredible the minutes devoted to them on the news. The driver appears, again and again, accident after accident, hopefully with a lot of gory details and weeping family members. But this time it was *my* people and so they died and God took them together. I've wondered a thousand times how they would have been able to bear life without one another.

I felt guilty for their deaths.

When night fell, the day of the funeral, I forgot my whole vocabulary and became stuck on one word: *die*.

Die, die, die.

Until, disturbed as I was, I got the fear that my poor mother, may she rest in peace, was turning in her grave because of this eldest daughter who would prefer to disappear and avoid the responsibilities that were awaiting her. To tell the truth, there weren't many while my grandpa was alive. He took charge of everything, and the house was paid for, and between his pension, some meager savings my parents had, the money given to us by the bus company responsible for the accident, and the odd jobs Alicia and I did, we got by. For a long time I endured a state of permanent bewilderment. In front of me and behind me this bewilderment floated and I don't know how else to describe it. I thought it was right to live like this because pains have the right to prevent you from forgetting them.

After my parents passed, everything was tinged by death, absolutely everything. I was very young to embark on that journey and I used to avoid the big questions and I also avoided facing my awareness of the end. I think that death decided to install itself by my side as a threat, without touching me, but invading me all the same. I would rush to my younger brother's bed during the night to check that he was still breathing, or if Alicia was late coming home, I sat by the phone waiting for the fatal call, or if a friend said she'd arrive at six and she wasn't on time, I decided she must have been run over on the street. Even the poor stray dog we'd adopted suffered my obsessions. I locked him in the patio so he couldn't get out and have something happen to him.

That's what I did instead of crying over the accident.

After my parents' death, I stopped being my grandpa's favorite. He devoted himself to raising my younger brother, feeling that the Lord had commissioned him with the task of making him a man, which made life easier for us. We had enough problems. The naps ended and the bedrooms were redistributed. Alicia and I moved into my parents' big bed, and Grandpa remained in his room with my brother. So the years passed and in spite of the fact that we all tried to live normal lives, I was broken. I spent many years on the wrong side of silence because I couldn't do anything else.

My grandpa died after Alicia and I had finished high school and I was in my third year at the institute. He got stomach cancer and it was a fairly short illness because it was detected too late for treatment. I devoted myself to caring for him. He was old, worn down, and defeated. That was my impression, and I made every effort to make his final days pleasant. I didn't leave his side until the end.

On his deathbed, I asked him something, the only thing I dared ask.

What didn't my mother protect me?

Because I did the same to her.

When I finished high school and was studying at the institute, I decided to ask myself the questions that I'm sure all women ask. What about marriage? What about kids? What about the future? Although I didn't tell anyone I didn't like children. When I was around them something happened to me, which I was able to detect with my sister's kids the countless times I'd taken care of them. I was gripped by a strange, hidden temptation to treat them badly, to take advantage of their physical inferiority and leverage my authority over them. I liked their defenselessness and I wanted to take revenge. As they grew up, I was sure I would never be a good mother and that it was better not to have children. But since there needs to be a father for that anyway, and in that area I was a perfect nonentity, it didn't seem to be a particularly pressing problem. While I was studying advertising I made friends with Toño, who was as timid as me and no great shakes. He still had zits on his face, his black hair was rather wiry, and he had slightly small brown eyes. He couldn't have weighed more than a hundred and thirty pounds and looked like a rat. A mouse and a rat, made for each other. The poor thing was no threat to anyone and acted as if he knew it. Poor Toño, he was such a good person, so polite and kind to me. I got over the fantasy that we could make a good couple because he didn't scare me, or I him, and it was obvious that he was terrified by women. Perhaps it was whatever experience he'd had with his mother or his family, he never told me. But the thing is that we worked well together and studied at my house or at his and we talked about nothing but nonsense and we had fun. One time, after seeing a movie, we were walking along a dark street and I think Toño suddenly felt obliged to play the macho, never mind any desire to. He threw me against a wall and put his hand under my blouse, all this without us ever having kissed. I was frightened. I was frightened and asked him to move more slowly. The poor guy sweated and felt stupid and from then on we took things nice and slow, testing the waters. I won't say it was a successful experience, just satisfactory. We made an effort and I was left with my conscience clear that I had tried, at the very least, and that I wasn't making decisions without entering the battlefield. From then on I could say, I'm not interested in sex, I don't like men. Even though I only said it to my pillow, I still said it, and that made me feel better.

Now, if I had decided that I did like men and my intention had been to couple up, my situation would be just the same. If having a man means prestige, an addition that hangs off you, an overcoat of fine cloth that drapes elegantly over your shoulders, not mattering whether it keeps you warm, then I'm left cold. People look down on you if you're alone. But where are the men? I can't see them. Women like me form a real army. Women in their thirties who are alone, who get out of bed of their own accord and sleep in that bed without a wrinkle on the sheet. Women who, despite working and going out into the world every morning, have nowhere to meet men. Where do all those potential men no one knows about hide? All my coworkers are married or live with someone and if you get involved with one, I'm speaking on behalf of my female colleagues, it's just in terms of a one-night stand or at most, a couple of nights. Then everyone feels guilty and angry for drinking too much and for having gotten involved in a fleeting affair with someone they're forced to see every day. No one has anywhere to meet anyone and time passes and you start acquiring an edge of desperation or confirmed spinsterhood, which scares off any potential candidates. Those candidates, by the way, are extremely scarce and aren't exactly a paragon of imagination or originality. Those who are don't get involved with department store employees or modest office workers. Women of my type don't get very far because nothing is free. To get anywhere you have to pay for the ticket and the ticket can be your name or your appearance or your bank account or your occupation, but you have to have some kind of ticket in your hand and I have none. On the weekends this army of women to which I belong is almost always bored and in the end they like working because at least at work they are surrounded by people and hustle and bustle and they forget the depth of their solitude. They say that in this country more people are depressed than anywhere else. Statistics don't lie and women my age in this situation bloat those figures, which is sad because they are right at that intermediate phase during which they're supposed to be forging their future and starting families. It turns out that the future slips through their hands. That's why, despite everything, I thank the Lord that I'm not another one of them and I have chosen spinsterhood. This way I get less hurt.

* * *

I was rather struck by a story I read in the newspaper about a woman who killed her husband in defense of her daughter. No one killed for me, not even close. It hurts so much that no one protected me. I would have liked to have met that woman from the news and rested my head on her shoulder and let her embrace me.

I think it's healthier not to marry or have children. That's preferable to embarking down that path only to mess them up irrevocably and damage everyone. I've made a huge effort to draw closer to the good side of life and imagine myself as a small sunny place where no one has anything to fear, and I expend a lot of energy on a daily basis defeating the dark parts of my soul, which God knows I have. I fear them and hate them because I try to be that ray of light but at times underground forces come up and drag me into the darkness. Perhaps my deep-seated inclination is that of a snake, who doesn't know it but who one day will shed its skin. I feel that I'm lying in wait, as if I'm not the owner of who I am and that one day I'll wake up having turned into that snake and I'll go out into the world to spread my venom like a heartless, destructive reptile. All the composure of my thirty-one years will go down the drain, confirming that prayers aren't enough and the abuse to which I was victim twisted me forever.

I only know one thing. Everything that has happened to me and everything that will happen is my fault.

NATASHA

*I*t gave me great pleasure to see you all chatting so animatedly in the garden, as if you'd known each other your whole lives. I thought of Anna Karenina, and that happy women are all alike, and every unhappy woman is unhappy in her own way.

Natasha is resting. She'll be around later to say goodbye to you.

I'm not sure of her intentions in bringing you all here today. She never notifies me of what she's going to do, so I can't offer you any insight. Did she want to get you all together to say goodbye? Perhaps. To introduce you all, so you can rely on one another in case she isn't there? It's likely. Or perhaps she was just eager for you to put your problems into words and, in so doing, understand how much you have advanced, how much you've healed. This is all speculation on my part. I'm only her assistant, and what I have learned about human nature I have learned by talking to her, watching her. I've spent so, so many years by her side that I know each of her gestures by heart, the undulations of her voice. But I don't have her wisdom, or her training. I never studied. I only spent a couple of years in the Faculty of Arts and the only thing that has ever motivated me is reading literature. As you know, there are people who aren't born to be protagonists but rather to coexist with those who were. That turned out to be the case for me. As a reader, you're never the protagonist of anything, just a qualified witness, and that's what my work with Natasha involves.

A few days ago I found among the papers on her desk the speech that architect Renzo Piano gave when he was awarded the Pritzker. Natasha had underlined the following phrase, which begins with the famous ending from *The Great Gatsby*: "*So we beat on, boats against the current, borne back ceaselessly into the past.* I find this a splendid image, an emblem of the human condition. The past is a safe refuge. The past is a constant temptation. And yet the future is the only place we have to go."

It was then that I began to understand the invitation she extended to you today.

All these years by her side in Chile have been a gift. In Buenos Aires, when she suggested I join her, I didn't hesitate. I had nothing. No one was keeping me there, and little by little she became my family. The various wars had been leaving our people without a country, with no anchor, no sense of belonging. Errant Jews. True to that pattern, we crossed the border.

I think you'd all like to hear Natasha's story. As a therapist, she is too modest to tell it herself, but she has authorized me to do so.

She was born in 1940, in Minsk, Belarus, which at that time was Russian territory after having been Polish, Lithuanian, French, German, occupied countless times. It must be difficult for Chileans to understand the hazardous life of those countries. You have gotten used to a history of rootedness, we, of uprootedness. For five hundred years your country has had the same name. First you were a dependency of Spain, then you became a republic. Yours is a territorially neat history. We in Central Europe have gone from pillar to post, the borders constantly shifting, and life changing after each war and each treaty. The man who was my husband, for example, was born in Galitzia, the land of Joseph Roth. That was his origin, although he didn't know whether to call himself Polish, Austrian, Ukrainian, or something else altogether.

But let's return to Minsk.

It was a terrible time to be born, that's what Natasha always says. She had just turned one when Nazi Germany invaded. The city was brutally bombed, nothing was left standing. It's hard to know how any of the inhabitants survived. Some say it was at that precise time and place that the extermination of the Jews began. Rudy, Natasha's father, liked to tell us how they saw those special bodies of civilians, lawyers, government employees, and priests arriving in Minsk, marching next to the German army. Their only duty was to kill Jews. The first massacres date from then. They went from house to house during the night, taking Jews out of their beds. Men, women, children, old folks, they brought them all together at a certain place in the city and transported them into the woods where they were executed. Later they came back to bury them, trying to erase all traces.

Within a few days of the invasion, the Nazis fenced off a specific part of the city, thirty-four streets. Rudy used to emphasize, only thirty-four, they removed all the residents and replaced them with all the Jews. They had no more than a square meter and a half per person. The children had no space at all. In the ghetto, a hundred thousand human beings coexisted, brought from different locations in the Reich. But Rudy and his family, like cats, had nine lives. My bones weren't ready to become ashes, he used to tell us. He owes his survival to a love story. Yes, sometimes love saves lives.

Rudy came from a fairly modest family, the son of a carpenter from whom he inherited his skills as a craftsman and his workshop. Not all Jews were rich, he liked to remind us. Although he received a religious education from his family and studied the Talmud and the sacred texts as a teenager, by the time he reached adulthood he was, deep down, an unbeliever. This meant that Natasha's view of life was like Rudy's, broader and more secular than that of their family and neighbors. It wasn't religion that tied him to his people. That's why it isn't at all strange that his great love turned out to be a goy.

Marlene, daughter of a local aristocrat who had fallen on hard times because Belarus was now part of the Soviet Union, commissioned him to make furniture for her future house. It was only a few months before she became engaged to a local gentleman, a textile entrepreneur who was also part of that depressed but nonetheless aristocratic class. All this happened before Natasha's mother appeared on the scene, but I'll tell you the details because of their importance later on. Rudy and this woman fell madly in love. It was intense and, of course, prohibited. The girl's father, loyal to his oligarch spirit, roundly opposed the relationship. In his eyes Rudy had no redeeming features. He was poor, uncultured, and above all, a Jew. Marlene intended to free herself of her engagement to run away with Rudy, but when she realized she was pregnant, by Rudy, of course, and that her romance had no future, she married the aristocrat and passed off her baby as his daughter. This doesn't mean that she gave up Rudy. He supported his lover every step of the way and invented increasingly unlikely ways of seeing his daughter, albeit from afar. He even became a door-to-door salesman of small items of furniture so that he could walk along the street where she lived.

Later, he met a humble woman, Natasha's mother, and decided to marry her. It was more of a rational than a passionate decision. When Natasha was born, her sister was already five.

Two days after the Nazi invasion, a horse and cart pulled up in front of Natasha's parents' house and Marlene got out. This woman was a stranger to Natasha's mom, but there was no time for explanations. With the shrewdness of someone who isn't being persecuted, Marlene understood that Rudy's destiny was seriously under threat and she decided to save him, which meant saving his family too. She took them to the country, to an estate her father owned, which the Soviets hadn't yet snatched. In so doing, she fired the caretaker and installed Rudy in his place. The surprising thing is the speed with which she acted. Five days after the invasion, Jews no longer had any possibility of movement.

As the war progressed and the Germans remained in the USSR, Marlene's stays at the estate lengthened, and she always brought her young daughter, Hanna, with her. We don't quite know what happened between Rudy and Marlene during those encounters, or how humiliated Natasha's mother must have felt.

Although they lived in great isolation, the echo of horror still reached them, sometimes in the form of rumors, sometimes as information. Jews were murdered by the hundreds each day. They arrived at the ghetto from all over and if they didn't die at the hands of the Nazis, they died from hunger and sickness. Epidemics were the order of the day in those subhuman conditions. Rudy found it despicable to pretend that he was aligned with the White Russians under the orders of an old oligarchy, erasing everything from his accent to his customs, changing his appearance, inventing another personality in order to deceive the Nazis, but he had to do it. Deceive them he did. Amid such uncertainty, the only thing that was stable for little Natasha was her relationship with Hanna. In the solitude of the estate, marked by the cold, fear, and lack of food, the bond between the two girls was the only light. Even though the adults took great pains to hide what was happening from them, a body frozen through lack of coal or an empty stomach couldn't be kept secret. Huddled together in the same bed, Hanna and little Natasha embraced and turned their backs on the horror.

Natasha was only five when the war ended, yet she claims to have clear memories of that time. When they showed the movie *Doctor Zhivago*, she spent days and days evoking her childhood. That house in the middle of the snow, where Zhivago and Lara hide, do you remember? That house reminded her of the estate, and the cold. It's just as well there was no snow in Buenos Aires.

The day the war ended, when Rudy understood that he wouldn't see Marlene and Hanna for a long time, he took the two girls by the hand, led them to the kitchen table, and sat them next to the stove. He gave each of them a gold chain with a precious stone hanging from it. Under the midday sun, the alexandrite shone with a bluish-green light. Then he held them against the fire and, to the girls' surprise, the color changed to a deep red. He fastened them around their necks, first Hanna, then Natasha. Alexandrite has healing properties, he told them, and will help you develop intelligence. Wear it always, in remembrance of this war. As you know, Natasha has never taken off hers.

Marlene returned to Minsk, taking Hanna with her. Natasha never saw her again. Later on Rudy managed to cross borders and, through West Germany, arrive in Argentina, as many of his compatriots did. That's when the second incarnation, as Natasha calls it, began.

On the other side of the world, Rudy continued to work as a carpenter. The first years were hard. Money was scarce, but given that they had always been relatively poor, that didn't lessen his energy. At least we're not scared anymore, he would say calmly. Because he was a true artist, things went well for him in the long run and he had a proper shop, with carpenters at his command and important commissions. Argentina was a very wealthy country at that time, full of promise and wonderful opportunities. Natasha started attending a public school, as all immigrants did then. Public education was good, not to mention the fact that there were very few private schools and those that did exist were very elitist. Her school was girls-only. At first, she struggled to understand what her classmates were saying, but she didn't take long to meet other girls in the same situation. The great immigration after the Second World War meant that she met girls from many other countries and quickly struck up friendships with Russians, Poles, Germans, Croats, and with the noisy Spaniards and Italians. Within a few months, they all spoke Spanish. Natasha became her family's interpreter. If they went to the market without her they had to use sign language to be understood. Her mother never managed to get a proper grip on Spanish because she worked at home and had little contact with Argentineans. She saw very few people. Rudy, on the other hand, as the years passed, ended up speaking with a minimal accent, a talent he had retained from his native country. Despite their Yiddish having been buried during the war years, in South America it became the family language once more and that was how the family communicated in private.

Natasha's parents were committed to the values of the age: the education of children as the great standard and the tool that would help them progress in life. Natasha had to have a good schooling, at any price. That was why, when she finished elementary school, they managed to get her into a good high school. At that time, the political climate was tense, marked by the increasingly iron grip that Perón exerted over the nation and its education. That high school changed Natasha's life. It was located on the still aristocratic Avenida Santa Fe and various lives blended together there, more cultured, more sophisticated than those she had previously known. She encountered girls who came from wealthy families, who traveled to the United States and brought back the first Bazooka gum.

Natasha left high school with very good grades and, influenced by some of her rather more well-to-do classmates, she decided to enter the Faculty of Humanities at the University of Buenos Aires. This annoyed Rudy a great deal. He thought it was nonsense, completely useless. Natasha promised she would study medicine in the future. In reality, what really interested her was psychology, not psychiatry, but back then there was no psychology degree as such that she could study. In fact, that very faculty spawned the first Argentinean psychologists of the 1950s and '60s, when therapies were reserved for psychiatric doctors. But she was not willing, at that time, to spend years studying medicine.

It's very Argentinean and very Jewish, that fascination with the world of psychology, and it has nothing to do with the founder of psychoanalysis, but with a passion for investigation, for origins and the effects of migrations. That's why we Argentineans and Jews are permanently leaving. We're errant, easily adaptable, and we have a compulsion toward diaspora. You find us living in the most unlikely places in the world.

* * *

I can clearly recall it. College classes had just started, I didn't know anyone, didn't know who to chat with, so I made the most of my free time reading on a bench in a garden. That's what I was doing when I was approached by a woman with a very Central European appearance—tall, slim, clear-skinned, high cheekbones, very blue eyes. Her hair, quite fair, was tied back in a ponytail. She was wearing a navy-blue skirt with flat black shoes and a short, fine white tank top.

Are you reading Simone de Beauvoir in French? she asked me admiringly, stealing a glance at the cover of the book.

Yes, I replied, somewhat amused.

Have you read *The Mandarins*?

No, this is the first book of hers I've read, I said, showing her the cover of *The Second Sex*. I don't know how much I like it yet.

That one's better. *The Mandarins* displays a certain meanness.

Is she some kind of pedant? I wondered. I was interested by the fact that she was talking about Simone de Beauvoir's mean side, that she dared to cast doubt on her. I invited her to sit with me on the bench.

She asked me why I spoke French.

Because I speak all the languages imaginable, I answered, laughing.

Where are you from?

From Simone de Beauvoir we moved on to my native land of Ukraine and Minsk and our tongues didn't stop. We were late for the next class. That's where it all began. She had just started studying French and like all self-respecting Argentines at the time, she aspired to speak and read it well, and she asked me to help her practice. She needed a bit of conversation to become fluent. I invited her to my house that weekend. If someone had said to me, as I was holding *The Second Sex* on my lap that sunny morning at college, that fifty years later I would be telling this story in front of her patients in Santiago de Chile, I wouldn't have believed it.

When Natasha was about to turn twenty-one, her mother died from lung cancer. It was a horrific death and she, the only daughter, felt the blow as though it were the loss of her life story. The fact that her mother died thousands and thousands of miles from the place she was born, and that Argentina had been unavoidably foreign to her, focused her mind on the concept of livestock being moved from one feeding ground to another with the seasons. Her mother's moans were in another language and each signal of pain triggered in Natasha's mind tragic landscapes, dazzling and distant, augmented by the mirror of the end. By devoting herself passionately to her mother's illness, Natasha felt that one day she should repay some kind of debt, without really knowing what. Rudy said to her, between injections, angry, impotent, Why didn't you study medicine instead of poking around in human nature? You might have saved your mother. The mind, it has no cure.

In the final delirium, her mother thought she was back in Minsk and was pacified. Natasha could not cry for her. We need God, she told her father in the cemetery. He didn't reply.

College over, Natasha decided to leave for France and keep her promise to her father to study medicine. France in those days vibrated with ideas and novelty. Movies, literature, and philosophy flourished. She did indeed study medicine and passed the boards, but she didn't enjoy any of it as much as she did reading about the different schools of psychoanalysis. She never subscribed to them as a form of therapy but she enjoyed the discussions with friends about those ideas. She spent most of her time living in a *chambre de bonne* on rue du Cardinal Lemoine in the Latin Quarter and there, says Natasha, her taste for austerity began. With so little space, she had nothing, and she didn't want anything. What interested her wasn't tangible.

The day she turned twenty-five, her closest friends organized a surprise for her, inviting her to the Folies Bergère, a place having nothing to do with her routine. Natasha had never been to a racy cabaret show. After the performance they ran into a young man dressed in an elegant black overcoat and white scarf. He knew one of Natasha's friends. His name was Jacques Henry, and he was a doctor, like them. Natasha's friend told him they were celebrating a birthday. He looked at the birthday girl and with a trace of mockery written across his face he asked, What's a Latin American medical student doing in a place like this? Should I be back on my continent leading the revolution? Natasha replied. He liked this answer, as well as her dark face and deep blue eyes. The others suggested one last drink to close out the night and they invited him along. They sat at a large table in La Coupole, and Natasha says it was one of the few times she has ever gotten drunk. She was feeling, in her words, "something strange," sitting next to this man who couldn't take his eyes off her and kept asking her tricky questions. At some point, unsettled, she asked why he wouldn't let her be. He replied, I like you.

The following day he invited her to a smoky café to listen to a young Greek singer named Georges Moustaki.

The day after that they went to see *Hiroshima, Mon Amour*. She didn't like the film. It's too slow, nothing happens, she told Jacques Henry. He couldn't believe she dared cast aspersions on the nouvelle vague.

Jacques Henry laughed at her and no one had ever done that before. She found it irresistible that, at last, someone wasn't taking her so seriously. Within a week, in spite of herself, she declared herself in love. They didn't waste much time. In a couple of months she abandoned her little tenth-story room on Cardinal Lemoine and moved in to a very pretty apartment on Place des Vosges. Are you rich? she asked him, disconcerted when she found out where he lived. His only response was to say that he was a good neurologist. She ended up marrying him several years later, for domestic reasons, as she calls them. She had to obtain French nationality. In Argentina, she explained, you need dual citizenship to fall back on, just in case.

Natasha wasn't, and never has been, a big fan of marriage. They lived fairly independent lives. Sometimes she left her lover alone for weeks and went to study at a friend's house at the beach. Jacques

Henry found this perfectly normal. He, in turn, would go to his parents' country retreat in Provence and was in no great hurry to return either. Both thought this was the only civilized way to coexist.

Although they tended to appear indifferent to one another, they did love each other. They never touched in public. It was difficult to imagine them being intimate. It was part of the rules. They provoked each other, they played a great deal, they fed their mutual intelligences. Jacques Henry liked to say, I'm stupid without Natasha. They talked a lot. Natasha despaired at the unknown recesses of her patients' brains. She was tireless in her discussions on the subject with Jacques Henry, her questions, her worries. Someone once asked her, If he hadn't been a neurologist, would you have married him?

She was also not a fan of motherhood.

When she became pregnant by accident, becoming a mother was the last thing on her mind. She was certified and worked in a public hospital, and she was starting to see private patients. Her career was devouring her. Jacques Henry intervened. Aware that it was his wife's body that was growing a life, and not his, he humbly requested, Let's make this an act of tenderness.

She had Jean Christophe, who today is a surgeon in Paris. He travels to this continent to see his mother as often as he can. He's handsome, has a sense of humor, and doesn't want to get married under any circumstances. He has already brought several women with him to visit and Natasha makes a show of giving them her seal of approval but still, at the age of forty, he hasn't been able to commit seriously.

One day in Paris, having returned from class to her small flat, which she kept even after moving in with Jacques Henry, she found a letter from Rudy in her mailbox. She climbed the ten flights of stairs delighted, savoring the anticipation of her father's news. Once she was settled with a cup of good coffee, she spread out the letter on her only small table. Hanna. Rudy told her about Hanna and reminded her of those years during the war when they lived together on

Marlene's estate. He told her that Hanna was her sister. This wasn't just a surprise to Natasha but a great shock. She had a great urge to talk to her father, desperate for more information. Since a call to Buenos Aires would cost her the same as food for a week, she had to resign herself to airmail. By the time Rudy replied, Natasha was beside herself and wanted to leave immediately to reunite with her sister. However, it wasn't that easy. Rudy only knew that Marlene's husband had left Belarus and settled in Moscow. Natasha, figuring that Hanna must be over thirty by now, was fearful of the errant spirit that her sister might have inherited too.

It was the start of the sixties, the height of the Cold War. Trying to locate someone in the Soviet Union was no small task. She began the *Recherche*, as I dubbed it, her great search. From that moment on Natasha obsessed over finding her sister. For Natasha, Hanna became like a tornado, a circular force, closed, potent, elusive. I've come to wonder how you live if you don't have something that drives you to action. It's what gives significance to a future that would otherwise be perfectly ordinary.

And so the search began. The *Recherche*.

The first thing that occurred to Natasha, quite rightly, was to turn to her Communist college friends. They were the *owners* of the Soviet Union in Paris, the most plausible interlocutors and messengers. They had only the name of Hanna's legal father, the textile entrepreneur Marlene had married. Almost a year passed before they heard news that he had died. He had fallen into disgrace with the regime shortly after the war, and Stalin had ordered him to be killed. That cut off an important lead or rather the only one Natasha had. I spent a season with her in Paris shortly after this occurred. She and Jacques Henry would sit at the kitchen table in the apartment on Place des Vosges, each holding a glass of red wine and reeking of tobacco. Jacques Henry smoked endlessly as they analyzed the scenario. The way in which Marlene's husband had met his end wasn't surprising. He was a typical representative of anti-Communist Russia, having tried to assimilate into the system in order to survive but who was denigrated and expelled by it. The problem was that, if he had fallen into disgrace, where could he hide his family or try to make them go unnoticed so they wouldn't run the same risk? Natasha decided to travel to the Soviet Union, but the only way to do so was to be invited with a delegation of French doctors. Her Communist friends arranged it for her, but this took another year. Nothing was easy and time took on another meaning in this search. I suppose that was the way she understood it because she didn't expend any gratuitous anxiety or adrenaline. The pursuit of this obsession had its own timing and she adapted to it.

Natasha's journey was a perfect failure. Her investigations were very badly received by the people who had invited her and she was unable to travel to Minsk to pick up the thread at the source. A regime like that was Natasha's worst ally. Her Communist friends promised to continue the investigation, and although she called them every so often and reminded them of that promise, she knew deep down that they wouldn't get far.

Life continued in spite of Hanna, though Hanna was at the heart of the obsession, but it continued all the same. At the start of the seventies, when Jean Christophe was still a child, Natasha decided that her marriage to Jacques Henry had ended. The passion had gone, that was her verdict. Without it they could be great friends but not a couple. Jacques Henry, with that characteristic touch of cynicism, fought her. He tried to convince her that passion didn't matter at all, that it would end someday anyway, that they should carry on. Sex? What the hell does sex matter? But Natasha had tired of Europe. She returned to Buenos Aires with her son.

Rudy was old and Natasha wanted to spend the last good times of his life with him. They shared a house. She established a private practice in a public hospital, which is the way she works today in Chile. She devoted herself to raising her son, caring for her father, and carrying out her work with passion and tenacity. Today, she looks back at that time with sweet nostalgia and her gaze softens whenever she remembers it, as if those large blue eyes fill with a mixture of placidity, affection, and rigor. Just like her.

We've all experienced a key moment in life that we can call a "turning point." A certain event unleashes another and then another and another. Suddenly our day-to-day has taken an enormous twist without us being able to remember, in the end, quite how or what produced it. In this case it was Rudy's death. Or the military dictatorship. The fact is that Natasha's life did an about-face and it was then that Chile appeared on the horizon. An important Argentine psychiatrist, Natasha's friend since her college days in Paris, had managed to get European funding to investigate female malaise in underdeveloped countries and had decided to move to Chile because in the early seventies its political and social situation was by far the most interesting on the continent. He was here for the coup d'etat. His investigation didn't strike Pinochet's military as political, so he was able to carry on working in peace. When things got too ugly in Argentina, he offered Natasha the opportunity to cross the border and work with him. But Chile's under a dictatorship too, Natasha objected. Yes, her colleague replied, *but it's someone else's*. He explained that if she came with her French nationality to work on his program, sponsored by the then European Economic Community, it would be difficult for them to bother her. He convinced her not to live with her heart in her mouth like her friends in Buenos Aires.

Videla's Argentina had become impossible for Natasha, and this offer surfaced at a time when she was seriously considering, in spite of herself, the idea of returning to Paris. Of course, Paris was full of Argentines, Chileans too. The whole of Europe was. But her friend's proposal made her opt for the other side of the Andes. After all, my real loyalty is to women, she said. She had already agreed with Jacques Henry that Jean Christophe would go to secondary school in Paris. Go on, she encouraged him, you don't need me anymore, the less mother you have, the saner you'll be. It was then that she said to me, Let's go. I was equally furious with and hurt by Videla's

Argentina but switching it for Pinochet's Chile seemed crazy. I was working with Natasha by then, I assisted in her research and helped her move her practice forward. I had acquired this rare serenity, like Baricco's character Novecento. He could have sailed on forever without disembarking. He had his music, I had my books, neither of us had any ambition. My marriage, like so many of our generation, had already ended. *Marriage is a criminal institution*, wrote Piglia. With matrimonial ties, one of the spouses always ends up being hanged. In my case, we had decided to separate before the hanging.

With no children and my siblings scattered around the globe, Natasha was the closest thing I had to a family. Once she left, I would've been left more or less orphaned in Argentina. A life by her side seemed a much better bet than a life without her. But I didn't shut up my apartment or make any definitive decision. I came to Chile to see whether I could tolerate it. The house on the beach at Isla Negra that Natasha's psychiatrist friend rented was an important factor in my decision to stay. Isla Negra as it was back then, before it became a Neruda fetish with tourists and buses and prints, was a solitary place. It received a very specific kind of visitor, the kind of people who found it a pleasure to wind up in the snack bar where we ate fried fish. We used to spend the weekends there and since we arrived in winter, my encounter with the Chilean sea was powerful. That sea at Isla Negra, its darkness, its chaos, its inaccessibility, penetrated my heart with an unexpected force, as did the pine forests and the immense rocks. It can't have been long before I told Natasha that I didn't at all miss the brown waters of the River Plate.

The following year I returned to Buenos Aires, I sold my apartment in Belgrano and swapped it for one in Providencia. For Natasha's part, she bought a small plot on the banks of the River Aconcagua. She fitted out the old house more or less the way it came, and we could continue to enjoy the grounds, adding magnolias, avocado, papaya, and chirimoya trees, medlars and eggplants and the pink and white crepe myrtles. Natasha has two enormous chestnut-brown boxers, Sam and Frodo. Their size is a result of the fact that they basically live off avocados. They are terrifying to a potential intruder. The contradiction between their apparent ferocity and their actual docility is very appealing. I go out to walk and play with them enough so as not to give in to the temptation of having one in my apartment. We became true residents of Santiago, complaining ceaselessly, about the pollution, about the traffic, about public transport, about the lack of stimuli. But deep down we were happy. It was enough to have a clear day after the rain for the majesty of the Andes to appear, right there next to us, for us to forget all our hatred for the city and to fall back in love.

But let's not forget Hanna. We'll return to Natasha's obsession.

During our Chilean years, she carried on doing the impossible to glean some news of her sister and although she faced one failure after another, she persisted in her efforts. My fear was that the constant indulgence of the fantasy would end up dissolving it. The idea of Hanna, because Hanna was no more than an idea, had become fragile, intangible. Nature, which does not forgive, had simply erased her. Some days, when we were in the country, Natasha asked me whether I thought she had died. I didn't think anything. But, of course, Hanna could have died. Sometimes I reminded Natasha that her sister was already over thirty when the famous *Recherche* began and most likely she was no longer tied to her father's destiny. She could have married, adopted her husband's name and become a good Communist, hale and hearty. She could live in Mongolia, I suggested, in Armenia, or in the Baltic. The USSR was so enormous and impossible.

One day the Berlin Wall fell.

A year later, the USSR came apart, the system collapsed, turning to dust.

Natasha closely followed what was happening, until it was possible to travel there. What strength and energy she showed during that time. At a weak moment, I felt it was my duty to accompany her but then I understood that the task was hers and hers alone. So that things would go well for her, I prayed to a God I don't believe in.

In Moscow, she settled into a relatively cheap hotel and prepared to stay for as long as necessary. She went from house to house chasing names that appeared to be linked to Marlene and her husband, assuming, of course, that she was already dead. Only one turned out to be distantly related, but with sufficient vagueness to insist that that branch of the family was from Minsk, not Moscow, that they'd lost trace of her, although they knew that he had been executed under Stalin. Then Natasha decided, as she did the first time, to go to Minsk. Before she left, she knocked on the doors of various embassies, the French, the Argentine, the Chilean, until she came to speak to the Germans. Weren't they, after all, the guilty ones?

In Minsk she experienced some highly emotional moments, getting to know the city and the neighborhoods that had belonged to her parents. She found relations who welcomed and sheltered her but they could scarcely help. They only informed her of what she already knew. The textile entrepreneur's family had fled the region after the war never to return. She figured out where the estate was, where she had spent so much time with Hanna, and went back there only to find it totally changed, not a stone or piece of wood that recalled the old house. Only an aged tree and remnants of an orchard produced an echo in her memory.

One day, in Minsk, she was called by an employee of the French embassy, an acquaintance of Jean Christophe, who finally gave her some news.

Hanna was no longer an abstract idea. Many years ago she had married a party employee, a Russian industrial engineer who had been destined for Vietnam at the end of the war. After unification, his job was to give technical support to the victors. Natasha felt very fortunate now that she had the name of Hanna's husband, although he had died in Hanoi some years later. It wasn't known whether his wife had returned to the then USSR. There was no record of it.

Vietnam.

From Moscow she left for Paris. Jean Christophe found her exhausted but by no means defeated. His reaction was, Another socialist country, *mon Dieu*, what a nightmare. They agreed that Natasha would return to Chile. Her employers were getting annoyed and I had to remind her that there are limits to how much leave you can take. From Paris they visited the Vietnamese embassy and the search started again. As expected, Hanna's husband's name appeared in the records, but not hers. Jean Christophe promised to continue. The French still feel rather *chez soi* in old Indochina, he told her, and you're no age to be traipsing from village to village, house to house. As soon as he had some free time, he would set off for the East. With that promise, Natasha returned to Chile.

Jean Christophe made countless trips to Vietnam and ended up becoming a real expert on the country, which he has come to love dearly. Of course, his first step when he set foot in Hanoi was to visit the Russian embassy. It was no longer the Soviet embassy. That was the excuse that masked the chaos and profound apathy he found there, just peevish, rather lazy bureaucrats to whom a lost widow, Russian or not, was nothing. What's more, he was told by an official with a certain sense of humor that the Vietnamese weren't like the Bulgarians, they were always more autonomous.

When Jean Christophe found out that the life expectancy of women in Vietnam was seventy-two, he decided to hurry. Time was running out.

On one of his trips he met a female soldier and party leader, a plucky woman who had known Hanna and her husband during the time of cooperation. They had been friends and she knew that Hanna had a profound interest in children and an extraordinary capacity to connect with them. He learned that in the USSR Hanna had trained to be a teacher, but that she hadn't been able to do it while living in Hanoi. After her husband's death, she disappeared. No one had seen her again. In a socialist country people don't just disappear like that, Jean Christophe objected, there are controls, there has to be some record of her. If, when she was widowed, she married a Vietnamese man, came the reply, we would have no way of finding out, she would appear with a different name and nationality. If it had been a brother of yours, Mom, not your sister, we would have found him by now, Jean Christophe complained. A brother wouldn't have lost his name like women do. If she went with a foreigner and left the country, they suggested, there are no clues whatsoever. You can't honestly believe, Jean Christophe was told with a touch of irony, that we've kept a record of the identity of every single person who has left the country in the last twenty years. When he asked about the marriage register they looked at him the way you look at a child who's asking the impossible without knowing it. At least the Vietnamese friend gave Jean Christophe something of great value, a photograph, which now rests in a beautiful frame in Natasha's bedroom, next to one of Lou Andreas-Salomé. In it, Hanna looks about fifty, with a clear, clean face, like Natasha's when I met her. The photo is black and white but you can tell the eyes are blue. She is posing next to her husband at some official reception and is badly dressed, wearing a dark, badly cut suit, although the jacket is the only part you can see in the photo. Her hair is combed back into an old-fashioned bun. Even so, she is a beautiful woman.

Jean Christophe had to get back to his job in France, so they hired an investigator to start the search, photograph in hand. Finding someone lost for years among more than eighty million inhabitants is no easy task. Hanoi was scoured from end to end, every school, every kindergarten, every hospital. Nothing. The same in old Saigon, which took a considerable amount of time. The center of the country was the next goal, and Natasha volunteered to cover it herself. She wasn't keen on the idea of the detective. From the outset she was skeptical about his results because deep down, without saying as much, she believed that only affection would provide sufficient strength to find her sister, not an investigation. She took a vacation and met Jean Christophe in Da Nang. After some unfruitful searches they continued to Hué. Already slightly frustrated, they came to a halt on the seacoast of southern China, in Hoi An. At least the place was sufficiently charming and beautiful to distract them from any burdens. It was there, in a school, where the principal, taking the photograph in his hands and scrutinizing it thoroughly, said to them, In the outskirts of Hoi An, in the middle of the rice paddies, there's a very small school where some white women teach.

It wasn't easy to find the place. The school was indeed insignificant, almost lost in the surrounding countryside, in the middle of an impoverished hamlet, surrounded by rice paddies and a few gray, skinny, bony cows. It was tenacity that enabled them to find it. It was a low construction split into three rooms, with a long, covered courtyard, the floor of which was just dirt. A group of small children was playing in a corner, in a circle around a woman. Another group was sitting on the floor around another teacher, practicing an exercise with small pointed stones. In the middle of the courtyard, a third group of three children sat at a low table examining two open books. They all had their heads covered with enormous straw hats, the typical Vietnamese conical hats, which made them almost invisible. Natasha entered the courtyard. Excusing herself, she interrupted the woman at the table, who, when she turned her head upward to look at her, revealed her pale complexion. Her eyes and what showed of her hair under the hat were dark, but she was a white woman. She smiled at her.

Hanna, said Natasha, in a reedy voice, I'm looking for Hanna.

The woman smiled again and in rudimentary French replied, No, there's no Hanna here.

Natasha pointed at the other two women surrounded by children—the women were concentrating on their duties, indifferent to this Westerner who was talking to their companion.

Phuong and Linh, said the woman at the table, nodding to confirm her words. She rose, twisting her body, and lightly grasped her questioner's arm as if to guide her out.

Natasha didn't give up. Although she might have been guilty of rudeness, she drew away and walked toward the other two groups working there, toward Phuong and Linh. Jean Christophe, who told me the story later, watched this scene from outside under a blazing sun, as if he felt it inappropriate to intervene.

Natasha approached the second woman, the one who was sitting in a circle with the children, and looked directly in her face. She was very old, with white hair and pale eyes. As was the third woman, who was sitting on the floor watching the children's stone exercise. But both had dark skin, dyed by the air and the sun, unlike Vietnamese women who took great pains to keep theirs pale. Neither of the two looked like a Russian woman from Minsk. In silence, Natasha went from one to the other, watching them. Then she caught the bluish-green reflection. The woman sitting on the floor was wearing a high-necked tunic, the first two buttons of which were unfastened. There was the flash of a precious stone. Natasha crouched and touched the stone. Then she opened her blouse and touched her own alexandrite. The woman on the floor watched her with great curiosity. Natasha uttered her real name and she nodded her head, amazed.

Yes, Hanna.

The *Recherche* was over.

Marlene had never spoken to Hanna about her real father so the existence of this sister was a complete novelty. She hadn't forgotten the days of war on the estate and she remembered with great tenderness that child called Natasha with whom she had shared such a terrible and crucial period. She had not forgotten Rudy or when he gave them both the alexandrite chain, which, at his request, she had always worn around her neck. It was so familiar to her that she no longer saw it and she never dreamed it would ever be the most irrefutable sign of recognition.

She was a frail, very slim old lady who lived in a cabin near the sea and devoted herself to teaching languages to children. She went by a different name. She had indeed married a Vietnamese man, with whom she lived for many years, a fisherman, and she took his surname. She hadn't changed her first name because she wanted to hide it but because Linh was easier for the locals.

I won't tell you Hanna's story. I'll just tell you, so that you understand Natasha's next steps, that Hanna is seventy-five now, her life has been hard and her body has suffered equally. *Ruined*, that was the word Natasha used to describe her. An errant Jew, like all of us. If not, how do you explain the fact that she didn't go back to Russia when she was widowed? Doesn't she believe in roots? Natasha asked me. I replied, No, the same as you.

Natasha wanted to bring her back to Chile, but Hanna's refusal was adamant. Nothing would take her from Vietnam. It was her country now.

Today, Hanna is dying. The poverty and frugality, her general living conditions for the last twenty years, have consumed her. She's old and tired, ready to go, if you can ever be ready for that. Her sister will be there for her and close her eyes for her.

I have no Hanna. But I have my books. They have a wonderful quality. They welcome anyone who opens them. Several of my authors have grown old with me and they are more real to me than people of flesh and bone whom I can touch with my hand. Natasha often came to my cubicle, tired after a long day's work, to talk.

"Tell me about life out there."

"By *out there* do you mean the characters in my books?"

"Yes, them. Tell me what they're doing, what they're saying, what they're thinking."

The thing is that literature, like psychoanalysis, faces the complex relationship between knowing and not knowing.

Edward Said, that admirable Palestinian writer, talked about the "late style." The term is generally used for artists. It's the final stage, when the creator lets go of the reins and starts to do what he wants, with no consideration of or coherence with his previous work. By releasing the moorings, extremely valuable work is often created.

I think Natasha has entered her late style as a psychiatrist and she will experience it as she pleases. A good indicator is that she has allowed me to tell you her story. She will leave for Vietnam and she won't return until she has buried Hanna's bones. The hospital, her research, her practice, her patients, they will all play a lesser role from now on. Her obsession has finally met its endpoint. She'll do what she has to do, and she'll do it with the appropriate solemnity.

When the poet Gabriela Mistral left for Mexico, the writer Pedro Prado wrote to his Mexican friends: "Don't make noise around her; because she's fighting the battle of silence."

I venture to say the same to you.

EPILOGUE

*B*ack straight, head raised, Natasha pulls back the curtain at the window and fixes her gaze on the group of women who, one by one, are climbing into the van that has come to take them home. It is twilight and the garden, languid but also majestic, is empty. The workers have gone to rest and the enormous trees frame the nine figures against the mountains. In an instant, they are gone.

She has said goodbye to each of them. She has embraced them and, with a murmur, released them.

She remembers when, during her childhood in Buenos Aires, Rudy's dog gave birth. She spent hours kneeling on the floor watching the puppies and she was struck by the way they needed each other to survive. It must have been the warmth they were seeking. They climbed over each other, pressing their bodies together, curling up against one another. One day she picked them up, one by one, and took them to a room where the fire was going and settled them all around the hearth. Don't get too attached to that image, Natasha, Rudy told her when he found her lying on the floor cuddling the dogs. The value of human beings is their capacity for separation, for being independent, they belong to themselves and not the pack.

Natasha allows the curtain to drop. They've gone. She imagines them walking away from her, their steps lighter than before, watching the stars, not those that we already know but those that are being born, the product of the deaths of others.

In the end, she tells herself, moving away from the window, after everything, in one way or another, we all have the same story to tell.

ABOUT THE AUTHOR

© Gabriel Renie

Marcela Serrano is the daughter of writers and is an award-winning Chilean novelist. Her debut novel, *We Loved So Much*, won the Literary Prize in Santiago. Her subsequent novels, among them *The Hotel of the Sad Women* and *Our Lady of Loneliness*, met with much success, landing her the Sor Juana Inés de la Cruz Prize and a runner-up nod in the prestigious Premio Planeta competition. She is widely considered one of the best Latin American writers working today. *Ten Women* is her first novel to be published in English.

ABOUT THE TRANSLATOR

© Beth Fowler, 2010

Originally from Inverness, Scotland, Beth Fowler earned her degree in Hispanic Studies from the University of Glasgow, including a year teaching English in Santiago, Chile. She began working as a freelance translator in 2009, and after winning the Harvill Secker Young Translators' Prize in 2010 began to move her focus from commercial to literary translation. Her first novel translation, *Open Door* by Argentine writer Iosi Havilio, was published in 2011. She lives near Glasgow with her husband and son.